THE WISH THIEF

LAND OF MAAR
BOOK ONE

THE WISH THIEF

VLAD GLAVEANU

To Alice, Zoé and Arthur,
our little dreamers

Contents

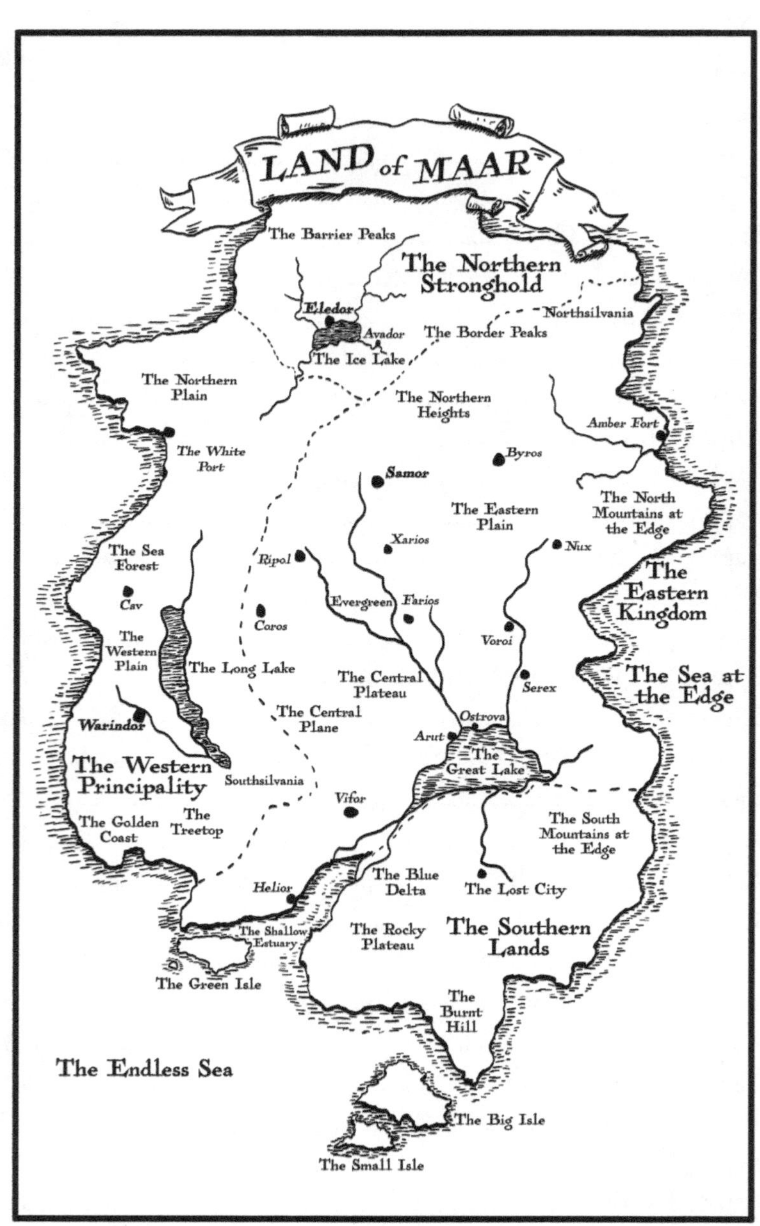

LAND of MAAR
The Barrier Peaks
The Northern Stronghold
Eledor
Northsilvania
Avador
The Border Peaks
The Ice Lake
The Northern Plain
The Northern Heights
Amber Fort
The White Port
Byros
Samor
The Eastern Plain
The North Mountains at the Edge
The Sea Forest
Xarios
Nux
Ripol
The Eastern Kingdom
Cav
Evergreen
Farios
The Western Plain
Coros
Voroi
The Long Lake
The Central Plateau
Serex
The Sea at the Edge
Warindor
The Central Plane
Ostrova
The Western Principality
Southsilvania
Arut
The Great Lake
The Golden Coast
The Treetop
Vifor
The South Mountains at the Edge
Helior
The Blue Delta
The Lost City
The Shallow Estuary
The Rocky Plateau
The Southern Lands
The Green Isle
The Burnt Hill
The Endless Sea
The Big Isle
The Small Isle

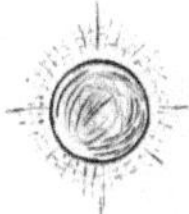

A T THE BEGINNING THERE was nothing and, from this nothingness, the first Wish Orb was born. This Orb, no bigger than a
pomegranate, concentrated within it all the life that was to come.
And it shined bright with its energy. When the time was right, the
Orb broke to reveal two grown Wish-Makers, each holding an Orb
in their hands. The woman used her one Wish to create the first
land and called it Maar. The man Wished to become ruler of this
land. The two had many children together, and their children had
even more children of their own. And their Wishes helped the land
grow. As the ruler got older, he felt his return to nothingness was
near. He looked at the land and its inhabitants and wept for not
having used his one Wish differently. His rule would fade, and his
memory would not endure. And so it is, since then, that the memory
of selfish Wish-Makers in Maar never lasts.

(*The Book of Wishes*, Genesis)

Chapter 1. The Outcast

Lia knew that, if she were patient, something worth talking about would happen in the quiet village of Ostrova. What she didn't expect was for it to start in Professor Filip's most hated class, the Metaphysics of Wish Orbs. Or, perhaps, that's exactly where it was meant to happen.

Seated at his desk, in front of three rows of benches packed with teenagers, Professor Filip – the headmaster – kept repeating what everyone already knew. This was his trademark 'teaching method', after all. Repetition in a monotonous tone, which was ready to turn venomous whenever students paid too little attention.

That day he took it from the beginning: 'All the people in Maar are born with a single Wish Orb.' How else could it be? 'Their Orb first materializes in their hand after birth and it is, at that age, no bigger in size than a pigeon's egg.' Lia had a hard time imagining Orbs so small but, then again, she had not seen newborns for a while.

'The Orb then disappears for several years. And it is only when the child starts to want something and understands that this wanting is a wish that the Orb materialises again in their hand. This time it is about the size of a hen's egg.'

Now that she did remember! Her grandfather Alfred had told her not to leave the garden and go running on the street when she wished to do exactly that. How startled she was by the round thing that showed up inside her tiny fist. Startled even more when that round thing began to shine, brighter than daylight. It was neither hot nor cold, like a smooth piece of lit glass. She wanted to look inside but couldn't because it was too bright.

She was later told that it was the brightest they have ever seen in the village. Her grandfather was so excited by this apparition that he took her out for a walk on the street, sitting on his shoulders. She loved the strange ball for it.

But it wasn't long until Lia understood that the shiny Orb she could make appear and disappear at will was not a play thing. No, quite the opposite. It was something that belonged to everyone else rather than her. In fact, she was constantly warned about it. Don't give it to anyone, don't touch another person's Orb, don't throw it in the air, don't check if it can float, don't use it to make light at night, don't taste it, don't paint on it, don't roll it on the floor…

'You only have one Wish and you must not make it until your Rite of Passage,' Filip went on, while half of the class fought to stay awake.

Oh yes, the dreaded Rite. Dreaded in Lia's eyes, anyway.

'The Rite is prepared by your family together with a representative of the Wish Order.' Filip loved referring to himself that way, even if Lia knew from her grandfather that he only got this role in the village because no one else wanted it.

'It's less than two years before your own Rites and, after completing this class successfully,' (he just had to say that when Lia's grades barely amounted to a pass…) 'I will start discussing with your parents or grandparents about the ceremony.' Lia was the only one in her class who was living with her grandfather.

And then it happened.

Filip was explaining the correct way of breaking an Orb in Wish-making – you throw it to the ground with your right hand, who makes up these rules anyway? – when the class got an impromptu demonstration.

Eduard, the young man who sat on the back bench and had barely said a word the whole year, leapt to his feet. '*I Wish for a pair of mighty wings, to carry me away from here, over land and sea,*' he shouted, his voice commanding the attention of the whole class.

And there it was: his Orb appeared in his hand. He smashed it to the floor (with the right hand, by the way). Its gentle, dim light was set free. Like a bird flying out, it floated around and then disappeared into thin air. A collective gasp followed and Lia, in spite of her hard-won reputation for always keeping her cool, took part in it wholeheartedly.

Eduard's shirt ripped open and a pair of enormous white wings burst from his back. He flapped them clumsily, sending papers and pencils flying around. His classmates jumped up and stepped back. Filip's mouth fell wide open, his eyes ready to pop out of his head.

Eduard looked as shocked as everyone else when he managed to control the movement of his wings. A smile of pure joy lit up his face. He started running on benches towards the open window next to the professor who shrieked and took cover. Eduard jumped through the window headfirst. He flapped his wings noisily and off he went, higher and higher, until he was the size of a seagull. Finally, he disappeared from sight.

Lia's classmates were all talking at once, Filip screaming over the crowd, other classes opening their doors and teachers pouring in, flying Wish beasts sent with messages to catch and bring the boy back. And, in the middle of it all, everyone was asking the question that was on Lia's mind as well: Why did Eduard do this?

***

Lia kept thinking about it all day and couldn't find a satisfactory answer. Nobody else she talked to could either, not even her grandfather.

That night, as she was lying on the rooftop of her house, waiting for Tudor to come, she kept wondering about Eduard. Did he manage to go far? It was his first time flying so he might have just crashed into the Great Lake, exhausted, like a big bird dropping from the sky. But what if he didn't? He Wished for mighty wings and that's exactly what he got. Maybe, just maybe, he managed to fly over the lake and reach the Southern lands, that savage part of Maar they were warned to stay away from. Ostrova fisherman knew not to cross the Great Lake and Eduard, even if he didn't come from a family of fishermen, must have known that nothing good awaits beyond the borders of the Eastern Kingdom. And yet, by doing what he did, he had become an outcast in his village and a fugitive from his Kingdom.

There was no coming back from that, was there? All because they were all born with a Wish to make when coming of age… One Wish that would decide their entire life: what they could do from then on and what they could not do anymore. The Wish that would turn them into full members of their community, of their Kingdom, and of Maar.

But only if, as the Book of Wishes said, the Wish was used to "help the land grow," if it was not "selfish". That was Eduard's crime. He did not help anyone but himself by asking for a pair of wings. He could not use them for swimming faster, or breathing under water, or taming wild cormorants like Ostrova's fishermen did.

Lia kept thinking about Eduard's fate while staring at the motionless lake in the distance, and at the pale reflection of the moon in it. Almost full, it was the only light piercing through the darkness. Distracted, she didn't hear her friend Tudor arriving.

'Sorry I'm late,' he said, struggling, as always, to get his broad shoulders through the round rooftop window. 'Florian and I couldn't find him. I hope he made it across the lake but...' They both knew there was very little hope for those who travelled further South.

'I know,' Lia said softly, thinking about the harshness of the Southern Lands. 'Thank you for risking your boat for the search.'

'Lia, I am worried for you,' Tudor changed the subject. 'I heard you had another fight with Professor Filip yesterday.'

His cousins, either Clara or Matei, must have told on her.

'You might find it funny to tell him in class that you have no idea where your Orb is, but don't cross him too much. He was appointed by the Cardinal and I have the feeling the Order is watching you closely. Your Orb is too bright for them not to–'

'Don't be ridiculous, Tudor!' she interrupted, trying to sound unconcerned. 'Nobody remembers seeing the Cardinal around here. Besides, doesn't the Wish Order have anything better to do then follow a teenage girl's every move?'

'A teenage girl from a tiny village, yes, but one with a powerful Wish Orb. A girl who makes fun of Wish-making and doesn't want to prepare for her Rite of Passage,' Tudor insisted. 'They must be worried about you making an unwise Wish... just like Eduard today.'

And so she contemplated, for the thousandth time, telling her friend she wasn't going to make an unwise Wish – because she didn't plan to make any Wish at all. She might be the first in the Eastern Kingdom, or even in the whole of Maar, to do this and they might have to define a new class of crime just for her. And they would – the Order never lacked imagination when it came to punishment.

But what was the point of upsetting Tudor, who had been so good to her and her grandfather, by saying that? She still had two more years before her Rite of Passage was supposed to take place and many things could happen before then. Maybe Eduard would come back and fly her away?

No, Tudor was better off thinking she'd grow a pair of horns than keep her "powerful" Orb shiny and intact for a lifetime. He had enough to worry about as the sole breadwinner for his two younger cousins, Matei and Clara. And yet, he was also the one who brought her and Alfred fish every evening, regardless of how much he managed to catch that day.

Lia tried to change the subject. 'You know you can keep the fish for yourself, for your cousins. They're the ones who–'

'Don't mention it, Lia,' Tudor said, his light blue eyes fixed on her. 'Just promise me you'll think about what I said.'

'Don't I always?' she replied with a smile. 'You know my biggest wish would actually be for you and grandfather to never worry about me again. I might even ask Professor Filip if this is a legitimate Wish to make and advise him about the urgency of the matter.'

Lia winked and Tudor couldn't help but smile, running his hand through his short, blond hair while slowly shaking his head.

'Perhaps he will even agree to be a special Witness for it, considering the enormous challenge this Wish would come up against. It would be something like the first Wish but, instead of the world being created, it would just give you two peace of mind which, if you ask me, is an equally mighty achievement.' Tudor laughed along with her.

The two of them spent the next couple of hours chatting about how to find Eduard before Filip or the Order did. It was going to be hard. The Order had men whose Wishes made them fast, strong, and eager to prove themselves. Lia kept hoping her grandfather could help. She would talk to him in the morning about it. But, if she wanted to be coherent the next day, they had to stop talking and go to bed. Only a few hours left before dawn.

Lia gave Tudor a drawing notebook from her grandfather's library for Clara, who loved making sketches. Then she walked him to the door, said good night and returned to her bedroom.

Her room was simple and lacked the decorations people her age usually adorned their place with. Apart from the bed and a tiny table by the window, she only had a set of drawers and two bookshelves. Under the bed, in a wooden box, she kept her most prized possession: an old, scruffy toy. Lia took it out, as she always had done whenever she had a bad day. The donkey that looked like a rabbit, or the other way around, had belonged to her mother from when she grew up in Ostrova. Alfred gave it to Lia when her parents left. From her father, all she had was her red-brown hair. Lia caressed the toy, then put it back in the box gently.

She had been living with her grandfather for as long as she could remember. Her parents, Lia was told, were killed when she was only a baby, while travelling through the Barren Lands of the South. And now Eduard was there – if he hadn't fallen in the lake in the meantime – risking his life for a dream.

He had looked so happy to have his wings, why would other people blame him for deciding his own fate? And who was going to decide hers?

Restless, Lia thought about her Wish and wanted to see her Orb. In an instant, she held the luminous Orb in her hands. The size of a ripe pomegranate, it was mature enough for her to make a Wish if she wanted to, even before the Rite. Just like Eduard had done.

Lia peered inside the Orb, her dark eyes squinting, looking for answers. It had been a long time since she held it like that. Its light felt warm and strong, stronger than that of any other Wish Orb she had ever seen… Ah, how could something so small ruin one's life?

WISHES THAT ASK FOR personal riches and good health are selfish. Wishes that are meant to change the lives of others against their will, for better or worse, are foolish. A Wish to create more Wishes is wasted. And Wishes that ask for youth and glory, those are the most dangerous of them all.

(*The Book of Wishes*, The order of the realm)

Chapter 2. Grandfather

THAT NIGHT, LIA DREAMT that Tudor rather than Eduard had made the unwise Wish. She was terrified by the prospect of never seeing him again. As dawn began to break, she dreamt that Professor Filip was gathering feathers from the schoolyard. He didn't want anybody to see them and imagine what wings might look like.

In her dream, Lia ended up making her Wish: for feathers to fill the air in every classroom. She was happy, relieved to finally have a Wish to make. Her classmates were running around laughing, like little children playing in the snow. Filip panicked, hands in the air, grabbing fistfuls of feathers and shouting at everyone to close their eyes at once.

She woke up at sunrise. Exhausted but still smiling at the thought of the professor's antics, Lia dressed quickly and washed her face with cold water. She was surprised to see in the mirror that she didn't look as tired as she felt, though her face was paler than usual, making her brown eyes look even darker and accentuating her freckles.

Alfred was busy in the garden behind the house when Lia got downstairs. It was late summer and the apples were starting to turn red, to her grandfather's delight. Beneath them, rows of onions, potatoes, cabbages and carrots were ready for picking. It was Lia's favourite time of the year. She had helped Alfred with the harvest for as long as she could remember and their small garden supplied food for her favourite meals throughout autumn and winter.

Her grandfather usually woke up before her and spent the early hours of the day gardening or, during wintertime, writing by the fire. He loved his garden so much that Lia often wondered why he hadn't made a Wish that helped him with it. Instead, Alfred had chosen to focus on his writing. As there were no historians in that part of the Kingdom, he had Wished to become the "living memory" of Ostrova and the northern shores of the Great Lake.

'Good morning, Grandfather.'

Alfred smiled as he entered the kitchen and took off his muddy gloves. 'Good morning, my child. I trust you won't get in trouble today at school,' he said without warning. 'I saw Professor Filip walking around, preoccupied, and I would hate for you to add to his burden.'

It was hard to tell if her grandfather disliked Filip or not – he certainly could not have disliked him as much as Lia did.

'And why is Professor Filip so worried?' she asked.

Alfred sat down at the table and held her hand in his. 'Filip is strict, but he alone cannot condemn Eduard. This is why we have the Village Council. To give everyone a fair trial.'

Lia knew. Alfred, almost ten years ago, when he was the school's headmaster, had argued in front of the Council against passing any judgement about Wish-making before listening to the accused. His arguments were so convincing that the Cardinal himself followed his lead and turned it into the law of the realm. Since then, it was rare for people suspected of unwise Wishes to disappear. Until yesterday.

Alfred himself spoke in defence of such people, like the girl in the nearby village, Arut, who Wished her touch would feel as soft as silk. Or the young man in Amber Fort, who wanted to be invisible for a while but forgot to mention how he could become visible again. Or the boy from Samor, the capital city, who Wished for more Orbs and, as foretold by the Book of Wishes, got nothing in return.

Only the girl with the soft touch was pardoned and, even then, she had to move to another part of the Kingdom and find a use for her Wish.

Lia thought about the other two while helping her grandfather set the table. Where were they now? Were they imprisoned for what they did? And how unfair was it if that were the case.

The smell of breakfast distracted her. Fried eggs from the neighbour down the street, milk from Filip's cousin who raised cows and fresh bread from Nicolae. Nicolae was Ostrova's famed baker, who had used his Wish to create the best bread oven in the Kingdom, one he was proud to pass on to his sons.

'Grandfather, do you think the Order might forgive Eduard for his Wish and allow him to come back?' Lia asked, spreading egg yolks on her bread.

Alfred was silent for a moment, as if weighing the likelihood of it happening.

'The Order is not about forgiveness, Lia,' he said in the end.

'You mean they are unforgiving?'

'No, simply that forgiveness is not a virtue they are concerned with. Their main focus is justice. The justice that will encourage people to act wisely, whether they like it or not.' Was Grandfather criticising the Order? She had never heard him talk so harshly about it before.

'Can't the King intervene and teach them some compassion?'

'The King's compassion is reserved for those living at the Royal court, my child,' her grandfather said with a sad smile.

She wanted to ask more but Alfred told her to finish her breakfast otherwise she would be late for school. Again. And if she was late again, Filip would be unforgiving – not unlike the Wish Order.

'Please, take care today,' he said. Her grandfather had always worried, especially about her behaviour at school, but now he seemed to be worried about something else, something bigger.

Before Lia could ask what it was, he added softly: 'You know I promised your mother and father before they left that I would look after you.' And he smiled again. One of the big smiles that filled Lia's heart and helped her forget she had no mother or father to look after her. The smile that made her feel safe in a world of Kings, and Cardinals, and angry headmasters. Her heart swelled with affection for the old man.

'I love you, Grandfather.' She gave him a hug before running out the door.

She knew she had to speed up when the metal goose of the postman, his Wish creature, flew by her carrying letters in its iron beak. Eduard could have helped with this task, if only they would let him… On her way to school she counted two other jobs he could be good at: picking fruits from high trees (instead of using their neighbour's strange and ineffective Wish horn, inherited from his great-grandfather, to blow wind at the trees) and sending messages between fishermen on the lake, telling each other about the movement of fish.

At the school gate, Lia stopped for a moment to catch her breath. It was better not to show she had been running.

Lia didn't have many friends at school, nor did she try to make any. Most of her classmates found her strange and were put off by her habit of getting in trouble with the headmaster. Ever since Tudor finished, the year before, the only other people she spent time with at school were his cousins, Matei, two years younger than Lia, and Clara, one year younger than her brother.

As she entered the schoolyard, Lia spotted Clara sitting under the old oak tree by the side entrance, scribbling in her drawing pad. Lia loved Clara's drawings and asked to see her latest sketches. The young girl showed her a sketch of two dragonflies. They looked as if they were about to fly off the page. Just as Lia was getting ready to express her admiration, everyone in the yard stopped chatting and an unusual silence fell.

The student group split in two, as if struck by lightning. An old, short man, with almond-shaped eyes and a piercing gaze, hurried through the yard, his grey robes floating behind him. The man headed straight towards them at first only to disappear, a moment later, behind the side entrance of the school.

Lia was about to ask the others who he was when she heard the high-pitched voice of Professor Filip sending everyone to class. When he saw Lia, Filip hesitated. Then he shook his head and rushed through the side entrance after the man.

What was that about? The stranger must be there because of Eduard. This required further research.

Instead of going in to another dull music class with Miss Mioara, Lia headed towards the staircase leading to Filip's office. She knew from the days when her grandfather was headmaster that this was where teachers held their council. Students were not normally allowed there, but Lia had the misfortune of knowing it in detail from the many times she had been disciplined behind closed doors.

She could hear her heart beating as she slowly climbed the wooden stairs, keeping to the poorly lit edges, trying not to make a sound.

'The boy was warned, your Excellency, trust me, I myself had a talk with him just the week before–' she heard the professor say.

'Which proves your methods are not adequate,' the stranger interrupted. 'And this makes me doubt even more your ability to educate her in the spirit of our community. You have been extensively prepared, Filip, but, from what I hear, you are not doing a good job.'

'But, Excellency…' Filip's high-pitched voice was fading. Lia heard the tinkle of something small being dropped.

'I might have to step in and either have you replaced or remove her from the village. And the second option is more difficult than the first.'

Lia imagined the headmaster looking down at the carpet as she had done so many times before. She wondered if Filip was memorising the carpet's geometrical pattern – she, at least, knew it by heart.

'Your Excellency, I will try my best. She is, however, very stubborn. You are right that until now I wasn't able to make much progress, but I do believe that–' Again, the headmaster wasn't allowed to finish his sentence.

'I do not care what you believe,' the stranger cut Filip off. 'This is not a matter of trying one's best, headmaster. We trusted you and now I hear about boys deciding all of a sudden to fly away! Do you realise what it would mean for her to make such a Wish? What the loss would be? And I know Alfred feels the same.'

Lia gasped. Were they… talking about her? Were they worried she might do the same as Eduard?

Lia turned to run down the stairs when she felt someone – or something – watching her from the shadows. As she peered along the dark corridor, she saw an enormous dog staring at her. She held back a scream.

In the shadows, the dog's bright yellow eyes moved towards her, slowly, accompanied by a soft growling.

Heart hammering, Lia stepped back but lost her balance and fell.

Before she rolled down the staircase, a pain erupted in her arm as it was pinched and grabbed. The dog held on to her with his teeth and, flapping a pair of massive, bat-like wings, dragged her back to the corridor and dropped her next to the teacher's room.

As Lia lay there, gasping for breath, the door opened, revealing the stern face of the man in grey.

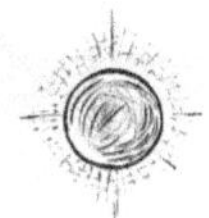

"PITY ME FOR NOT having been born a Wishfull, master, for what power do I really have to change my miserable fate?" asked the apprentice.

"Only fools cry for not being Wishfulls and envy them. Don't you know they are the most powerful and the least free of us all?"

(A Dialogue; text forbidden by the Wish Order in the 5th century)

Chapter 3. The Thief

THE SCHOOL YARD WAS remarkably silent for that time of day. The only sounds came from Miss Mioara's music class. The class Lia had missed; the one she wished she hadn't.

Outside the teacher's room, Lia kept her eyes on the enormous winged dog that was now sitting beside the visitor, both of them looking at her with the same intensity. From behind, the pale face of Professor Filip emerged and, as he saw her, he looked tense and then strangely relieved.

The first to break the silence was the stranger.

'I do not remember inviting you to our reunion but, now that you are here, you might as well join us.'

His tone was polite yet chilling. He took a step back from the door as if to invite Lia to enter. The dog went to its previous resting place, wrapped in the darkness of the corridor.

With its wings folded, it looked both terrifying and ridiculous. Why would anyone Wish to have such a monstrous pet by his side?

'I… I am here to… I am sorry to interrupt,' Lia mumbled, lifting herself up and edging towards the staircase. A frown from the old man and a low-pitched growl from the dog told her she had to stumble into the office instead.

The wooden door closed behind her, separating them from the winged beast in the hallway.

The room looked different. Nothing had changed place. The old furniture was all there, the books remained on the shelves, and the dark green curtains still framed the window. Still, it was a highly unusual scene.

For one thing, Professor Filip was not occupying his position at the desk, on the big chair that Lia mistook for a throne when she was younger (as a child, she often imagined her grandfather was the king of Ostrova). On the contrary, Filip was standing close to the corner she usually found refuge in. If she ever dreamt of seeing the headmaster frightened, this was certainly her moment. Somehow, she didn't enjoy it as much as she thought she would.

Lia decided to keep quiet and see what the others had to tell her. It was clear that Filip had taken the same decision and they were both waiting for the visitor to address them.

The visitor, on the other hand, didn't seem in a hurry to say anything. Instead, he turned towards the window and looked outside at the empty school yard.

'Do you have anything to tell us about Eduard, Lia?' he said finally, turning his piercing gaze towards her.

Lia was not surprised that he called her by her name. She wanted to ask how he knew her and her grandfather but did not dare interrupt.

'You know Eduard may have committed a crime against his community,' the visitor continued, 'and if you or your friends are hiding information about him, you are participating in this crime.'

His voice was still soft but, from the way he pronounced the word crime, you could see he was a man who enjoyed his job – passing judgement on others – and was good at it. Lia looked him in the eyes yet remained silent.

'We will find him, of that I can assure you, even if we have to search the seas, land, and skies,' the old man said and looked towards the door where, on the other side, the frightening winged creature kept guard.

Was he planning to send that monster after Eduard? Although it didn't draw blood, she could still feel the beast's teeth marks on her arm.

'Don't you dare harm him!' she shouted, startling herself but apparently not the stranger, who seemed to take pleasure in her reaction. It was Professor Filip who responded, from the other side of the room:

'Measure your words, insolent brat, it is the Cardinal you are talking to.' His face was livid, grasping to restore the little authority he had left.

What? This was the Cardinal? She knew the Cardinal was the head of the Wish Order and the right hand of the King, but she never imagined him like the person standing in front of her. She looked at him again, as if trying to check if Professor Filip was lying or not. What she saw was a flash of anger on the visitor's face.

'Headmaster, our conversation is over,' The Cardinal spat. 'Leave me alone with your student and wait for me in your classroom. I assume you have students to attend to somewhere, don't you?'

Filip bowed and then scurried out, leaving Lia alone with the Cardinal. It was the first time she would have preferred the company of the headmaster.

Lia did feel remarkably unafraid though, all things considered, having made peace with the idea that she would probably be expelled from school for what she just said.

She was ready to tell the Cardinal again not to harm Eduard when, to her surprise, the old man turned towards the headmaster's table, picked up an open chocolate box and asked if she wanted one. She said no but did not thank him.

What did this strange man want and, most of all, why was he interested in her in particular?

'Of course, Eduard will not be harmed,' the Cardinal said with a tight smile. 'I am the high representative of the Wish Order, Lia. We serve the King's people, not harm them. Didn't Professor Filip manage to teach you this in class?'

For a moment, she thought that maybe the Cardinal wanted to check if the headmaster was good at his job but dismissed the idea as silly.

No, he was here because of her. Could she pretend she didn't overhear that part of the conversation? Better to distract him and talk about Eduard.

'Will the dog be sent after him?' Lia asked.

'Yes, we might need to send Alar to find and bring him back, but not to hurt the boy in any way. As you know, child, your grandfather was the one who advocated listening before condemning. What we all want is to do the best, Lia, both for the village and for Eduard.' He looked like he wanted to add something else but changed his mind. 'The fearsome dog you mention is a symbol of care and loyalty towards the Kingdom and all its citizens. Alar is the visible side of my Wish to serve them.'

The emblem of the Order was two dog heads under an eight-ray sun. The very thought that someone would Wish to have such a monstrous creature around made her shiver. It also strengthened her belief that sometimes making no Wish was better than the alternative...

As if reading her mind, the Cardinal continued: 'Our Wishes need to reflect the care and love we have for our community and our land, otherwise both will disappear, and the world will turn to chaos.' He paused, waiting for his words to sink in.

'Imagine if all your friends in Ostrova Wished to have wings like Eduard did, and fly away like him, abandoning family and friends. What would happen to the village?'

'We would turn from a village of fishermen into one of people who fly, hunt birds, carry messages to other villages, trade with faraway places,' Lia answered back. This was actually something she wanted to talk to her grandfather about, if he ever got to prepare Eduard's defence.

The Cardinal's features twisted in a repulsive grin. He turned again towards the window.

'You are quite right. But this is something Eduard cannot decide alone. And this is why we need him back, to see if his Wish was indeed wise or unwise. Would you be ready to tell everyone your dream of changing Ostrova, Lia? Would you Wish yourself a big, strong pair of wings?'

He turned towards her and looked her in the eyes. Lia forced herself to hold his gaze and not to blink.

'I would try to convince the others that following one's dream is not a sin to be punished,' she said, her heart racing.

'And what is your dream?'

'I have no dream,' Lia answered boldly.

Who would have thought that she would end up confessing this not to her grandfather, nor Tudor, but the mighty head of the Wish Order?

The Cardinal sneered. It was clear he took it as yet another sign of rebellion instead of accepting her confession for what it was.

'You might have no dream here in Ostrova, but the world is larger than that, Lia. You can see for yourself if you come to visit the Order. If nothing else, it should convince you that our goal is not to punish but to help.'

What a dreadful prospect!

'I will not come. My Grandfather won't allow it. And I would rather run away than travel anywhere with you and your rotten dog,' Lia snapped.

She had crossed the line again but she didn't care. It was better to stop the madness right then and there.

Lia knew very well that the old man standing in front of her, not much taller than she was, was the emissary of the King. He had the power to take her away, even put her in prison for disobeying.

The Cardinal continued to fix her with his narrow, inquisitive eyes. 'Very well,' he said, after a long pause, 'I will discuss this with Alfred. I am not trying to take you away with me out of cruelty, but in order to protect you from a much greater evil. You are unaware of this, Lia, but you, and others like you, are in danger.'

He moved to put his hand on her shoulder, but she took a step back.

The Cardinal went on unperturbed: 'People have been disappearing throughout the Kingdom recently. They start their day normally, they go to school or work but then, before sunset, nobody can find them.

'We suspect a Wish Thief is abducting them in order to steal their Wishes. All the missing so far are young people who have not yet had their Rite and who, we suspect, have a Great Wish to make.' He paused again.

'This applies to you, Lia. You are among the Wishfull of our Kingdom. I know it, Filip knows it, and your grandfather does as well. We all need to work together to make sure you understand both the danger you are in and the responsibility you have towards yourself and others. I *have* to make sure of this.'

'You're lying!' Lia cried, shaking with anger. Her Orb was much more luminous than others' but that didn't mean her Wish was going to be different, did it? 'You're making things up to make me leave home and follow you and your ugly beast. Well, let me make it clear again: I am not going.'

She yanked the door open but the enormous dog stood up and blocked her way, barking. Lia stood her ground, too scared to reach for the stairs but determined not to go back to the Cardinal. Between these two evils, she was prepared to choose the dog.

'It's alright, Alar, let her pass,' she heard. The dog stopped barking and stepped aside.

Lia ran down the stairs. She felt the beast and its owner watching her as she stormed into the schoolyard and out of the main gate, not daring to look back.

Swallowing back tears, Lia ran. She thought about making her Wish there and then, just like Eduard did, and flying away, but she couldn't do that to her grandfather. Or Tudor. Yes, it was Tudor she needed to see but it was close to midday and he would be out fishing. If only he knew what had happened…

Lia plonked herself down by the lake, under an old willow tree, hidden from sight and away from the main road. She tried to calm down, but the voice of the Cardinal and the words "danger" and "responsibility" were echoing in her head.

She didn't feel in danger – except from the Cardinal and his beast! The evil old man made it all up about her being a Wishfull, probably with the help of Professor Filip.

Anger boiled in her veins. She had to warn her grandfather. But how could she tell him that she met the Cardinal and shouted at him several times?

Lia stumbled to her feet and walked by the lake, deep in thought. It was a beautiful afternoon, but she barely noticed it. Birds and dragonflies were flying around, reflecting the autumn sun on their wings. It would get cold soon. Winter was on the way and this small paradise would be gone.

If something happened to her, this might be the last time she saw the village in the autumn. Her shoulders hunched in misery.

The seat of the Wish Order was far away, up north, close to the tall mountains that separated the Eastern Kingdom from the Northern Stronghold. These were places she had only heard about in stories. She had no desire to see them in person. Her parents would have thought differently, perhaps. She had been told they were always up for an adventure: a trait she had not inherited.

Truth was, she didn't really want things to change. And no stupid Wish Thief would make her change everything. Who decided people needed to break their Orbs when they reached a certain age? And that the Wish Order should have the power to control the life of everyone in the Kingdom?

By the time she realised how far she had walked, it was late. As the shadows became longer and the lights of distant houses began to twinkle, Lia started heading back home.

OLD WISDOM GAVE US one Orb Wish and one alone. For what would unlimited Wish Orbs help a person achieve besides replacing carefulness by rashness, restraint by excess, virtue by foolishness?

(The Book of Wishes, The order of the realm)

Chapter 4. At Night

L IA TOOK A SIDE road on her return. She wanted to make sure she wouldn't meet Professor Filip or, worse yet, the Cardinal on her way back. Seeing the latter twice in the same day would surely amount to tempting fate.

At the edge of the forest, Lia did stumble upon familiar faces though. Eduard's mother and sister were travelling in a small carriage loaded with their belongings. Were they leaving? Lia called out and begged them to stop. Her calls had the contrary effect. The two women, startled, hurried even faster deep into the woods. In a moment, they were gone.

This has to be Filip's doing! Afraid for his position, he probably found a way to scare them into leaving before they could even talk to the Cardinal. Now Eduard had even less the chance of coming back and having a fair trial.

It was up to her, Tudor, and her grandfather to help him. Alfred needed to know what was happening at once. Maybe he could send someone after Eduard's family and bring them back? And he would certainly stop the Cardinal from ever trying to take her away.

More determined than before, Lia started running home.

The full moon helped her find her way back to the village. Once there, she was greeted by the usual veil of faint lights, resembling a swarm of fireflies, that hovered gently above Ostrova's streets at night. She used to love this Wish as a child, before she learnt the Order gave its permission for it.

Their house was at the other end of the village, isolated from other houses, far from the school and the small pier. Her grandfather wanted it that way as he enjoyed a good walk.

To her surprise, when she got home, Lia found everything submerged in complete darkness. *Grandfather isn't home*, she thought. This would have worried her greatly on any other occasion, since Alfred lived by a very strict daily routine, but he was probably out talking to the Cardinal.

Once more, Lia regretted having spent all day outside and not looking for her grandfather at once, to tell him everything. But it was too late, she was going to find out sooner or later what fate they decided for her. And then they will hear what *she* had to say about it.

Lia entered the small hallway leading to the living room and reached out for the lamp on the side table. It wasn't there. Odd.

Her eyes were getting used to the darkness and the soft light of the moon, peering through the big windows of the main room, helped her move easily in the familiar space.

She called out to her grandfather twice. There was no reply.

Lia picked up another oil lamp in the kitchen. Its delicate light reminded her of a Wish Orb. She made her way to the living room, determined to sit at the table and wait for her grandfather's return. It was important for him to hear her version of the day's events.

Before she could reach the table, Lia tripped over something and almost dropped the lamp. It was the chair from her grandfather's desk, lying on the floor in the middle of the room. What on earth was it doing there?

She didn't have time to think about it before the lamp's feeble light revealed the state of her grandfather's desk. His papers were scattered everywhere.

Lia instinctively took a step back. Someone did this. Certainly not Alfred. His Wish had been to become the community's living memory. Besides her, his Chronicles were what he cared for most in the world.

Boom, boom, boom. Her heart beat so fast it felt like it would soon break out of her chest. Someone must have broken into the house.

Someone was still there! Lia heard soft footsteps coming from upstairs. She froze. Whoever made a mess of Alfred's work was just a few metres away.

'Who's there?' Lia asked, trying hard not to betray her panic.

The footsteps stopped. Then, all of a sudden, a man rushed downstairs. She could only see his eyes; the rest of his face was covered. Lia gasped and darted to the other side of the big living room table, putting some distance between herself and the intruder.

Boom, boom, went her heart.

They both stood still, staring at each other. She couldn't tell if he was planning to harm her or not. If anything, his gaze seemed strangely empty, as if looking through her.

'What do you want?' she asked, almost in a whisper. There was no reply. The stranger made a jump towards the table and Lia immediately took a few steps back. She touched the windowsill. It felt ice cold.

Lia was surprised at how clearheaded she became all of a sudden. Time stood still as she began planning her escape.

She had three options. One was to make a run for the front door, in case the burglar came around the table. She could also run sideways, to the kitchen, where she had the backdoor to the garden. This was more difficult to do, considering the distance, but at least she could grab a knife from the kitchen and try to defend herself. Her third option was the most challenging but would surely confuse the man standing in front of her: she could try to get past him, up the staircase to her room, then onto the rooftop. On its right side, covered in ivy, there was a ladder and…

Bang! Before Lia could choose her move, she heard a loud noise and felt glass falling over her from behind like ice shards. She instinctively covered her head. Someone had just broken the window and was trying to grab her through it. Lia screamed and moved towards the table.

Touching its surface, she felt a piece of glass under her hand. She grabbed it without thinking. Her body was in control.

Meanwhile, the first intruder was already by her side. His arms wide open, he was just about to catch Lia. She raised her hand and struck him over the face. Her body, her body was saving her. She heard a roar and the stranger stumbled and took a few steps back, falling down.

Lia rushed to the front door. When she grabbed the handle, she felt the door open from outside. Rats! On the other side, another burglar was trying to get in. She pushed the door closed with all the strength she could muster and locked it.

It's over! No. There is the upstairs.

Returning to the living room, Lia saw the man who had broken the window trying to get in. The burglar she had struck was still to the side, covering his face with both hands.

Before she could rush upstairs, she heard a voice swearing. The man trying to climb in had cut himself on a glass shard. Lia didn't feel any pity for him.

Then, a soft light appeared in his hand. A Wish Orb?

Lia saw it quickly before the intruder threw it to the ground, in the middle of the living room. A faint vapour of light emerged from where the Orb fell, and quickly faded into the surrounding darkness. A Wish had been made. Another Wish. She remembered Eduard's face in a flash.

No time to think about it. The house quaked, and a sudden noise of cracked wood filled the air.

The next thing Lia saw were several tree trunks piercing through the floor. They looked like dark brown arms growing out of the earth underneath, reaching for her.

Her heart was racing. How could this happen? A gigantic plant was sitting in the middle of the living room. Someone had used his Wish to make it appear. And all to get her!

For a split-second, she considered using her own Orb to make the moving plant go away and stop the burglars. It was absurd.

Before she could dash upstairs, one branch of the enormous plant grabbed her left leg and started dragging her to the middle of the room. Lia screamed and began twisting and turning, like a trapped wild animal.

She tried to hold on to her grandfather's office table but couldn't. When she let go of it, the force threw her all the way to the main table, on the other side of the room. Strangely, she felt little pain on impact. The plant was still wrapped firmly around her ankle.

In her fall, Lia had kicked the small lamp off the table and it had broken on the floor. The wood and Alfred's papers started burning and the fire spread to the moving plant. The room was glowing, red and yellow, and the branch wrapped around her leg began shaking violently.

Boom, boom, the heart went. Her body was back in control.

She was fighting the burning branch trapping her foot. Through the smoke, Lia could hear the cries of the two intruders beside her. Instead of trying to escape, they jumped up to set her free. All three worked together.

No time to think about it.

Not until Lia saw something even more surprising than a Wish ritual performed in her house: the same burglar held two more Orbs in his hands.

After making a second Wish, the fire was put out and the plant had stopped moving. With its branches fallen to the ground, it looked like a giant octopus lying lifeless in the middle of the room.

The only visible source of light left was the third Wish Orb held by the intruder. Lia could not take her eyes off it. How…?

The two masked men grabbed her, ready to take her out of the half destroyed, smoky house. Lia thought she heard the burglar who had several Orbs whisper in her ear:

'Everything will be alright. You will be with your grandfather soon.'

She didn't fight anymore. She couldn't. Her body had given up.

As they carried her out, Lia felt a deep sadness. If these men were taking her away she would never see Ostrova and her home again.

And Tudor. He would come later to find both of them gone and a gigantic, burnt plant in the living room. He was going be worried sick…

But at least she would be with her grandfather. She could tell him how sorry she was for everything. It was all her fault. She should have never answered back to the Cardinal. She should have taken his offer. She…

As they were about to reach the door, the three of them heard loud noises coming from outside. It sounded like a fight. A loud bang and a howl ended the commotion. Lia remembered a third burglar was waiting there.

Before she could guess what was happening, the front door got smashed open and, in the bright moonlight, she saw Tudor rushing in with a wooden bat in his hands. Her heart jumped again.

Tudor was breathing heavily, his right sleeve ripped off and his eyes burning with rage. He was now a foot away from her and the two intruders. Lia had never been happier to see him and, without thinking, shouted his name.

The two men holding her were equally surprised, but clearly less excited to see her friend than she was. They stepped back and pulled her with them.

The man she managed to cut with the broken glass roared and jumped forward just to be swiftly thrown back by Tudor's fishing bat. He landed on her grandfather's desk, breaking it in two. Lia took advantage of the confusion and tried to set herself free from the last stranger still holding her. She couldn't.

She saw again the Wish Orb in the burglar's free hand. He was ready to make another Wish. This would be the end of Tudor, the end of them both. It could not be.

Lia threw her weight on the intruder, making him lose his balance. They all saw the Orb fly half across the room and smash into the wall. It had been broken. She held her breath. Nothing happened. The burglar hadn't made his Wish in time.

Energised by this unexpected victory, she bit his arm and set herself free. Tudor was ready to club him when Lia stepped in. She grabbed the burglar by the collar, shook him vigorously and asked what he did with her grandfather. Why wouldn't he say, why?

The sound of horses in the distance stopped her. More than one rider seemed to be galloping up the road. In the dark, Lia and Tudor looked at each other and understood. Then they heard the sinister laugher of the burglar on the floor. It was certain, others were coming for her.

Tudor was the first to react. He grabbed Lia by the hand and dragged her towards the kitchen saying: 'We have to go, now!' Lia resisted at first. She wanted to know what had happened to her grandfather. But there was no time. They had just a few moments before being outnumbered again.

Tudor and Lia got out through the kitchen door. They crossed the garden in a hurry, stepping over her grandfather's carefully tended squashes and carrots. Lia had tears in her eyes. As they were about to enter the forest, she looked back at the place she had called home for as long as she could remember. It felt as if she would never come back to it.

Tudor made the sign to hide. Silently, he pointed at a large winged creature flying above them, heading towards the lake. Lia knew very well what it was and whom it belonged to.

O UR DUTY IS TO care for each other. Not for a single or special
other, but for all others. Family and friends might bring us joy,
but it is only community that gives our life purpose. Wish-making
needs to respect this higher goal. No Wish should be made to help
family or friends. They come and go from our life and, in helping
them, our Wish is wasted. It is community that lives on and so our
first duty is to serve it and its custodians, the Wish Order and the
Kingdom.

(The Book of Wishes, On Wish-making)

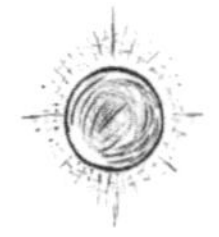

Chapter 5. In the Forest

THE ROAD WAS DARK and wet. The old, familiar forest felt deserted, cold, uninviting. Tudor led the way, holding Lia by the hand, regularly looking back to see if anyone was chasing them. There was no sign of that but, to be sure the riders could not reach them, Tudor took the two through the thickest part of the woods. Only Wish beasts could follow them there, but not the flying kind. Lia walked behind him, paying little attention to her surroundings.

All she could think about was her own guilt that her grandfather had been taken and she might never see him again. A few times she had the impulse to go back to the house and face the intruders but couldn't find the strength to do it. All she could do was follow Tudor.

As her thoughts became more organised, she remembered the Cardinal and his warning about people disappearing all over the Kingdom. Him saying he would protect her. What a liar! He must be behind all of this, plotting her kidnap, not even dirtying his own hands or getting his beastly dog involved. The creature probably saw it all and went back to its master.

But why take her grandfather and ruin his work? This was unnecessary and cruel. Most of all, who would ever use Wishes to do this? This is beyond unwise and if the Order's head approved it, then...

Lia still struggled to accept that one of the burglars used more than one Orb to catch her. Perhaps she had imagined it all. Nobody has more than one Orb and, even if someone took the Orb from another person, it would be impossible to use it for Wish-making. Something terrible had happened in her house that night and she was unable to make sense of it.

Without her noticing, they left the small road and started going directly through the trees, deeper into the woods. The light of the moon was barely piercing through the thick branches above and she was unable to see where they were heading. But she trusted Tudor's lead. They both knew that part of the forest very well; even so, it all looked unfamiliar to her on that night. Even when Tudor materialised his Wish Orb and shed a bit of light around, she could hardly recognise the place.

Her mind was stuck on the thought that she couldn't go back. There was nobody to go back to in Ostrova. Nobody who would believe her or protect her and her grandfather. Not if the Cardinal was involved.

He and his beast won't win! She resolved to find her grandfather and rebuild their lives away from the Order's reach. If only she knew where Alfred was...

After what felt like half an hour of walking, Tudor stopped in front of a stone wall covered in moss and wild fern. It was the last remnant of an ancient border the two of them had discovered in the forest many years ago. Their secret meeting place, the one they never shared with anyone else, not even Tudor's cousins or Lia's grandfather. The old wall and the abandoned stone shed attached to it were theirs alone.

As years went on, they stopped meeting there. Finally, they stopped thinking about the wall altogether. School and chores replaced playing and wandering around. The old shed and their childhoods remained somewhere in the past, the shared memory of what was and would never be again.

'You found it…' Lia whispered. 'I didn't think we would ever come back here.'

'Sit and rest. You have been through a lot tonight,' Tudor insisted, cleaning the bench along the shed's wall of dirt and dry leaves. She stopped him and used the bright light of her own Wish Orb to inspect his arm and face for signs of injury. Luckily there was just one big bruise on his left cheek. Tudor was not bothered by it.

'I cannot thank you enough for saving me, Tudor. My grandfather and I…' Lia wanted to go on but couldn't. She knew exactly what she wanted to say, had rehearsed it a few times in her head while walking through the forest. She took a deep breath.

'Now leave me here and return to the village. Matei and Clara must be awfully worried about you. They need you. They need you more than I do.' Tudor tried to say something but Lia stopped him.

'No, please, listen to me. I have been giving this a lot of thought.' She paused again for a moment. 'This is my problem and only I should deal with it. I think Grandfather and I have been targeted by the Wish Order and the Cardinal. I saw him in the village, he wanted me to go to the Order's Seat… He and his men will not stop until they catch me, Tudor.' Her voice started shaking but she carried on. 'I cannot go back to the village, I am not safe there, not without Grandfather. But I am not giving up. I will find him…' Tears were forming in her eyes. She couldn't look at Tudor anymore.

How could she ever leave him? And yet, she had to. It was not fair to mess up his life as well.

'Lia, I had some time to think about this too.' The firmness in his voice stopped her. She wiped away the tears budding in her eyes.

'First of all, you must know I am not going to leave you alone. We are in this together, do you understand? Yes, the men who tried to catch you will not give up. You won't be able to defend yourself against all of them.'

Lia wanted to intervene, but he didn't let her. Although stubborn and impulsive at times, she would always listen to him.

'Besides, Lia, it is not possible for me to return to Ostrova either. If you are right, and they are looking for you, then they know I helped you. They will try to catch me as well in order to get to you.'

Lia covered her face with her hands. Tudor was right. She did call out his name back at the house… She couldn't bear to look at him, she had made so many mistakes and he was paying the price.

'No, don't cry, there is nothing to cry about. I am the one who wants to help you. I am here with you because there is no other place I would rather be. You and your grandfather are like family to me, to us, you know that very well.' His voice broke down, heavy with emotion. Lia hugged him.

She felt so moved by his loyalty and, at the same time, so guilty for everything. For the way their lives had changed in just one day, for her part in it. Perhaps if she had listened more, if she had been more careful, if…

They spent the next moments in silence, in the abandoned shed lit by the gentle lights of their Wish Orbs. It was close to midnight. A soft, autumn wind rustled the leaves and the cries of foxes echoed through the trees.

They both felt safe there, as they once did in the village. It would make a good shelter, Tudor said, at least for the night. Yes, Lia agreed, they could use the shed while trying to find out more about what happened to her grandfather. Perhaps someone saw the thieves take him.

She started telling him everything that happened the day before, how she overheard Professor Filip talking to the Cardinal, how the Cardinal wanted to take her away, and how the winged dog they saw flying above them was his, the beast he Wished for, the one he had threatened to send after Eduard. Surely the dog will look for them, they had to go into hiding.

But what about Tudor's younger cousins? Lia tried to convince him once more to go back for their sakes. He could talk to Armin, the head of the Village Council. But, but would he believe Tudor and Lia's story? And, even if he did, would Armin and Professor Filip dare to go against the Cardinal? No, most probably going back would mean being sent to the dungeons of the Order…

'I need to return quickly and bring Matei and Clara with me,' Tudor decided. 'If I leave them now, the Village Council will decide their fate. They are both underage and not close to going through the Rite. Someone will be appointed to take care of them. Most probably Filip. I cannot let this happen.'

'But Tudor, if you bring them here, it will be so hard for them. They will miss their home and drop out of school… This whole mess might take a long time to solve,' Lia protested. 'Are you ready to change their lives this way because I am not.'

'We will all manage,' he said with all the confidence he could muster. 'Remember that Matei and Clara are good at taking care of themselves and they know the forest well. They can go back to school as soon as everything is cleared up.' She didn't believe him and suspected he barely could believe it himself.

Tudor told her to rest while he was away.

'Don't even think about it!' Lia replied. 'I am most certainly coming with you. You risked your life for me and now you are risking your only family. The least I can do is help.' Tudor was ready to contradict her but, seeing the determination in her eyes, backed down. Lia was going to join him back to the village no matter what and there was no point in discussing it any further.

Luckily for them, the night sky was becoming cloudy and, without a full moon, the forest was pitch dark. Since Tudor and his cousins lived in a small house by the lake, on a side road that was not usually lit at night, it was unlikely they would be seen. They had to hurry, though, and leave at once; the sun would rise in just a few hours.

***

When they arrived at Tudor's place, they didn't have to knock. Matei and Clara opened the door for them. They had been up all night, waiting for their cousin's return. It was hard to miss his absence, if anything because the three of them shared two rooms in a small hut made of straw, typical for poor fishermen in Ostrova.

Once inside, Matei, who greatly resembled a taller and slimmer Tudor, was the first to speak.

'Tudor, Lia, thank the Wish-Maker you are here,' he said. 'We didn't know what had happened to you! We didn't know whether we should wait here or go looking for you. In fact, we were just about to leave now!'

Unlike the eternal patience his cousin seemed to possess, Matei was not known for his reserved nature. Quite the opposite. His body and movements gave the impression of someone animated by metal springs and ready to jump.

In stark contrast, his sister Clara had a distinct air of restraint, quietness, almost melancholy about her. She also looked different than the boys, so much so that people couldn't tell they belonged to the same family. Her black hair, pale skin and violet eyes were the legacy of her late mother, a woman famed in Ostrova for her beauty.

'You were ready to leave the house?' Tudor whispered, trying to make Matei lower his voice as well.

'Yes, because we didn't know what had happened to you, Lia or her grandfather,' he said in a slightly softer voice.

'We started packing a few things,' Clara added, pointing to an open, half-full bag on the floor.

'Do you know anything about my grandfather?' Lia asked quickly.

'What I know is what Clara told me and what I saw myself,' Matei said. They all looked towards Clara, but she encouraged Matei to go on with a nod. 'After the two of you met at school and saw that weird old guy come in, followed by Professor Filip, Clara went to her classroom. It wasn't long after that she saw you out the window, Lia, rushing to the gate. You looked upset so she decided to go after you.'

Clara looked at Lia as if to apologise for following her or, at least, for having tried to do so.

'But, when she got out of the schoolyard, she couldn't see you anywhere. And then Professor Filip came along. He was talking to the stranger and apologising for your behaviour.' Matei couldn't hide his pride for Lia's actions, whatever it was that she had done to upset the two men. 'Clara hid behind the main gate. And this is how she overheard their conversation.'

Lia and Tudor looked at each other. Matei went on, happy to see the story captivating everyone there.

'The stranger was scolding Filip, imagine that! He sounded furious. He said you and your grandfather might be in danger and that Filip had only made things more difficult by not knowing how to guide you. He also said that he will have to deal with your grandfather now, before leaving the village, and that he wanted to make sure Filip would take care of things after he left.' Matei had spoken so fast that he needed to pause for breath.

'The bastard!' Lia shouted. She was shaking. 'He is the danger, he made all this happen, I am certain of it.'

'We don't know...' Tudor tried to say, but Lia wouldn't let him finish. She was on the verge of crying again and sat down at the table, feeling helpless. She had to know everything that happened that day, anything could be a clue and might help her find Alfred.

'My grandfather...', Lia managed to say before her voice broke.

'I am sorry but I don't know where your grandfather is,' Clara answered the question Lia couldn't formulate. 'After I heard the conversation between the old man and Professor Filip, I hurried to find Matei, but he was out fishing with Eric. It was only later in the afternoon that they returned to the pier,' Clara said softly.

Matei took over telling the story once more. 'My sister and I rushed to your house and, when we arrived, we saw your grandfather and the stranger arguing in the garden. I have never seen your grandfather shout at anyone before but this time he raised his voice. We couldn't make out anything they were saying, except your name.' It was about her, Lia thought, her grandfather confronted the Cardinal for her.

'We decided not to interrupt. Anything we could have told him, your grandfather already knew from the visitor. We came back in the evening instead and when we did…' He looked at his sister.

'What did you see? Was it my grandfather?' Lia asked, her heart beating faster.

'Your house was a mess…' Clara replied. 'The front door open, one window broken, books and papers thrown everywhere on the floor, half burnt, and…' she stopped as if looking for words to describe the scene.

'A giant plant had grown inside the house' Tudor finished her sentence. 'We know, Lia was there when all of this happened. But you were very lucky not to meet anyone else, especially the burglars who tried to kidnap her. I don't want to think what would have happened if you had.'

'We didn't see anyone, true. But we did find something in the house. On the broken table in the living room, someone scrawled a symbol. Two dog heads under an eight rays sun,' Matei added, this time in a whisper.

'The sign of the Wish Order…' Lia said. She stood up. 'You did very well to start packing. It's time to go, there is nothing for us here and the Cardinal made sure we wouldn't get any help. When our neighbours enter our house tomorrow, they will see the sign and know the Order had been there. Nobody will dare ask questions, they will all think my grandfather and I have been taken away.'

She was trembling with anger but there was great resolve in her voice. 'And when the Order comes back, they will come for you since they know Tudor is the one who helped me escape. We are all better off going now.' She took a deep breath. 'I am sorry…'

'No, Lia, it is not your fault,' Tudor said and took her hands in his. 'Don't apologize again. We are coming with you because we want to, because we are your friends and because we want to rescue your grandfather. It's our fight too from now on,' he said with a confident smile as Matei cheered and Clara nodded.

'There aren't many people who would miss us here anyway,' Matei added as if to persuade Lia none of them would regret leaving.

They had to leave swiftly, though. The four of them finished packing everything they thought could be useful. A few warm clothes, two light blankets, matches, rope, some food, and a map of Maar given to Matei by Lia's grandfather on his birthday.

Matei and Clara saw it all as a great adventure about to begin. Tudor was by her side. Their optimism almost made Lia forget her troubles.

As they reached the abandoned shed in the forest, the sun was up, and her heart was full of hope: they would be alright as long as they were together.

And together they would find Alfred, she was certain of it.

WHEN YOU ARE LOST, let the Orb's light guide you. When you are sad, rejoice in the Wish you've made. When you are fearful, look to the world your Wish helped build.

(Popular saying in Maar)

Chapter 6. The Cave

THE FOUR FRIENDS WOKE up late, after having spent most of the morning making themselves comfortable in the stone shed. Lia was the last one to wake and, when she did, it was to the smell of grilled fish. Matei and Tudor had paid a successful visit to the nearby river. Compared to their lake cousins, the fish were small, but there were plenty of them.

After a breakfast of fish and some bread packed for the road, Lia started telling Matei and Clara everything that happened the day before. They were as surprised as she was to find out that the man in grey was the Cardinal of the realm. Most of all, they found it hard to understand why the Wish Order would get involved in abducting an old man and trying to capture his granddaughter. The Cardinal said that Lia had a Great Wish to make – all her friends suspected as much – and that people like her had been disappearing from around the Kingdom, but could his story be trusted?

'Perhaps they were kidnapped by the Wish Order and forced to make certain Wishes by the Cardinal,' Lia wondered out loud.

'I doubt even he would go to such lengths…' Tudor said. 'Why would he? The Cardinal has enough power to force anyone into making the Wish he wants. The King gave him this authority. And he also commands the Guard of the Order. If you are right, Lia, then the riders we heard are probably the Order's.'

'What if he is trying to force people into making Wishes they don't want to make? Wishes that are forbidden? Like… like making trees grow out of someone's floor!' Lia insisted.

'But is that forbidden?' asked Matei, who was listening from the door.

'Well, it is certainly an unwise Wish, a Wish that doesn't really help anyone, right? Only someone forced into making such a Wish would do this. And then using another…' Lia fell silent. She was about to tell them that a second Wish has been made by the same burglar, and that he had a third Orb in his pocket. Would they believe her though?

'Did you ever hear of anyone having more than one Wish?' she asked her friends instead.

A long silence followed. Clara, who until then sat quietly by what once was a window sill, was the one who broke it.

'There's the story of Plyoc, the boy who had three Wishes to make. It's in one of the old books from your grandfather's library. He let me read it. I always wanted to ask him what he thought about this story. I assumed it was not a book we should talk about, you know, one of the banned ones.'

'What is it about?' Lia asked. 'I don't know it, but I do know Grandfather kept some banned books in his library. He always had them under key and told me there would come a time to read them, when I was ready. I guess you were ready for this one,' she said with a smile. Clara smiled back and went on telling the story.

'What I remember is that Plyoc was a normal boy, living in a far-off land, perhaps in the Kingdom of the North. Or maybe the land beyond the Endless Sea, I'm not sure. He was born to make three Great Wishes, and his two older brothers became jealous because of it. In fact, they were so jealous that, when the time came for them to make their own Wishes, all they could Wish for was to destroy one of their young brother's Wish Orbs. And so, Plyoc had only one Wish left to make.'

Clara fell silent for a moment. Either she couldn't remember the ending or maybe she was looking for a better one.

'So, what happened?' Tudor asked.

'Yeah, don't keep us hanging,' Matei added impatiently.

Turning towards them, Clara said with a smile: 'What happened is that Plyoc used his last remaining Wish to re-create the wasted Wish Orbs of his two brothers. Can you imagine?'

'Ha, now that was unexpected,' said Matei. 'I would have turned them into mice for robbing me of my Wishes,' he announced while showing the rest just how tiny the two brothers would have become.

'Yes, in the end he actually made their own Wishes come true, for free,' added Tudor. 'They wanted him to have no Wish of his own, and this is what happened. It is kind of sad for Plyoc in fact…'

'Unless…' said Lia.

'Unless what?' asked Tudor.

'Nothing,' she replied. But thought that Plyoc might have wanted it that way. Maybe it was his own Wish not to have any "Great Wishes" to make, certainly not three of them. And he made this Wish come true by forgiving and helping his brothers. A seemingly selfless act.

Perhaps she should do the same and use her own Wish right there to be reunited with Grandfather! Yes, Wishes should never act against the will of others – it was against the laws of the Order – but surely her grandfather would rather be with her than wherever he was. And they would all understand why she did it. Or would they?

Above all, she was afraid of Alfred's reaction. He certainly would not want her to use her Wish this way and he would probably know why she really did it. Lia couldn't bear imagining the disappointed look in his eyes.

'What a weird story, Clara,' Matei went on, visibly amused. His good mood was contagious and Lia was grateful for it. 'Well, if I had three Wishes to make, I would certainly Wish never to go tired, thirsty or hungry ever again,' he said counting each Wish on his fingers.

'How nice to always think of yourself', Clara teased her brother.

'Speaking of hunger,' Tudor intervened, 'you know the forest won't feed us unless we make it, so how about we all go back and find something tasty for dinner?' His proposal was received with enthusiasm.

Matei and Tudor went back to the small river to try their luck again. Lia and Clara, on the other hand, decided to gather any fruits and mushrooms lying around. The four friends agreed to stay in earshot of each other. After Matei swore to defend them all by Wishing to become a human fireball, if needed, each pair went on its way.

Lia was glad to be in Clara's company for a while. It gave her time to think. She had no idea where to go from there. If only she knew where her grandfather was, if only she could be sure he was taken by the Order...

The two walked in silence near a ravine in the forest. One looked for mushrooms, the other for wild berries. Lia remembered the place well. She used to play hide and seek there with Tudor a few years ago, when she was Clara's age. At the end of the ravine, there was a small cave.

It was inside this cave that Lia had spent her only night away from home, when she had her first – and only – big fight with her grandfather. He had retired as headmaster and his successor, Professor Filip, was already making her life miserable. She could not stand going to school anymore and told her grandfather exactly that.

For the first time in her life, she saw him become furious with her. Lia remembered shouting that she was a grown-up and she could make up her own mind about her own future. Alfred disagreed. Not as long as she lived under his roof.

And so, she ran out of the house, not taking anything with her and not knowing where she was going, punishing her grandfather by not returning home the whole night. She'd regretted it ever since. Even at the time she knew he and Tudor would be looking for her, so she had started wandering deeper and deeper into the forest.

It was a summer night, without moon, rainy and cold. Lia's clothes were drenched in water and she was shivering, ready to return, when she saw the entrance to the cave. It was a lucky discovery. She was able to make a small fire inside and had time to calm down and think, until sleep took over.

She had a long, dreamless night. All Lia could remember was that she woke up suddenly from it, determined to return home.

If only she could fall asleep there again and then return home. Last time Lia was in the cave she felt confused, scared and angry. Not much had changed. Maybe a quick visit back would help her find peace again?

Even though she knew it was a silly idea, she asked Clara to check on the boys. Seeing her friend disappear behind the trees, Lia hurried towards the cave's entrance. She wanted to be there, alone, just for a few minutes.

As she went in, the coolness and darkness of the place took her by surprise. Lia remembered the small fire she had made years ago and, sure enough, found its mark on the ground near the entrance.

What if others had discovered the cave in the meantime? What if they were still there, watching her from the darkness, ready to strike? You are being silly again, she thought.

In just a few moments she was able to see better inside. Everything in the cave looked just as she would have expected. The stalagmites and stalactites towards the back created a wall that looked like wet tree trunks coming together. She wondered what was beyond them.

As Lia moved deeper inside the cave, she slipped and fell. Then, looking up again, she couldn't believe her eyes. Could this be?

She was no longer in a cave but back inside the forest. Yet it was certainly not the forest she had left behind a moment ago. The trees of this forest were entirely made of water. Sand and small shells, like the ones she sometimes discovered by the lake, made up the grass. It felt like full summer.

Am I dreaming? Lia asked herself as she stepped on the yellow, warm sand. A strange breeze caressed her cheeks, and the sound of seagulls echoed from the canopy of giant, liquid trees. None of the seagulls were anywhere in sight.

Lia was torn between fear and an overwhelming desire to explore what could only be a Wish world. Professor Filip gave such worlds as examples of what one should never Wish for: a selfish, arrogant Wish that makes you the creator of a universe nobody needs or cares about. They were also warned about getting trapped inside Wish worlds and never finding the way out…

For the first time in her life, Lia decided to trust Filip and go back. She gasped as she looked behind her. The cave was gone. She was surrounded by plants made of water, standing under the hot afternoon sun.

Her heart started beating fast. The stories were true! She was alone, stuck in a strange place she might not be able to leave. Unless, unless she managed to find the creator of this world… who might be anywhere, perhaps far, far away. Or dangerous – the kind of person Filip warned them about.

She began calling for someone, anyone. But all she could hear back were the invisible seagulls, mocking her cries from above.

At first, Lia decided to stand still, in case the cave magically reappeared around her. As this didn't happen, she started moving around, determined to find a way out.

This new forest seemed to extend in all directions for as far as she could see (and she was able to see quite far since all the trees were rather transparent). As she moved, Lia became fascinated by how much the trees resembled real ones, in all details but one – their substance. She started touching them. Her hand went right through their trunks and come out on the other side.

Strangely, she was not getting her hands wet either. It was as if the water was meant to stay inside the trees and, as soon as she tried to catch some of it, the drops quickly found their way back to the safety of the tree trunk. The trees attracted all the water and kept it in place, Lia thought.

To test her hypothesis, she started running into them, splashing trunks and branches, excited to see the water naturally coming back, recreating the familiar shapes.

An hour must have passed while she explored the seemingly endless world of water-plants, unseen seagulls, and yellow sands. As hunger started to kick in though, Lia realised that she might end up starving if she couldn't return to the real forest she came from.

Her friends must be extremely worried. They probably thought she had been taken by the Order. Who would look for her in the small cave at the end of the ravine? And, even if they did, what good would it do for them to be trapped with her in this other world?

Perhaps she could use her own Wish to escape. She knew from Grandfather that no Wish can cancel another person's Wish. So, if the creator of this world wanted to keep visitors inside, then she couldn't undo this.

But what if this wasn't the case? What if this was not a Wish world but simply another world she just happened to stumble upon? That would make it an ideal hiding place, if only she could find the way out. Her Wish could help her locate the entrance and find it again in the future.

As she reached this conclusion, Lia made her Orb appear.

And as soon as she did, the trees around her started shaking violently. It was as if they were ready to move, take their watery roots out of the sand and run away. She felt the ground quake.

For a split second, a deep silence surrounded her. Lia felt faint with fear.

And then, at once, the trees started collapsing, one by one. The water inside them fell to the ground and, because they were so tall, and because there were so many of them, the water level started rising alarmingly fast. Lia held on to her Wish Orb while being pushed around by gigantic waves.

She screamed, but no sound came out. The fear was chocking her.

There were no more trees around, only water. Water so high Lia could not see its surface while her feet remained on the sand. She started to move her arms and legs frantically, trying to push herself upwards. It didn't work, she wasn't able to raise herself from the bottom.

Lia was a strong swimmer, that was sure, but she couldn't hold her breath much longer. With a last effort, she looked at her Wish Orb and thought about getting out, back to the cave, then threw it to the ground. The Orb floated gently down and rested on the sand. It didn't break.

This was the end.

Lia opened her mouth. She felt the taste of water, a taste she knew well from all the sunny days spent swimming in the lake, Tudor by her side.

No more air in her lungs.

But then breathing. In and out.

How could that be? She was breathing – perfectly in fact – under water.

She started looking all around her for an explanation. She was fully immersed. Her Wish Orb was still intact, laying on the sand.

As she picked it up, Lia heard a small but strangely commanding voice say: 'Put that away.'

A WISH IS NOT a desire, for desires often cloud our mind. A Wish is not a plan, for plans often fail. A Wish is not a gift, as gifts can be returned. A Wish is not a dream, for dreams we have no control over.

(*The Book of Wishes*, On Wishes and Wish Orbs)

Chapter 7. The Future

LIA STARTED WALKING AROUND, surveying the yellow sands, trying to find who could have spoken to her. She was afraid to open her mouth again under water. Could her words even be heard?

Maybe if she did what she was asked, the person would talk to her again. As instructed, Lia made her Orb disappear.

'Very good,' the voice said.

It was coming from below, from the sand at her feet. She looked closely but everything was yellow and bright. Except for a few dark spots that, upon close inspection, belonged to a tiny salamander.

The black and yellow creature matched so perfectly its environment that it was no surprise she had missed it at first. How many other living creatures had she failed to see? Lia looked around carefully.

'You are from the Outer world,' the salamander spoke again.

'I… Yes…' Lia replied, astonished both that a tiny salamander could talk and that she herself could speak under water.

She knew Wish animals could be made to speak, but never expected to be addressed by one. It was, after all, forbidden by the Order to create talking animals; not only would the Wish-Maker be sent to prison, but the animal would be sacrificed for breaking the law of the land. That was the case, at least, in the "Outer world."

'What… who are you?' Lia said, but soon regretted asking the question. The tiny salamander was clearly not happy to be interrogated. It turned its head away and stayed silent.

'I am sorry, I didn't mean to offend you in any way. It's just that I am lost here and you are the first… well, the first being I found in this empty world.'

'Empty?' the salamander interjected. 'Is this what you call empty? Little girl, there are millions, no, tens of millions of *beings* like me here. But what would you know? A person from the Outer world – someone who only notices those things that are big enough to crush her.'

Lia could see they got off to a wrong start and wanted to change the topic. Then she remembered how the conversation actually got started in the first place and asked:

'Why did you want me to put my Wish Orb away?'

'Oh, that,' answered the salamander, for the first time interested to talk about something. 'Your Orb is strong, child, and it is disturbing the dreams. Didn't you see that? Look at the chaos you've created around you.'

It was true, the trees had vanished the moment she made her Wish Orb visible. But why? And what did they have to do with dreams? Lia was about to ask precisely that question when she saw the salamander turn around and look into the distance. Initially she thought it might have lost interest again in the conversation, but then she saw a human-like shape appear on the horizon and move quickly towards them.

It was an old man, as far as Lia could tell, dressed in a strange outfit and walking very fast for his age (and for someone walking under water). He seemed to be wearing a long blue cape and, on his head, a tall hat made of leaves. She would certainly not have wanted to meet this strange looking person anywhere else but, there, she was ecstatic to see him. Maybe he was friendlier than the tiny salamander.

When he reached them, Lia realised he was a really tall man, made even taller by his pointy, leafy hat. The cape, through the water, looked magnificent, displaying shades of blue and green that Lia had never seen before.

'Hello,' she said hesitantly.

'There is no point talking to him' answered the salamander, who was climbing the cape of the old man. A small yellow dot in a sea of blue and green. The stranger waited patiently for the tiny creature to make its way up, reach the hat and find a cosy place between the leaves.

He didn't seem to have noticed Lia at all, so she proceeded to telling him that she was from Ostrova and that she found herself there by accident after exploring the inside of a cave in the nearby forest.

The old man looked at her intensely. His dark green eyes were kind and inquisitive; yet, he kept quiet.

A seagull finally appeared. It was flying or, rather, swimming above them where Lia could no longer see the surface of the water. The stranger suddenly became animated, flapping his hands and making seagull-like sounds. They were so accurate that, at first, Lia thought he had a seagull hidden somewhere inside his cape.

But no, the old man was capable of imitating seagulls perfectly. And, as if to demonstrate his many talents, he started making other bird noises too. The stranger's excitement was contagious, and Lia found herself enjoying the little performance. Even the salamander didn't object to any of it.

'He is excellent at this,' Lia said, talking to the only being there who was able or willing to communicate with her.

'Yes, you can say so,' answered the salamander.

'What was his Wish, to imitate birds?' she asked out of curiosity.

'His Wish? Do you still think you are in the Outer world? Child, we do not speak of Wishes here. And, most of all, we don't give them shape.' Lia apologized again for her mistake and reminded the salamander that she didn't know anything about the world she was in, including how to leave it.

'What would you want to leave it for?' asked the tiny creature.

Lia was surprised by the question. After learning Wishes were forbidden there, why was she in such a hurry to leave? Wasn't that what she always wanted? On the other hand, how could she live there, with nobody around other than seagulls, the strange old man speaking their language, and the moody salamander? What about her friends and her grandfather?

She told the salamander that she had friends in the "Outer world" and that they were waiting for her. They were probably very anxious about her absence. Besides, she could not continue staying under water forever; even if she could breathe there, that was not something she would get used to.

The old man, who had been looking up all this time, turned to Lia. With a sign of his hand, the water split right between them and started quickly moving away. Before Lia could blink, there was no more water around, just the yellow sand under their feet. Everything was bathed in light, even if there was no actual sun to be seen in the sky.

'Much better,' said the salamander. 'My skin was getting all wrinkly.'

The old man replied with a chirp.

He must be the master of this place, Lia thought. And the salamander was probably his voice. Perhaps she could convince it to help her get out.

'Excuse me,' she said timidly, 'this is all very nice, but I am still not that eager to live here… would it be possible to return to the cave in the forest? Will you help me?'

'You are truly a child of the Outer world' said the salamander, sounding disappointed. 'Everything you wish for needs to be done. You are lost, you wish to go back. You are alone, you wish to be with your friends. Wishes, wishes…' it said mockingly. 'Do you ever allow yourself to dream, Lia?'

'How do you know my name?' Lia said, beginning to fear it was all a plot orchestrated by the Cardinal. He had also asked her about her dreams. She took a step back but there was nowhere to run or hide.

'We know your name because we know your dreams, from when you were a young child. A child who fell asleep in a cave,' said the salamander, trying to reassure her.

'You know about that? You saw me then, sleeping in the cave?' Lia asked hesitantly.

'No, we did not see you because we are not of the Outer world, but we were there, in the dream you probably don't remember. And we talked for days, even months, who knows,' replied the salamander. The old man made new seagull noises, as if to confirm what had been said.

'That is impossible. I only spent one night in the cave. Actually, it was even less than that. And I remember this because, as soon as I woke up, I went back home.' Lia was getting angry. She could see the two were making up things just to keep her there.

'And how do you think you made up your mind about that?' asked the salamander softly.

'I… I just did!' Lia replied confidently, even if she started doubting herself. Had she visited this world before? In her dreams? It all sounded very unlikely but, then again, she was there, and she was awake (or was she?).

'If you say I met you in my dreams back then, why I am seeing you now, fully awake? I certainly did not fall sleep in the cave this time.'

'Both then and now you were running away, no?' said the tiny creature. It certainly knew more about her than Lia wanted. 'And both then and now you refuse to let yourself dream. Still, this is what we have to offer,' the salamander concluded.

'Dreams? What need do I have for them when my grandfather was taken by the Wish Order and my friends are alone in the forest, worried sick about me?' Lia asked, losing her patience. 'I want to go back!' she shouted.

The old man, who had been humming, stopped and looked at her. His eyes were full of compassion. For a moment, she remembered the look her grandfather gave her when she was upset. A look she might never see again.

He slowly took his big cape off and Lia saw that it had the same delightful colours on both sides. As he laid the cape on the ground, carefully, she felt something important was about to happen. The salamander was equally quiet, perhaps in anticipation.

The old man left the cape down for a moment and then, with a sudden movement, lifted it in the air and placed it back on his shoulders. In the sand under it, an eye of water as blue and clear as the cape itself had appeared. Lia looked inside the clear water but could not see the bottom. An endless pit had just opened in front of them.

'What is this?' Lia asked, not really expecting an answer. The salamander didn't miss the question, however.

'It is the stuff of dreams, like everything else here.'

'Is it in my dream?' Lia asked again, starting to question whether she was actually dreaming or not.

'How typical, everything needs to be about you, dear child,' the salamander answered mockingly. 'This, what you see around you, doesn't belong to one dream or one person, and it was certainly not made by you or for you,' it continued. 'However, you would be wrong to dismiss it, like most Outer world people do, as a simple dream.'

She was actually thinking that. Or at least hoping it was a simple dream and that she would wake up in the cave, or in the stone shed in the forest or, even better, at home, with Grandfather by her side.

'You wanted to see your grandfather Alfred and your friends. Well, then, just look, look in front of you' said the salamander, pointing its tiny head towards the round, clear surface of the water.

At first, Lia could not see anything other than a deep shade of blue and her own face reflected in it. But then, as the water began to quiver gently, as if moved by a calm breeze, she started to notice the inside of a house. It was her home, the living room and, at the desk, her grandfather working.

'What is this?' she asked, but the salamander kept quiet. The old man seemed to have lost interest in her once more and was closely inspecting the sand instead.

Lia recognised the scene reflected in the water. It was the day she had that big fight with her grandfather, the one that led her to spend the night in the cave. She saw her grandfather getting more and more upset with her reaction. Lia couldn't hear what they were saying to each other and was grateful for it.

Missing the sound of their voices made her focus more on Alfred's face. The sadness she saw in his eyes was greater than the anger she remembered. Involuntarily, tears started rolling down her cheeks, yet she couldn't look away.

Lia asked the old man in front of her: 'Do you know where he is now?'

He replied, but with the song of a blackbird. Perhaps he wanted to tell her things about her grandfather. Or maybe he was mad or didn't know anything at all. In any case, the surface of the tiny pool of water between them became agitated once more, as if a stronger wind was blowing through it.

Lia could see her grandfather again. This time, however, he was standing in a dark, small room, looking at the ground. He did not move. He could not move. His hands were chained to the wall.

'Where is this?' Lia asked, her voice rising in panic. With a jump she was by the old man's side, grabbing him by the cape and asking loudly 'Where is he?' Neither he nor the salamander replied. She looked back and saw the sign of the Wish Order reflected in the water. There was no denying it, her grandfather was a prisoner in the dungeons of the Order!

'*Dreams show you what was, is, or will be,*' the salamander said, finally breaking the silence. '*It is not what you wish for, but what you came to see.*'

Lia wanted to get out of there as soon as possible. She had to go to the Order's fortress and set her grandfather free, there was no time to lose.

'*And if your travels take you to places far and wide,*' she heard the salamander continue, each word echoing ever more loudly. '*Remember who's beside you, and those you left behind.*'

These last words were not spoken by the salamander anymore. When Lia looked up, she saw the old man talking, in the voice of the salamander.

She didn't have time to wonder about it because the light started to dim fast. The transition from day to night was so quick that just a moment later, a dark, moonless night embraced the whole land. The only source of light was coming from the small pond in front of them.

And, as she looked at the surface of the water once more, Lia saw her friends, Tudor, Clara and Matei, being chased by soldiers. She was overwhelmed by terror at the sight of the soldiers getting closer. Lia wanted to shout but they couldn't hear her, just as she didn't hear them.

She couldn't bear looking at the water anymore. All she did was ask 'why,' without hoping for an answer. The stranger and his salamander were both gone. But the voice of the salamander (or was it that of the old man?) was echoing everywhere around her, a voice deeper and more powerful than anything Lia ever heard before.

'*The Outer world loses its shine, as Wishes wilt and people pass. He looks for you and if you're found, your Wish will fade, and his will last.*'

The echo of these last words was deafening.

Then there was darkness. No more light in the water, no more water or sand. Lia felt dizzy and had to sit down. As she started touching the ground, she felt wet, slippery stones. She looked around and, in a new, dim light, she could see the cave wall. She was back. The sun was up in the sky outside.

A whole night must had passed, Lia thought, as she slowly found her way out, shaken. Her friends were probably gone. The image of them being chased was haunting her as she started running through the ravine, desperate to reach the stone shed in the forest.

'They are alright, but not as lucky as they were this morning,' Lia heard a voice say behind her. She almost screamed.

It was Clara, emerging from behind a tree.

Fear turned to joy, overwhelming joy. She hugged Clara and kept telling her that she was back.

Clara seemed surprised and, smiling awkwardly, said 'I am back, yes, from seeing the boys…' Lia checked if she was joking. No. She didn't seem to have noticed her absence for half a day. How was that possible?

One thing was certain, Lia wasn't ready to talk about what had happened in the cave. Her friends wouldn't believe her. She barely believed it herself.

When she finally accepted that nobody had noticed her absence – more than this, that she had not been absent at all – Lia decided not to mention anything of what she had seen. She needed time to think about it all.

Her grandfather was being kept prisoner and her friends were at risk of capture as well. Unless she did something about it.

That evening, the four of them gathered around the fire and made dinner. Matei and Tudor were in a particularly good mood and their continuous chatter made it easier for Lia not to participate. When they wanted to decide what to do next, she said it had been a tiring day for all and it was better to talk about it in the morning.

THE FUTURE

At night, when everyone was asleep, Lia silently packed a few clothes, some food and water, and took the map of Maar with her. She whispered 'forgive me,' and quietly walked out into the forest.

63

THE BOOK OF WISHES was put together from earlier writings by Eugen, the first Cardinal of the Wish Order soon after its establishment in 299, during the rule of King Septim the Weak. At the time, the King ruled from the Castle of Samor over the entire land of Maar and its four provinces, Eastern, Western, Northern and Southern. King Septim couldn't govern Maar alone towards the end of his days and, lacking legitimate heirs, decided to name Eugen as his successor, effectively uniting the new and powerful Order with the Crown. This decision was contested by Roland, the lord of the Southern province, who threatened to leave the common realm should Eugen become King. The South and the North did not recognise the legitimacy of the Wish Order and feared the ambitious Cardinal and his Wish Council. Eugene, the first Cardinal-King, waged war on the South, a war that lasted 30 years and rallied all the other provinces against the East. At the end, the Eastern Kingdom was born as the largest and most powerful in Maar, having defeated and burned to the ground all of the cities in the South. Valer, the Cardinal-King at the time, wanted to do the same with the rebellious North and West, but royalists in the East, led by young Elena, the self-proclaimed granddaughter of Septim, killed him and reclaimed the throne. The Wish Order was separated once more from the Crown and the new Cardinal, Mihai, swore his allegiance to Queen Elena of the East. Even if the precepts of the Book of Wishes continued to guide all Wish-Makers in Maar, the power of the Order was confined to the Eastern Kingdom alone, cut away from the Northern Stronghold, the Western Principality, and the now wild and barren lands to the South.

(from *The Chronicles of Maar*, by Alfred from Ostrova)

Chapter 8. The Council

T HE ROOM WAS WELL lit by a chandelier made up of hundreds of candles, hanging high above a long, rectangular table. The table itself had been cut from a single block of wood and its legs displayed the carved heads of mythical beasts.

Eight chairs were placed at the table, three on each side and two, taller than the rest, at each end. They were all painted in shades of silver and gold and had carved emblems on top. One of the tall end chairs displayed two dog heads and, above them, a golden sun. The opposite one, the tallest in the room, showed three Wish Orbs, each one bearing its own crown.

Except for the flickering candles above, drawing lively shadows on the stonewalls, nothing moved or made any sound in the room. At the window, the Cardinal, hidden from sight behind thick curtains, stood perfectly still, looking out into the night.

He was so deep in thought that he didn't hear the footsteps outside or the gentle knock on the door. After a few moments, the knock was repeated. As if awakened from a dream, the Cardinal came from behind the curtains and said loudly 'come in'.

A young man appeared and, after bowing to the ground, told the Cardinal that the magistrates were in the waiting room, ready for council.

'Invite them in,' he replied and moved towards the tall chair with sculpted dog heads under the golden sun. Holding the gold painted sun with one hand, as if to regain his balance, the Cardinal waited in silence.

His eyes fell on the large tapestry on the opposite wall. It was an embroidered map of the kingdoms of the land. The Eastern Kingdom's cities and borders were shown in gold. The Northern Stronghold and its capital city, Eledor, appeared in silver. To the west, between the Eastern Kingdom and the Endless Sea, the lands of the Western Principality were depicted in copper. To the south, all city names had been removed, leaving only empty, iron marks in the barren lands. The Endless Sea was shown in blue-green with the help of thousands of small turquoise stones. At the top of the tapestry, embroidered with rubies and gold, a single word stood out: MAAR.

The door opened and six magistrates came into the room. After each of them bowed in front of the Cardinal, they swiftly found their assigned places at the table. 'For the King and the Order,' they said at once and waited for the Cardinal to take his seat.

He did not. Instead, he walked back to the windowsill and continued to look outside as if expecting someone else to join them.

'Magistrates,' he addressed the group after a moment of silence, 'this is a difficult time for the Order and for our Kingdom. Our very existence is under threat.' He spoke softly, yet firmly, as he moved back to the table and sat in the tall chair marked with the Order's symbol. The others allowed themselves to take their seats.

'We have been fighting against selfish, unwise Wishes for more than three hundred years and yet, today, we face a much more cunning enemy than ever before. An enemy that endangers the peaceful lives of all the people of Maar.'

He looked around the table to study the effect of his words on the audience. 'Today we received the news that the same evil is now spreading from Eledor to Warindor. In how we deal with this wickedness rests our survival, or our collective doom,' the Cardinal said gravely.

'Your Excellence,' someone intervened from across the table. It was a younger man with red hair and a matching, rosy face. He sat in the chair ornamented with a six-winged eagle, the symbol of the Northern Heights.

'If I am allowed to speak,' he continued after the Cardinal gave a gentle nod, 'there have been only two cases of Wish theft in the Heights.'

'Only two?' the Cardinal asked dryly. 'Well then, maybe we should all learn from you, Joreas. Do tell us why you think the Thief was so merciful with your mountainous province. Advise us, please.'

Joreas had clearly lost his nerve but could not back down. He started timidly but became more confident as he spoke.

'Well, I think advising is a strong word… but in the Heights we have our Wish vultures circle around villages and roads, hovering above even the most inaccessible areas. I have my Tars fly above the border with Eledor almost every day. He is instructed to stop anyone who carries Wish Orbs and to alert our soldiers.'

'Interesting' said the Cardinal. 'And how exactly does your… bird see Wish Orbs hidden from sight? Say, under cloths or in a bag perhaps? And does Tars also patrol the border at night?'

Joreas started looking around the table for ideas. Nobody dared come to his rescue, so he bowed his head and did not reply.

'Well, now that we clarified how effective the Heights are in stopping the Wish Thief, let me share with you a little experience from a recent visit I did,' the Cardinal said, sounding both annoyed and strangely satisfied. 'It was in your part of the realm, Istol,' he added, looking towards a tall, round man, sitting on a chair ornamented with two fish and a waterlily.

Istol murmured something but the Cardinal continued, 'I was in the small village of Ostrova, trying to take care of one of our last Wishfulls. Do you know who I am talking about?'

'Yes, your Excellency, it must be Lia, the granddaughter of Alfred, the former schoolmaster,' Istol replied without any enthusiasm.

'Indeed. Unfortunately, I was unable to convince her to come with me, largely because of the incompetence of the current headmaster – the one called Filip, a person you assigned to the job?' the Cardinal asked. The magistrate was caught between the need to deny ever having met Filip and the impossibility of doing so.

'I ordered him to leave office as headmaster,' the Cardinal said. 'I hope you will agree with this, my dear magistrate of the Great Lake.' Istol nodded vigorously.

'Moreover,' the Cardinal announced, 'I tried to reach the child, but she disappeared. I have placed her on our list of missing Wish bearers and, as a subject of the Order, and a Wishfull one, she is to be found at all costs and brought directly to me.'

Trying to mask his anger, the Cardinal went on with his story:

'It seems Professor Filip, and even her grandfather, of whom many of you know, didn't manage to instil in her the desire to become a good citizen of the East. And this, my friends, is the first evil we had always battled against. She, and others like her, must not join the ranks of the lost, nor be robbed of a Great Wish,' he added firmly.

'Your Excellence,' the only woman in the room interrupted. As the high magistrate of Farig, the easternmost province, her chair was carved with a magpie carrying three moons in its claws.

The Cardinal looked across the Council table in surprise. When he realised who had spoken, he regained his composure.

'Lady Aril, go on.'

'Thank you, your Excellence,' she replied and stood up.

Tall, with dark blue eyes and a hair so blonde it almost looked white, Lady Aril left her chair and walked confidently towards the tapestry on the wall. The robe she wore, displaying a deep shade of purple, contrasted greatly with her pale complexion. All the eyes were on her when she turned around. The Cardinal was smiling while the magistrates waited in silence.

'If you allow me, Sire,' Lady Aril continued undisturbed. 'I think we have something to learn from Lord Joreas.' The head of the Eastern Heights gasped, surprised to be mentioned and, even more, agreed with.

'Of course, the low number of thefts in the Heights can only be attributed to luck,' she continued, sending Joreas a casual smile, 'but we can learn from monitoring key points in our kingdom. Here is what I propose.'

And, with a swing of her hand, Aril sent small lights floating towards the wall, lights that started hovering across different places on the map of the Eastern Kingdom.

'These are the main passage points of our realm,' she continued, looking directly at the Cardinal. 'Some of them are well known, like crossroads and boarders, others we know less and some we have just discovered.'

'And how did you learn about them?' Joreas asked, infuriated. She ignored him and continued talking only to the Cardinal.

'Your Excellency, given the growing danger, I have been tracking for a few months the meeting places and side roads across the Kingdom. All I need is your approval for the Council's riders to be placed there, ready to be our eyes, ears and, most of all, our hands and swords.'

She went on to describe each one of her chosen places, offering precise details regarding their location and justifying her picks. At first, the other magistrates were incredulous and several of them interrupted to question her about locations within their own realms. As she went on, they fell silent, one by one. The Cardinal himself seemed to enjoy the presentation and, on several occasions, nodded and encouraged her to go on.

As she finished, Lady Aril finally addressed the whole Council. 'Nothing should stand in the way of protecting the Wish-Makers of our Kingdom, as you gentlemen surely agree.' She looked around the table, then back at the Cardinal. 'We shall crush the Thief who threatens our world. And we shall protect our Wishfulls. Even if some don't realise it yet, they depend on us.' She added the last part in a soft voice, as if for the Cardinal alone.

He walked towards Aril and stood beside her. The difference in size between the two, with the Lady being at least one head taller than the old man, would have amused anyone but the magistrates sitting at the table.

'I entrust you with placing our men throughout the Kingdom as you see fit. You can also use Joreas's vultures and all the other men and beasts the Order has at its disposal.' Joreas puffed but did not protest.

There was a murmur among the members of the Council while Lady Aril elegantly bowed and said: 'I am here to serve, Sire.'

Joreas seemed ready to speak again when a strong knock at the door was swiftly followed by three soldiers entering the room. They were part of the Royal Guard, their dark red vests visibly displaying three golden Orbs and crowns, the emblem of the King. The first to enter announced loudly:

'His Majesty, the King, Lord of the Eastern Kingdom.'

A moment later, a bearded, middle-aged man walked in and went straight towards the Cardinal and Lady Aril. Dressed in plain, dark green clothes, the Eastern King had a wide gold belt around his waist and wore a white crown. His demeanour was that of a determined man who did not like to waste time.

His entrance had an electric effect on the members of the Council who, with the sound of chairs being moved back in a hurry, stood up. The Cardinal and Aril bowed and waited to be addressed.

'Cardinal, if you have a moment,' the Eastern King said loudly, wanting to be heard by the other members of the Council.

'Certainly, your Highness, certainly,' the Cardinal answered. He turned towards the Council table and told the magistrates they would meet again in two days' time. Meanwhile, they should all follow Lady Aril and her plan. She bowed to the Cardinal, the King and, with another swing of the hand, extinguished the small lights still hovering over the Kingdom's map.

At last, the King and the Cardinal were alone.

'Let us pass to my private chamber, your Majesty,' the Cardinal said and led the King through a side door into a smaller room. The walls were covered in old manuscripts and lit by four big candles on a wooden desk. A large, stained glass window let the moonlight in, giving the room a feeling of antiquated serenity.

'Aron, I will be brief,' said the King. 'I want to make sure you and the Council are doing your best to stop this criminal from stealing Wishes in our Kingdom. In particular, I want to know how you plan to protect the two Wishfulls we have left.'

The Cardinal hurried to answer the question. 'Your Majesty, believe me, we share the same concern and the Council is restlessly working to…'

He could not finish his thought. Impatiently, the King interrupted.

'Restlessly but not so effectively, Aron. Otherwise we would have caught this Thief. I gave you my riders, free hand to use the Kingdom's army if necessary, and what came of it?'

'My Lord,' the Cardinal mumbled, grasping for words, 'you can rest assured that they are being put to good use. As we speak, riders are placed throughout the Kingdom, allowing us to monitor whoever passes, north to south, east to west. I myself have been visiting places in the Kingdom where the Wishfulls live, trying to put them under our protection.'

'And have you?' asked the King eagerly.

'Not yet. I couldn't find them, or they had disappeared already…' the Cardinal admitted, avoiding the King's gaze. 'But I took measures, Sire, and punished those who didn't know how to raise and protect such rare treasures of our Kingdom.'

The King stepped towards the stained-glass window and kept quiet for a moment. The Cardinal sat down, forgetting to ask for the King's permission.

'Aron,' the King spoke again, 'we have known each other for many years. You have been like a father to me and I have always trusted you fully with heading the Council. But lately, I have heard some disturbing rumours.' He continued to look outside.

'Like what, your Majesty?' asked the Cardinal with the tone of some-one who was not looking forward to receiving an answer.

Turning towards him, the King said curtly: 'That the Thief might be working from within the Order.'

'What?' the Cardinal stood up and approached the King, looking directly in his eyes. 'Sire, are you doubting me?!'

'No, not you,' the King said. 'What I am simply saying is to watch out for this, Aron. If there is suspicion, you should know about it, and make sure it doesn't reflect reality,' he added and turned back to the window.

After a moment of silence, the Cardinal said in a low voice. 'As you wish, your Majesty. I will see to it that the Council's reputation is clean. As clean as it has always been.'

'I trust that to be the case, Aron,' answered the King. 'We cannot afford to fail in our task. And we cannot allow criminals to infiltrate and corrupt the Kingdom's highest Council.' The King approached the Cardinal and placed a hand on his shoulder.

'We stand and we fall together,' he said. The Cardinal nodded.

'Then we agree. You will start interrogating magistrates, one by one, from tomorrow. We must know how the Wish thefts happened in their lands. You will be fair but strict and any suspicion you have you will report directly to me.' The determination in the King's voice did not allow for contradiction.

'Then,' the King continued, 'you will place a high ransom on the head of the Thief. Three bags of gold if the Thief is captured alive, two bags if he or she is brought dead to the Council. Any useful information will be rewarded with five gold pieces from the Royal treasury.'

The King asked the Cardinal to write down his offer. After he finished, King Alexandru signed it and ordered for it to be copied and placed in all towns and villages of the East.

'This will be effective, Sire,' the Cardinal agreed. 'I will be sure to use the Council's nighthawks to spread the news fast, up to all our borders.'

'Very good,' approved the King. 'But we shouldn't only think of the Thief but also its potential victims. Most of them seem to disappear into thin air… We have to stop this from happening, Aron.'

'Yes, your Majesty. What would be your suggestion?' said the Cardinal, suspecting the King had a plan.

'The Council will round up all vulnerable Wish bearers and the two Wishfulls known to us, and place them under the Order's tutelage. I have given orders this morning to use the castle's West Tower for this purpose. This way our guards will be able to keep them safe.'

The Cardinal's smiled as he nodded in approval.

'Excellent Sire, excellent! I was about to bring into our custody one of the Wishfulls, the one from the village of Ostrova, but she refused my offer. Nobody knows where she is now. As soon as we find her, she will be placed strictly under our, I mean, under your Majesty's protection,' he quickly corrected himself.

'Look for her. And any Wish bearers that we know are defenceless,' replied the King. 'Sometimes, unfortunately, good intentions are not understood the first time around,' he continued, shaking his head.

'It will be done,' the Cardinal replied. 'It will be done from tomorrow morning. No! From tonight. We had planned to place soldiers and riders across the Kingdom to inspect all travellers. Now they will also be able to bring in anyone who needs our protection without delay.'

The King nodded his agreement and the Cardinal continued. 'And, if I may, Sire, allow me to be the first to talk to the Wishfulls before sending them to the Tower. I am sure I will be able to explain everything to them and turn them into well-behaved guests.' The King said that was not necessary, but the Cardinal insisted.

The King wrote his order in the Cardinal's presence, signed it, and left the room without saying another word.

As the door closed behind him, the Cardinal's smile dropped. He held the King's orders in his hands and, shaking, read each one more time. Then he collapsed in his chair, drained of all energy.

A sudden sound from outside made him jump back to his feet. He ran to the stained-glass window and opened it. Carrying the night breeze, the winged dog flew inside the room, making the candle lights tremble.

The Cardinal dropped the orders, he was not concerned with them anymore. He took the big head of the winged beast in his hands and asked, out of breath, 'Where is she?'

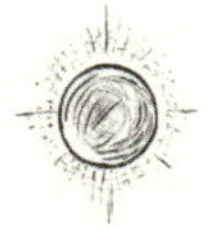

A *Wish Orb* is a shiny sphere, roughly the size of a pomegranate, made up of the energy of the Wish to be made by the Wish-Maker. The greater the shine, the more powerful the Wish, the bigger the good that can be achieved through it. The brightest Orbs, usually announcing a Great Wish, belong to people called *Wishfulls* and are very rare. Only the Wish Order can legitimately identify Wishfulls and keep a record of their existence. A *Wish* is a statement of request made by the Wish-Maker though which he or she acquires a desired skill, object or being. Wishes can be *wise*, when they are meant to help not only the Wish-Maker but the community as a whole, or *unwise*, when they selfishly help the Wish-Maker alone. Wishes can also be *wasted* when no statement is made upon the breaking of the Orb, when an unclear statement is made, or when what is requested exceeds the energy of the Wish Orb. In order to avoid selfish or wasted Wishes, it is paramount for *Wish bearers* – all those who hold Wish Orbs – to prepare their *Rite of Passage* – the ceremony of making the Wish – together with the community and a representative of the Wish Order.

(from the Metaphysics of Wish Orbs school textbook)

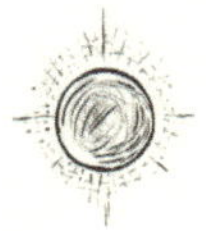

Chapter 9. Evergreen

TEN DAYS HAD PASSED since Lia had left her friends, fast asleep, in the forest surrounding Ostrova. And there was no time to lose. She had travelled day and night towards the capital, the Eastern Fortress of Samor, where the Order and the Royal Castle sat next to each other. And where her grandfather was held, she was certain of it. Everything she knew led her to that conclusion. She had seen him there with her own eyes, in the dream world inside the cave.

The journey had been difficult. Lia couldn't use any of the main roads or bridges of the Kingdom, fearing the Order's many soldiers, beasts, and spies. She also had to eat and sleep once in a while. Every two days, she would stop in villages on the way and offer her help in exchange for a plate of food and shelter for the night.

The day before she had been gathering apples from an orchard in Farios, in the rich valley midway between the Great Lake and the Eastern Fortress. She was uneasy at first about passing through the region. As a fertile and sunny land, it was densely populated and crossed by the redbrick road connecting the northern and southern parts of the Kingdom.

But avoiding it would have meant two extra days of climbing steep hills and she was in a hurry. Besides, the coming autumn made plenty of work available along the way.

The Maric family was happy to have Lia help them collect fruits from their large orchard, spread from the main road up to the hilltop, and spend the night in their home. It had been a good year, with just enough rain during the summer months, and most of the apples and pears were ripe for picking.

Madam Mariana, the family's head, was a short and plump woman of great vitality and strength. As most people in Farios, she didn't speak much and, when she did, it was slow and decisive, often ending in healthy laughter. Valley people were famous in the East for their calm demeanour and humorous approach to life. Accustomed to the harshness of freezing winters and torrid summers, these families of hard-working people yearned for the simple, uncomplicated existence they had learnt from their parents and their grandparents before them.

The Maric family were no exception. They welcomed Lia with an open heart and did not ask her any questions about where she came from or where she was going. Mariana was just grateful that she was there, as the five adults of the family – herself, her son, her father and her two sisters – could barely manage to collect all the fruit in just a few days. After all, the Marics were famous for their excellent jams and could not afford to let fruit rot away in the orchard.

Although Lia initially wanted to spend the night and leave early the next morning, Madam Mariana convinced her to stay one more day and help them finish the work. She even offered Lia to spend the whole autumn with them, to make jams together and sell them in Farios. Lia refused as politely as she knew how.

'Why are you in such a hurry, girl? You are our guest now and you must know one thing about Farios hospitality: we never let our guests leave tired, hungry or sad,' Mariana had told her the night before.

Her son Afilon, two years older than Lia, greatly resembled his mother. They were both short and robust and had the same simple and good-natured way of interacting with everyone.

Madam Mariana found a way to place them near each other during fruit picking. Lia could not help but think that Afilon's mother was looking for a daughter-in-law on top of an extra pair of hands in the orchard.

From the few words she exchanged with the boy, she learnt how excited he was about having his Wish Rite at the end of the week. All his family would be there to witness the occasion. Most of all, Afilon was happy about his Wish. To her surprise, he was eager to tell her about it as well, despite the custom of not sharing one's intended Wish with strangers.

He wanted to have a flute whose songs would instantly heal trees harmed by pests, diseases, and the biting cold of winter. This was his Wish. Simple and handy, just like Afilon was.

She would have liked to see him make this Wish but couldn't risk it. A representative from the Order was going to be there for the occasion and she didn't want to be seen by anyone remotely connected to the Cardinal.

Lia had seen an announcement placed on the door of the town hall the day before, when she was looking for work. By Royal decree, the Order had the King's permission to gather Wish bearers and Wishfulls in the Eastern Kingdom and offer them "protection" from a wicked criminal – the Wish Thief. This unidentified Thief even had a good ransom on his or her head. A great way to make some money, Lia thought, if only she could denounce the Cardinal without being immediately imprisoned by the Order.

Mariana and her sisters had prepared a copious breakfast that morning, as they did whenever there was hard work to do in the orchard. Besides bread and cheese, they had fresh milk and different kinds of jams and marmalade made from the last harvest. Lia offered to help them, but she was assigned only the job of setting the table, again with Afilon.

'It's going to be a good weather today it seems…,' he said awkwardly.

'Yes,' she answered with a smile.

Her mind drifted to Tudor, where he was and what he might be doing. He and his two cousins must have returned to Ostrova. And, hopefully, Tudor was able to continue his job as a fisherman and Matei and Clara had gone back to school. Were they also thinking of her? Did they hate her?

'Which one?' she heard Afilon ask.

'Excuse me?' Lia said, having missed his question.

'I asked if you would prefer the pear or apple jam?' he repeated, this time holding the two jars in his hands.

'Ah, apple, thank you!' she answered hastily, without thinking. Satisfied with the answer, Afilon said it was his favourite too.

'Don't bother her, boy,' Madam Mariana said and winked. 'Better think about what needs to be done today,' she scolded her son and then turned to her father to make the plan for the day.

Lia hoped Mariana understood she was in no way an eligible bride for her son. He was thrilled by the prospect of making his Wish and she couldn't care less about hers. All she wanted was to find her grandfather. And maybe, one day, meet Tudor and his cousins again and ask for their forgiveness.

'We can start with the pears at the back of the garden,' Afilon's grandfather proposed and received unanimous support. 'It's much better than being near the road, with all the noise and hassle. This way they will leave us alone.' The other nodded, it was only Lia who couldn't figure out who "they" were. So she decided to ask.

'The folk from the Order,' Afilon's grandfather answered casually, biting into a juicy apple. Lia's eyes widened but nobody seemed to notice.

'It's the second time they've come this month. Their vultures flew over the village the whole of last week. In fact, they stood right on top of our house two days before you arrived,' he continued calmly as if describing a common scene in Farios.

'And that weird woman,' Afilon intervened. 'She really scared Ado, didn't she, Grandpa?' Ado was the family's dog, sitting under the table, curled around Lia's feet.

Afilon and his mother both laughed about it. Lia was certainly not in the mood but smiled graciously.

'And why are they coming here?' she dared ask. The others fell quiet. For a moment, Lia thought they would start asking her questions. In fact, nobody was in any hurry to answer, just like they were in no hurry to do most things. In the end, it was Madam Mariana who broke the silence.

'They are looking for Daria and Dragomir, poor souls…' she said with compassion.

'Who are they?' Lia said, both relieved and curious.

'They are brother and sister. The milkman's kids, just two houses down from ours. Simple and honest children they are. But they ran away last month and now the Order is looking for them,' Mariana said for the first time with sadness in her voice. 'And all because Daria is supposed to be a Wishfull… May they be safe, wherever they are.' She sighed and stood up, ready to gather the dishes and breakfast leftovers.

Lia shivered at the thought of the Cardinal looking for anyone. She was surely on his mind too and, as such, on the mind of his beastly creature. She had to leave that day, that very moment in fact. But she didn't want to raise any suspicions and, most of all, endanger Mariana's family in any way.

After breakfast, Lia helped Afilon wash the dishes while planning her escape. Based on the map she had, the best way was to leave through the garden and continue up the hill, despite the difficult climb. That would take her closer to the Silver River and, from there, it would be only five days walking until she would reach Samor.

Madam Mariana interrupted them with the announcement that representatives of the Order had summoned all the villagers to the town hall. She apologized to Lia for this disruption and assured her she would be paid for the whole day and could wait for them in the house.

That was her chance to get away. As soon as the family left, Lia packed her few things, took some water and bread for the road and wrote a note thanking Mariana for everything. Looking back and listening for any noise from the valley, she started climbing the steep hill at the end of the orchard.

The day was getting hotter and, under the autumn sun, insects were calling each other loudly from the half-burned grass. Heavy fruits made the branches of trees bend under their weight. Lia used to love this time of year. She would help her grandfather in the garden and then go for a swim with Tudor and his cousins. The green leaves in Ostrova turned yellow, then brown and red, framed beautifully by the deep blue of the water and light blue the sky.

The top of the hill was in sight and, crossing it, Lia found a smaller valley, tucked between three high hills. The river was behind that valley, making a small canyon before rushing south, away from the Eastern Fortress.

There was no road to take so she had to find her own path through the rocks and bushes. Crossing was riskier, since there were no trees to conceal her presence from the Order's winged creatures. But she had to go on.

***

It was only towards the evening that Lia managed to find refuge in Evergreen, the forest beyond the hills of Farios. As a child, she had heard stories about those woods, known for being the oldest in the Kingdom, maybe in the whole of Maar. Looking at the map now, Lia could see Evergreen extended from Farios up north, close to the Wish Order. There was no other way but to cross it.

Evergreen was not any old forest, but one Easterners were well advised to stay out of. Lia grew up with legends about the fantastic creatures hiding within it, beneath its twisted trees or at the bottom of its shallow waters, legends of forest spirits and terrible witches. The kind of stories that kept children in Maar awake at night.

One story told of the Cyclops who supposedly crafted the Wish Orbs of the Kings and Queens of Maar by turning the waters of the Silver River into pure crystal. Another told of a three-tailed dragon that lived under a hill in the middle of the forest and only came out to devour those who didn't yet have their Rite of Passage. Lia wasn't afraid of meeting any of them, certainly not more than wasting time out in the open where she could meet her own dragon, the Cardinal's beast.

The night brought distant sounds and strange scents. She heard birds that normally only sung during the day and felt in her mouth and nostrils the fruity aroma of orchard apples. Small lights were gently floating high between the trees, descending slowly between the grass blades and tree roots. It was time to find shelter for the night, she decided.

And, just as she made up her mind and put down her bag, Lia saw someone in the distance watching her from behind. At first, she thought she had imagined it, but the stranger moved quickly out of sight, giving Lia the certainty that she had been followed.

What to do?

Her heart started beating faster as she quickly grabbed her things and hurried in the opposite direction. The sound of footsteps behind her was unmistakable. Someone was following her, stopping when she stopped and hastening when she started running again.

Who could it be? And why wasn't this person saying anything? The robbers that broke into her home didn't talk much either…

Lia's bag fell to the ground and spilled its contents. The water bottle broke with a loud noise. Torn between running away and needing her belongings, Lia scrabbled to pick them up. She could only grab a few of her clothes when, looking up, she saw the stranger fast approaching. If only she had taken a knife or any weapon with her!

She shouted 'leave me alone!' and abandoned the bread and the map of Maar. She started running down one of the steepest slopes of the forest. She didn't care anymore about her things, all she wanted was to get away as fast as her legs could carry her.

It was pitch dark in that part of Evergreen. The small lights Lia saw before were all gone and the woods had become gloomy and slippery.

And then she couldn't go any further. In front of her, a high stonewall, covered in giant moss, grass and fern, was blocking the way. Lia turned around, convinced that she would find the stranger standing right next to her.

Instead, to her surprise, she saw the moss open and, in the pale light of a small orange lantern, a woman appeared from behind the stonewall.

She extended her hand and whispered softly, 'come with me.'

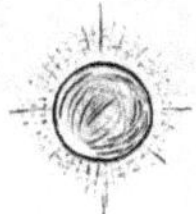

TRUE FRIENDS CANNOT BE Wished for.

(Saying in Maar)

Chapter 10. Shelter

'Evergreen, Evergreen, darkest place you've ever been,' went the nursery rhyme Lia remembered. She sang it with her friends when she was only four or five, playing in the forest surrounding Ostrova. A cheerful song that meant little to them. A funny name she only knew referred to another forest, far away. Not a place she might find herself in one day. Lost in its darkness.

As stunned as she was to see someone emerging from the stonewall, Lia was not eager to stand around and wait for whoever was chasing her to catch up. On the spot, she decided to trust the woman and, holding her hand, passed through the thick layer of vegetation and arrived on the other side.

Her companion walked fast and Lia followed. In the dim, orange light of her lantern, the woman appeared slender, middle-height and possessing a strange beauty that made it almost impossible to guess her age. While her mouth was small and her nose narrow and pointed, the woman's eyes were mesmerising. Captivated by her gaze, Lia forgot her fears and followed her deep into Evergreen without asking any questions.

Before too long, the two arrived at a small house made of stone and wood, hidden behind a line of tall pine trees. From the outside the house looked small but, once inside, Lia discovered the place was quite spacious. The main corridor led to a big living room with two bedrooms on each side and a kitchen at the end.

'There is so much space because the house is partially underground,' the women told her as she helped Lia take off her mud-covered jacket. 'I will wash this for you if you don't mind,' she said and went into one of the side rooms.

Lia didn't have time to thank her. Left alone, she started exploring the living room. Everything looked clean and tidy. Wood was burning in the fireplace. Nonetheless, Lia still felt cold. She picked up a brown, woollen blanket from a tall chair by the table. The blanket smelled of wild flowers and felt soft on her skin.

Around the walls, Lia saw nicely carved bookshelves and potted plants. It instantly reminded her of Grandfather's library. She approached one of the shelves, curious to see if the woman had any of the same books. Most of all, she was interested to know if she had any maps of the Eastern Kingdom to replace the one she lost in the chase.

One of the living room walls was entirely covered by a large, dark-green cloth. It was similar in colour to the cloak worn by her host. Lia touched it and, as she did, it slowly fell to the ground revealing an enormous mirror the size of the wall.

Surprised by her finding, Lia explored the room in the mirror and then looked at herself. She realised she had rarely seen her whole body reflected before. She found herself thinner than she remembered, no doubt from all the walking.

'I see you found my little mark of vanity,' said the woman, entering the room. She was now wearing a yellow dress with a floral pattern, her hair raised in a bun. Around her neck, Lia could see a bright piece of jewellery that seemed to sparkle in the reddish light of the fire.

'Please don't touch it though, it is such an old thing it might fall on you,' she said with a smile.

'I am sorry, I didn't get the chance to introduce myself before. My name is Lady Laurnic but all my friends call me Crina,' she continued in a joyful tone as she approached Lia to shake her hand.

'Nice to meet you,' Lia replied in a more reserved manner, wondering which friends Lady Laurnic referred to. She seemed to live alone and there were certainly few neighbours in Evergreen. At least of the human type.

'And your name?' Lady Laurnic asked after a moment of silence.

'Um, Lia.' Was she supposed to give her name?

This was all rather strange and, for as grateful as Lia was for being rescued, the thought dawned on her that she'd now ended up in a house with a person she knew nothing about.

'Very nice to meet you, Lia. You have a beautiful name,' Lady Laurnic said and gestured for her to step away from the mirror and sit at the table. 'I am happy to answer any questions you might have. I think we can agree we met in pretty unusual circumstances.'

Her penetrating dark eyes inspected her from head to toe. Lia remained silent.

'OK, I will start then. As you can see, I live alone in the forest. I have been here for many years now. I am from one of the villages just north of Evergreen. As a child I always loved nature and, in the end, I thought to myself, why not? Why not live here, where days and nights are filled with the songs of birds, where flowers grow big and wild right at your doorstep, and you are visited by deer in the cold days of winter. Tea?' she asked pointing to the small kitchen to her left.

'I… yes please,' Lia replied, surprised by the question.

Lady Laurnic stood up gracefully and walked towards the kitchen. One could see from the way she moved and talked that she was not an ordinary girl from a village. She was probably once part of the nobility of the Eastern Kingdom, which made her choice of living in Evergreen even weirder.

Lia wondered especially how this woman, living in the depths of the forest, happened to be there exactly when she needed her most. Was she connected to the Wish Order?

'You have no reason to fear me, Lia,' Lady Laurnic said as she came back from the kitchen with a big, blue teapot and two ceramic, hand painted cups. Again she had anticipated Lia's thoughts.

'You have been through a lot tonight and it was lucky I found you when I did. You see, the trees of the forest not only offer me joy but also protection. It is hard to believe but, somehow, they let me know when there is danger around. That is how I found you,' she said, looking Lia straight in the eyes.

It was indeed hard to believe that trees could warn anyone but, then again, Lia had seen stranger things in Evergreen. And she needed to trust someone or she would never be able to leave the forest.

'Lady Laurnic…,' she said, with an indecisive tone.

'Please, call me Crina,' the Lady replied with such kindness in her voice that Lia suddenly felt more confident.

'Crina…' she continued, 'thank you for bringing me into your home. I am so grateful you came to my rescue tonight. And I don't want you to feel offended, but I need to leave this forest tomorrow morning. By the looks of it, if there is anyone who can help me with this, it's you.'

Lia expected her host to resist or ask questions.

'Certainly. I will do everything I can to help,' Crina replied resolutely as she poured tea in both cups. 'You just rest now and, tomorrow morning, I will guide you out of the forest,' she continued reassuringly. Lia smiled, nodded and thanked her.

She was still captivated by the grace of the women standing in front of her, from the elegance of her movement to the way the folds of her yellow dress fell to the ground. And her necklace had the most miraculous little stone Lia had ever seen. It seemed to be glowing in the dark.

'If I may, why do you have such a big mirror?' Lia asked.

'Ha, I saw it didn't take long for you to discover it,' Crina answered half-jokingly. 'You are young now, Lia, but you will see, as you grow older or, I should say, as you become more mature,' she added with a wink, 'small signs of old age start to show. Noticing them takes time and you need good mirrors for it.'

'Do you mean you find yourself old?' Lia said and, as soon as she did, regretted her question. Crina laughed.

'No, not old, but I am getting there,' she answered with a slight melancholy in her voice.

Lia never had time to look in the mirror, but not because she was young; she was simply not interested. This habit of Crina's was probably yet another sign of her more distinguished upbringing, Lia concluded.

After the two women finished their tea, Crina took her guest to one of the bedrooms. The bed was already made. The room was simple but decorated with taste. Lia noticed on the small bedside table a blue vase with fresh flowers and a basket full of apples, just like the ones she had picked in Farios.

As they said goodnight, Lia thanked Crina again for the hospitality. Lying in the bed, soft and comfortable, she realised she hadn't had a proper night of sleep in a long time.

Despite all the stress of the day, Lia smiled thinking everything had a way of turning out fine, even in the most unexpected ways.

***

The next morning, she woke up late to the smell of freshly baked bread. The sun was up and, out the window, Lia saw the two rows of tall pine trees going around the house. Evergreen, the place that terrified her so much the night before, looked like a normal forest in daylight, not so different from the one back home.

If Crina was indeed going to be her guide out of there, she might be able to reach her destination, and hopefully her grandfather, in a week's time. For a moment, she wondered where it was that she was going exactly. The smell of breakfast was enticing but the warmth of the bed made it hard to stand up.

Crina entered the room carrying a wooden tray with a loaf of bread, butter, and a bowl of fresh milk. She was wearing a red dress that went very well with her brown hair and dark eyes, all accentuated by the small bright stone around her neck. Lia wanted to ask what kind of stone that was but Crina was busy telling her about how she baked the bread (apparently there was a secret to it) and Lia decided it was impolite to interrupt her.

While she ate, Lia learnt about the house and the forest. Crina told the story of how the King himself once passed through Evergreen and his expedition lost all of their horses. And how the Wish Order never managed to find any of the people hiding there. Maybe it was one of those people who had chased her the night before, she suggested.

'Who do you think that was, Lia?' Lady Laurnic asked directly. Lia didn't know how to answer.

To explain why she might have been followed would mean telling the whole story and Lia still wasn't entirely sure she could trust Crina. On the other hand, her host had saved her and was her best chance of continuing the journey so, for better or worse, she had to confide in her.

Lia explained how it might have been someone sent by the Cardinal and not a criminal chased by the Order. That the Order had captured and imprisoned her grandfather and they were trying to catch her as well. Lia did not mention that she possessed a Great Wish. She wasn't even sure she had one, it could all have been invented by the Cardinal for all she knew.

Then Lia said her friends tried to help her, especially her good childhood friend… her friend… Tudor! She stopped talking, shocked that she'd had difficulty recalling, even for a moment, Tudor's name. What kind of friend was she, after all he and his cousins had done for her?

Crina noticed Lia was upset but probably thought it was hard for her to continue such a sad story. 'Do not worry, my dear, remember you are always welcome here, for as long as you want or need.'

Despite a beautiful, sunny morning, towards noon it started raining heavily. Lia decided she should wait to leave in the afternoon or even the next day if the weather didn't improve.

'It is only a short autumn rain. But it can get chilly,' Crina said, looking out the window. She gave Lia books and maps to look at, and they even found a copy of the same map Lia had lost the day before. Crina took a pair of scissors and cut it out of her atlas, handing it over. 'It is yours to keep, my dear.'

The afternoon came but the rain did not stop, on the contrary. It looked as if it was turning into a full-blown thunderstorm and the two made lunch together. After the meal, they sat at the table and talked again over tea.

Lia got to tell Crina more of her story, especially her childhood in Ostrova. She told her she was missing home and that Crina's house reminded her of it. Except it had no garden.

'But of course it has a garden!' Crina cried. 'It is right outside your window, I am surprised you didn't see it this morning,' she added.

'You have a garden?' Lia answered, confused. 'I am pretty sure I looked outside and saw the forest. Pine trees…'

'Nonsense my dear, come, I will show it to you, it is exactly like the one you told me about,' Crina interrupted and eagerly took Lia to the window.

And there it was. A well tended garden, with rows of vegetables, roses and violets on the side and mature fruit trees at the back.

Lia couldn't believe her eyes so she decided to go outside to take a better look. Crina was happy to join her, especially since the rain was showing signs of stopping.

As they walked past the vegetables and flowers, Lia had the feeling something strange was going on. She could remember well the pine trees outside, two rows of them. Or did she? What if she imagined them? It was true that she was very tired and managed to forget several other things that day (among them, Tudor's name!). What if she'd missed the garden as well?

Crina started collecting ripe tomatoes and peppers and asked Lia for her help. 'If you want, you can take care of all of this,' she said in her usual, charming tone.

As the evening came, the two returned to the house. The bright light of the sunset made its way into the living room, giving Crina's dress a sparkling shade of red. The enormous mirror on the wall amplified the warm atmosphere, creating the illusion of space and cosiness.

Lia started looking at herself in the mirror. She rarely had the chance to do so. In the bright light of the sunset, her red-brown hair seemed to have caught fire. For the first time, she thought of herself as looking nice, perhaps even attractive.

'You are beautiful,' Crina said passing by her. 'But enough staring in the mirror, the dinner won't cook itself!'

As night fell, Lia felt more and more tired. She had barely done anything the whole day and yet her whole body was aching. Maybe she was recovering from the previous weeks of travelling? Maybe now that she finally found a good shelter, her body was telling her it needed to rest?

Crina was very happy to have her stay one more night; in fact, she said Lia could stay for as many nights as she wanted. She had been looking for a long time for someone to help her take better care of the garden.

Lying in bed, Lia was thinking about that offer when Crina came in the room to say good night. She herself looked tired and, as if reflecting her state, the usual glow of her medallion was barely visible now. Crina seemed concerned as well.

'If you worry about the garden,' Lia told her, 'I can help you tomorrow. I am actually good at it. Plus, it would be a small way to repay your generosity.'

'You are too kind, Lia. You know, in the short time since we've met, I feel like we developed a special bond. I might even say a close friendship. Or, rather, we are like mother and daughter,' she smiled but with sadness.

Crina sat on the side of the bed and gently caressed Lia's cheeks. 'I hope I am not overstepping, I mean, I don't think your mother would like to hear me say this,' she added jokingly.

'I don't have a mother. Or, rather, I never knew her,' Lia replied. 'Or my father. I was raised by my grandfather, but I probably told you the story already...'

'No, no problem Lia, you can tell me again,' Crina said, looking her in the eyes. 'I like to listen, you know.'

'Well, I miss my grandfather... He has been such a special person in my life. My father, my mother and my best friend, all in one. And he is such a clever man, too! He was the headmaster of my school for many years,' Lia continued, becoming sad as well. 'But now he is not with me anymore... he... he... where is he?' she asked, frightened.

'Where is he, Lia?' Crina echoed, starring at her intensely.

'I don't know! I cannot remember. I thought I knew,' Lia answered and took a deep breath, her voice waning. 'I was going somewhere for him, but where? I cannot remember.'

'It's OK, it's OK Lia,' Crina replied and hugged her. 'Sometimes we forget, it is alright.'

'No, no, I could not possibly forget this. Where is he? What is he doing? Where...' She couldn't finish asking. Her body had collapsed into sleep.

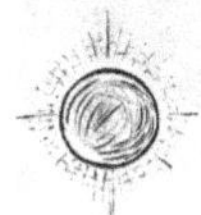

Wɪsʜ Oʀʙs ᴀʀᴇ ᴍᴀᴅᴇ of pure energy and this energy can be released only through Wish-Making. All other uses of it involve magic and are strictly forbidden by the laws of the realm.

(from the *Metaphysics of Wish Orbs* school textbook)

Chapter 11. The Mirror

L IA WOKE UP WITH a bad headache. She felt so ill that she could barely get out of bed. Crina helped her get dressed and made tea for the two of them. It was raining heavily outside and a grey mist engulfed the house, wrapping it in a thick layer of gloom.

'It seems this is not a good day to travel either,' Crina said, making her bed. Lia didn't reply. She held the cup of tea in her hands and kept looking out the window. The garden was all muddy. She would have liked to get out and tend the vegetables at least, but it was not possible.

'Does the rain ever stop here?' she asked. She had been unable to leave the house for two days now. Or was it three?

'It does stop, eventually. You just need to give it a bit of time,' Crina answered, refilling her cup. 'It almost feels like you are not happy living here with me, Lia…,' she added with some sadness in her voice.

Crina herself looked more tired than usual. Her long black dress and the dark brown silk scarf she wore around the shoulders made her seem much older than Lia remembered. Deep wrinkles around her eyes had appeared overnight. The white necklace stone had lost much of its shine and was barely visible.

'Today I want to leave,' Lia announced abruptly.

Crina gave her a mocking smile Lia had not seen before. Then she warned that Lia would be soaked in a second and her cold would get much worse. Crina insisted she wouldn't be held responsible for it. Then she stood by Lia and wrapped her arms around her.

'I don't have a cold. I don't need to be in bed. What I need is to move, to be out, to go,' Lia insisted trying to free herself from the embrace.

'My dear, we have been having this conversation many times now,' Crina replied with an exasperated tone as she let go of Lia. 'You want to go, but you don't know where. You don't even know where you came from, little less where you are heading!' she said, raising her arms in the air. 'You would only get lost in the forest again, and neither of us wants that.'

'This is precisely it,' Lia replied sharply. 'Maybe, somehow, if I go out, I will remember. I will see the road. I will see something. I don't know…' She buried her head in her hands.

Arguing with Crina exhausted her and that is all they had been doing lately. She started to wonder if Crina would ever let her go. No matter the weather, Lia had to leave. And soon. She could try to escape but she knew well enough that it wasn't possible to get far without Crina's help.

'Will you help me?' she pleaded.

Crina sighed. 'Help you do what, Lia? You don't know where you are going. You are clearly confused. And you are very weak,' she added emphatically. 'It would be irresponsible of me to let you go.' And, after saying this, she took the empty teacups and left the room, closing the door.

Lia was left alone in the dark. She had not seen the sun for days and Evergreen looked more and more like a place of eternal doom. She tried very hard to remember where she came from but could not...

Lia could see herself picking apples in a sunny place, a memory she felt was very recent. Or swimming in a deep, blue lake together with a young man. His face and blonde hair were familiar to her, yet she couldn't say why.

Most of all, she could not shake off the feeling that she was forgetting something very important. Something she had to do urgently. Maybe it was related to her meeting Crina in the forest? She didn't know... Crina told her she needed to rest and recover, but for how long?

***

The next morning, Lia could not get out of bed. Crina had closed the drapes, saying she needed to rest the whole day. Lia, on the other hand, insisted she wanted to get out of her room, but her host wouldn't have any of that.

Why was she doing this? Too tired to even think about it...

Crina sat by her bed, reading to her from a book of stories from the Eastern Kingdom. Once in a while, she would stop and check if Lia was sleeping. When she finally left the room, Lia could hear her lock the door behind her.

In the evening, Crina helped her guest to the living room, set her down at the table and went to the kitchen to make dinner for the two of them. The room had changed. There were no plants anymore and the dinner table was now placed in front of the big mirror that was no longer covered.

Lia could not help staring at it. When she arrived in Crina's house, she found herself pretty. Now, she looked weak and miserable. Dizzy as she surely was, Lia could see her reflection in the mirror move a little, look around the room and then back at herself.

She closed her eyes. She was too exhausted to try to understand what was happening and why. When she opened them again, she saw Crina in the mirror, standing at door, with a teapot on a wooden tray, eyes fixated on her. She was not moving and, for a second, Lia thought she was imagining her as well.

Crina did come inside though. She put the tray on the table, took Lia's temperature with the back of her hand and poured her another cup of tea.

'How are you feeling, my darling?' she asked, her face uncomfortably close.

'I don't know…,' Lia replied quietly. 'I feel tired. Very tired.'

'Yes,' Crina replied, slowly shaking her head. 'It is this bad weather. We haven't had this kind of weather for years. At least not after the flood. Oh, but you are too young to remember that, probably you weren't even born,' she continued. Lia didn't answer.

Crina stood up and looked at herself in the mirror. She was definitely looking much older as she put her hand on the frame. In the mirror, Lia could see Crina's necklace had lost its shine.

When Crina turned around, she had a big, forced smile on her face.

'I tell you what. It is a cold dark night and I am running out of candles. The firewood is wet from all this rain. We need more light to cheer ourselves up. Don't you agree?'

Crina paused to give Lia a chance to answer but she could barely nod her head in agreement.

'Well then, how about you bring forth your Wish Orb, Lia? Just for tonight. We can place it here on the table while we eat,' she added in a hurry. 'I used to do that as a little child, at home, on such rainy nights.'

Crina waited for Lia to reply but there was only silence. Her usual smile turned into an ugly frown but, before she could say anything else, Lia raised her hand. Inside it, her Wish Orb appeared, instantly making the whole room brighter.

Its light was so strong Crina gasped seeing it. Her eyes became wider and she seemed she was about to laugh. But only for a moment. Instead, she thanked Lia and told her to wait with the Orb until she brought dinner.

Lia did as she was told.

She held her Orb close to her face, as if trying to remember it. All she knew was that she didn't feel any excitement about having a powerful Wish Orb or having to make a Wish. She almost despised it. For her, having the Orb light up a room at night was as good a use as any.

Crina soon arrived with two plates of rice and vegetables. 'These are from the garden,' she said, taking the Orb from Lia's hand and placing it on the table. 'You need your hands free to eat,' she added, concerned perhaps of how Lia might take her touching the Wish Orb.

But Lia was too weak to say anything and most of the dinner was spent in silence. Crina tried to make conversation, telling her about how she started her little garden in the forest. She could see Lia was not listening. The girl was staring at the Wish Orb on the table. It looked like something that wasn't part of her life anymore and that made her feel sad.

'Did you like the dinner?' Crina asked as she took away the dishes. Lia hadn't eaten half of what was on her plate but nodded in agreement.

'You will have to go to bed now if you want to be up early tomorrow morning,' Crina said and helped her up.

'Why would I want to be up early?' Lia asked softly.

'Because tomorrow is an important day, Lia. The day you will remember everything and will be reunited with people very dear to you.' Crina took Lia by the hand and helped her move towards the bedroom.

Lia looked back at the Wish Orb on the dinner table.

'Oh, yes,' Crina said as she grabbed the Orb gently. 'I will take care of this for you until tomorrow.'

And, as she said it, Crina took off her necklace, removed its tiny stone and managed to attach Lia's Orb to it. The Orb was far too big for a necklace but, as with any Wish Orb, it was light to carry. Lia wanted to react but could not say anything. She felt as if she had suddenly lost something of great value but couldn't bring herself to do anything about it.

All she wanted was rest.

And tomorrow, yes, tomorrow, everything will be fine. She will remember. And she will find home.

***

Later on, Lia woke up in complete darkness. The drapes had been closed and the small candle on her bedside table had burnt out. It was impossible to tell whether it was morning or evening, day or night.

With great effort, she stood up and pulled apart the drapes only to find the same thick mist surrounding the house. Tall trees, just outside her window, had replaced the garden she saw days before.

Lia closed back the curtains. She didn't want her host to suspect she had been out of bed.

Crina only visited her twice that day and, on both occasions, Lia pretended to be asleep. She could hear Crina standing still in the room, she could feel her intense gaze upon her. One time, she was so close Lia could feel Crina's breath on her forehead.

Lia wasn't scared. She remembered how Crina took her Wish Orb the other day and imagined her wearing it around her neck. As long as it was in the possession of another person, Lia couldn't make it disappear anymore. Why did she care for it that much?...

All she wanted was to have it back and to leave the gloomy cottage. To get out of the forest once and for all. If only she had the strength to do it... Crina left another cup of tea on the side table.

101

Lia didn't drink it. Instead, she spilled its content behind the bed and lied down again.

***

'Time to wake up,' she heard Crina whisper in her ear. Lia instinctively replied she didn't want to and turned around to face the wall.

Crina grabbed her right hand and started dragging her out gently but firmly. Lia was too weak to fight her. Slowly opening her eyes, she could see Crina was wearing the same black dress from the day before, long and tight around the middle, and her hair was up in a bun.

Her face, strangely illuminated from below by her Wish Orb, showed nothing but coldness and determination. Crina was no longer pretending to care for her anymore and Lia had the feeling something terrible was going to happen unless she managed to get away.

But Crina was strong and quick, a strength and vitality regained from carrying Lia's Orb. She looked much younger as well, almost Lia's age, despite their large age gap. If anything, Lia was feeling older and more tired than ever before.

When they entered the living room, Lia saw it was completely empty, no more books or plants, no dining table and chairs, only candles placed on windowsills and the great mirror on the wall. The windows were all open and, through them, the smell of wood and fresh air filled the house. Outside it was pitch dark and, inside the house, despite the few candles, Lia couldn't see much either. So tired, so very tired…

'It's time you went home, Lia,' Crina said, placing her upright in front of the mirror.

Lia looked straight ahead and made out her own reflection. Crina was not there, even as she was standing right behind her. Instead, an old man appeared in the mirror, a man whose caring eyes and white hair were all too familiar. Yet, Lia could not remember who he was.

'He is there Lia, waiting for you.' Crina was pushing her closer and closer to the mirror. 'Don't you recognise him?' she asked. Without waiting for an answer, she added, 'it's your grandfather'.

'My…' Lia whispered.

'Yes, it is he, the man you were looking for, and he is home, waiting for you,' Crina said in a soft voice. The man in the mirror was standing close to a kitchen table. Through the open door behind him, Lia could see a beautiful garden, similar to the one Crina had at some point.

Was that man her grandfather? Was he the man she had been looking for? Everything was very confusing, and Lia was afraid. Her heart was beating fast and she started breathing heavily.

With her last strength, she tried to push Crina away and head for the door. Surprised by her energy, Crina took a step back but did not fall. Finding her balance, she grabbed Lia firmly by both her hands and dragged her right back to the mirror.

Holding her head up, she directed her gaze towards the image in the mirror. Inside, the old man, smiling, started opening his arms.

'He wants you to join him, Lia,' she heard Crina say in her ear. 'Be a good girl and go to him.'

Lia felt powerless and, touching the mirror for support, saw her hands could go right through its shiny surface.

The pain! It was as if her fingers got pierced by thousands of needles. Like touching fire inside the mirror. Lia quickly took her hand out.

Turning towards Crina, she tried to push her back one more time but all she could do was grab the Orb around her neck and hold on to it.

'No!' Crina shouted and slapped Lia so hard she instantly fell on the floor. Kneeling near her, Crina grabbed Lia by the collar and, in anger, told her she was never to touch the necklace again.

'I saved you. I took care of you. I am giving you everything you wanted, you insolent little girl! Isn't this your lost grandfather? I exchanged your Orb for making this Wish of yours come true and this is how you treat me?' she shouted as she shook Lia.

To her surprise, Lia didn't feel pain anymore, not even fear. Days of being sick in bed reduced her sensitivity and made her dizzy above all else.

It was her grandfather. And she saw her home in the mirror.

It all came back to her. She was supposed to rescue him from the Wish Order. She had been travelling with Tudor and his cousins before abandoning them in the forest around Ostrova. She tried to cross Evergreen and was rescued by Crina. And then… Lia closed her eyes, hoping she would wake up from the nightmare.

It was at that moment when she heard, loud and clear, a croaking noise coming from outside the house, followed by the sound of flapping wings. She felt Crina stand up to face the intruder.

When she looked next, Lia could hardly believe her eyes. A big raven had flown inside the house through the open window and was attacking the woman. She, in turn, was screaming and moving her hands up and down but the raven was still there, flying close to her face and neck.

Despite the blows it received, the bird managed to grab the Wish Orb and started pulling on the necklace. Crina desperately held on to it when it finally broke loose. She let out a mighty shout of anger as the black bird flew off with the Wish Orb in its claws.

It was gone, Lia's Orb was gone!

'What have you done to me, beast!?' Crina cried as she covered her head with her hands. That was her chance. Lia grabbed her by the legs and pulled hard. Losing her balance, Crina had nothing else to hold on to but the mirror.

She extended both her arms, as if trying to catch it by the frame, before she fell in. Lia saw, for an instant, the frightening image of Crina's old, terrified face as she disappeared inside the mirror.

Then there was silence. The raven had flown out of the room with Lia's Wish Orb and vanished into the night.

Crina was gone. Or, at least, she wasn't there anymore. Would she manage to get out of the mirror? If she did, she would certainly kill her.

Lia tried to raise herself up, with great difficulty, and look inside the mirror, her heart beating fast.

Before she had time to react, someone grabbed her by the shoulder and pulled her a few steps back. It was a man. Tall and slim, the stranger held a bow in his hands. He swiftly took an arrow from the bag around his waist, straightened the bow and shot directly into the mirror.

It broke with a loud, human-like screech and fell to the floor in a thousand pieces. The image of her grandfather and of Crina were both gone with it.

Evergreen, Evergreen,
Darkest place you've ever seen,
If you enter, just you know,
It will never let you go.

(Nursery rhyme)

Chapter 12. Raven

Lia didn't know who the stranger was or why he had broken the mirror, but she didn't feel like asking. All she wanted was to get out of that rotten place and the dark, gloomy forest surrounding it. And then sleep, sleep for a week, a month, a whole year.

'If I were you, I wouldn't go alone at night,' she heard him say as she turned towards the door.

Lia stood still, realising it was useless to leave in her state, without any map or any idea of where to go. She turned around to face the man who had spoken to her. He had his back to her and was busy preparing a torch.

The room felt even more eerie when lit by red and white flames. Pieces of Crina's mirror reflected light like fish scales scattered all over the floor, sparkling and hypnotic.

Was she really gone, or could she be hiding behind one of the glass shards? Gah, what's this thought? If only Lia could get away somewhere. And sleep. Yes, sleep. So tired.

As the stranger turned towards her, Lia saw his face clearly for the first time. He had dark eyes, dark, shoulder length hair and the skin tone of someone who had spent many days walking under the sun. The well-defined features of his face, with a strong jaw, thick eyebrows and long eyelashes, contrasted with his tall, slim body. Body of a teenager, face of a man.

He stood there, looking at her, saying nothing else. Half-suspicious, half-amused, as if evaluating if she was worth his help or not. And, in that moment, Lia was not tired any more. A rush of anger surged through her. He was the one who came in there, broke the mirror, and told her not to leave. What did he expect her to do now, beg for his help?

'Don't tell me, you are going to look after me now, right?' she said with as much sarcasm as she could muster. 'Or are you also here for my Wish Orb?'

The stranger didn't seem moved in any way by her anger.

'Well, the joke's on you because it's gone. The Orb is gone…' She wanted to tell him that a big raven came in and stole it. But, just as she thought of it, Lia heard again the sound of flapping wings and, to her amazement, the bird returned, carrying her Wish Orb in its claws.

It landed elegantly on the stranger's shoulder. He made a quick gesture and the Orb was in his hands.

Both raven and man gazed at Lia, as if waiting for her reaction.

Before she had the chance to jump at them – oh, how rage can animate the weak and the weary – the stranger threw the Wish Orb towards her. This was so unexpected that Lia almost missed catching it.

She felt a huge wave of relief to have it back. Anger turned into curiosity. Not wanting to show her feelings, Lia quickly made the Orb disappear and looked at the stranger more confidently than before.

'Is this your bird?' she asked. 'Why did it steal my Wish Orb?'

The stranger raised his eyebrows in surprise and smiled. 'Hmm, I don't know, let me ask the bird,' he said, trying to imitate her tone. He looked at the raven on his shoulder and the raven looked back at him.

Lia half expected the feathered beast to speak, but it didn't. Instead, the stranger continued to mock her by saying she should take better care of her Wish since no "birds" might be around to help her next time.

'I don't need any help,' Lia replied. Argh, the nerve of this guy! No, he has things to answer for and he will answer. Who on earth does he think he is? The Royal Wish Orb?

'Who are you, anyway? Why were you here at night? How did you find this place and why did you break the mirror?' Lia asked all her questions at once, slowly moving towards the man. He didn't budge.

The raven gave a load croak and flew towards her, making Lia trip and fall down. The creature then landed on the windowsill and gave her a menacing look. Still shaky and tired… but, by the Wish-Maker, she won't give him the satisfaction.

The man stepped towards her and extended his hand. Lia ignored the gesture and stood up all by herself. She stared at him and took a deep breath.

It was clear the stranger standing in front of her didn't mean to hurt her. He had even returned her Wish Orb. But his attitude really got to her, that was sure. Maybe she was just tired, though. Maybe she should try to start all over again. With a bit of luck, he might be able to get her out of the horrid forest.

'Can you guide me out of Evergreen?' she asked more calmly.

He nodded and pointed to the door as if showing her the way. The raven flew out the window and, as quickly as it came, it vanished between the trees.

'Can I trust you?' she asked reluctantly.

'I think you have no other choice,' the stranger replied. And he was right. His voice was kinder. Maybe he was making an effort too.

She packed her things, put on her warm jacket and came back to him.

As they both walked out, Lia was curious to look and see if the garden was still there. She couldn't find it. There were only trees, nothing else. When she turned around, the house had disappeared without a trace. She wasn't startled by this, as if half expecting it. And she was still too tired to think about any of it.

They walked in silence for more than an hour.

The stranger made her stop a few times as he carefully listened to the sounds of the forest. She could barely hear anything except the familiar songs of night birds. He seemed focused on making as little noise as possible. Lia did the same without being asked.

Was she so weak because of some kind of poison Crina was feeding her? Was it the tea, perhaps, that made her lose her memory? One thing was certain, the moment Crina and her mirror vanished, Lia started feeling better. Maybe it was all a dark spell or a bad dream. It certainly felt like one.

Waking up from this nightmare was partially thanks to the stranger walking in front and his weird raven (that was nowhere to be seen). They were not after her Wish Orb. If they had been, why did the raven bring it back? But could she be sure they were going out of the forest?

As the first sun rays gave the grass and leaves a peculiar, golden glow, her doubts returned and Lia thought about running away again.

'Who are you?' she stopped and asked bluntly.

A couple of metres ahead of her, the man stood still, turned around and fixed her with his dark, penetrating eyes. Lia noticed he was probably the same age as Tudor. His clothes looked worn out and he had the air of someone who had been travelling for many days.

'Why do you need to know?' he answered.

'What do you mean why do I need to know?' Lia replied, trying not to sound neither angry nor scared. 'I have been following you for some time into a dangerous forest and I know almost nothing about you. I don't even know where you are taking me,' she added.

He didn't seem surprised by her reasoning. Looking up towards the morning sky, he said: 'If you want us to reach the edge of the forest before it gets dark, then we better start moving faster.' And, having said this, he went on marching ahead.

What?! Lia was so shocked by his attitude that she didn't move at first, watching him disappear behind the trees. Then she remembered she didn't have food, water, or any idea where she was and hurried after him.

'Wait!' she shouted, trying to catch up.

When she finally did, Lia heard him whisper in a harsh tone. 'You better be quieter here or this will be the end for the two of us.'

She almost apologised but then remembered he didn't actually answer any of her questions. In a softer tone, she asked again what his name was. The stranger stopped and looked at her, as if to check whether she was worthy of such precious information.

'Why do you care?' he said abruptly. 'You can call me whatever you want.'

'Really? Well then, I can think of a few names that would fit you,' she replied. 'But I will call you Raven since you and your bird have so much in common,' she added, walking in the direction he was going.

'Like what?' he asked.

Lia smiled and answered casually, 'why do you care?'

It was late morning and the forest had radically changed its appearance. At night, danger seemed to be lurking behind every tree and Lia's companion had made them stop many times so he could listen carefully before moving on. In full daylight, she found his worries unwarranted.

Evergreen looked like any other forest she had been in. But, then again, Crina's garden also reminded her of her grandfather's. Perhaps it was wiser not to trust anything she saw there. So why did she trust Raven?

They didn't take a break for hours and Lia was bone tired and increasingly hungry and thirsty.

When they reached a small river flowing, half hidden underground, she told Raven to stop so she could have a drink.

'You don't want to drink that,' he said and handed her his own water bottle. Lia insisted she could get her own water. As she moved towards the river, Raven took her by the hand and held her back.

'What are you doing?' she asked, pushing him off.

'The water you are reaching for burns worse than fire,' he said and handed her his bottle again. Seeing her disbelief, he continued: 'The rivers in this part of the forest are protecting it from visitors like yourself. Try not to touch anything and you'll be safe.'

'Easier said than done,' Lia mumbled. She didn't care for checking if he was right or not; above all, she didn't like the tone in his voice. Lia drank and passed him back the bottle, but he told her to keep it.

She really couldn't make up her mind about Raven. Was he a friend, an enemy, or someone who didn't care either way? What if he just happened to pass by Crina's house at the right time? But then, why would his bird take and then return her Wish Orb? He must have known what was going on.

Moving on, always moving on.

***

At midday, Raven found them a resting place beside a large, fallen tree, close to the river they had been following for a while. Lia was completely drained of energy. She agreed to have lunch there and continue walking until the forest's edge. She even offered to go find them some fruits and mushrooms, but Raven warned her they should not take anything from the forest or damage it in any way.

'Well, then I am not sure we will have anything to eat at all…' Lia said softly as she collapsed on the grass.

'I have some of the bread you left behind,' Raven replied, 'it's a few days old, but we can throw away what is rotten.' He opened his shoulder bag and, to her surprise, took out Mariana's home-made bread. 'Ah, and here's your map,' he said and took out Alfred's map.

Stunned, Lia was about to ask him where he got them from when she suddenly realised he must have been the one who chased her in the forest.

'You! It was you, wasn't it?' she shouted. 'You are the one who ran after me and made me lose my path.' Her heart beat faster and she felt her cheeks getting red and warm. 'It's because of you that I was caught by that witch and almost got killed. It's all your fault!'

Raven waited patiently for Lia's outburst to end and, in his usual, dry tone, replied that she shouldn't have run away like that.

'But I was scared and you were following me! And you didn't say a word, why?' she said, raising her voice even more.

'Precisely because of this, you silly girl!' he replied angrily as well, a reaction that caught Lia off guard. She hadn't seen him lose his temper before. 'Because one is not supposed to go around screaming and shouting in this forest, didn't I tell you?'

Was he also afraid? Could it be?

'There are many things that watch you here in Evergreen, from below the water, from the grass and from the tiniest branches of every tree. The forest is watching,' Raven continued more softly.

Lia took a quick look around, trying to check if he was right.

'And if you want to have any chance of surviving, you need to keep your eyes and ears open and your mouth shut,' he concluded.

There he goes again! Scolding her as if she was to blame for being afraid of someone chasing her in the stupid forest. Yet… he had a point. She didn't know much about Evergreen but went in anyway. That was a bit foolish of her. If only he knew the whole story.

If it wasn't for Raven, she would be trapped inside Crina's mirror. Or worse. She had a lot to be grateful for, but his condescending tone – which seemed to come so naturally to him – prevented Lia from even considering thanking him. She took several deep breaths before continuing the conversation.

'OK, I guess you are right. I should have been more careful. I should be more careful now as well,' she admitted. 'But do tell me this at least. What were you doing in the forest and why were you following me?'

'I wanted to warn you about dangers like the one you met,' he replied.

Lia looked him in the eyes and could tell he was telling the truth. But there was clearly more to the story than he was willing to share with her. It was only by discussing calmly that she had any chance of getting to the bottom of it.

Just as she was about to ask why he was travelling through the forest in the first place, Lia heard the sound of flapping wings. Then she saw the raven flying fast towards them and carrying something in his claws. It was a dead rabbit that the bird placed on a rock at Raven's feet.

Sitting comfortably on the man's shoulder, the oversized pet observed Raven closely as he took out a short hunting knife and started preparing the rabbit for lunch. There wasn't much meat to share, but he worked fast and did not forget to give his bird its slice.

'Do you want me to make a small fire?' Lia tried to make herself useful.

'No. Remember what we just talked about, no breaking or burning anything. It makes the forest aware of our presence. This is why this rabbit had to be caught outside and brought here.' His tone was kind again.

It must mean they weren't far from the edge of the forest. Lia was uneasy thinking of Evergreen as an enormous, attentive and vengeful being. But she was even more curious to see how they would eat the meat. Did he expect her to do the same as the bird and have it raw with a bit of old bread on the side?

As he finished cutting it, Raven took the meat to the river and, under Lia's watchful gaze, placed each piece quickly in the running water using his knife. They all came out cooked, some even slightly burned. He had been right about the river after all.

The lunch was meagre and they didn't waste much time eating it.

During the meal, they were visited by small, funny looking creatures that came out from the trees and from under the grass around them.

Lia had never seen such animals: they looked like bear cubs, yet their whole bodies were covered in snake-like scales, shining yellow and green under the light of the sun and dark blue in the shade. They purred like small kittens and were equally curious about what Lia and Raven were having for lunch.

She tried to give them a piece of cooked meat, but they didn't seem to be interested by it. Instead, the tiny creatures started playing with the rabbit skin, chasing each other and growling. Lia was amused by the whole scene while Raven, predictably, told her not to get too close to them.

'These are Vaarians, guardians of the forest,' he told her. 'They look cute but can deliver a nasty bite even when young, so try not to touch them.'

She had never seen anything like those creatures before or even read about them. Neither did she ever find one in the forests around Ostrova. The only one who disliked the tiny beasts was Raven's bird. It flew to a nearby tree and watched them keenly from high up.

'Your bird seems frightened by them,' she noticed.

'Zyron is smarter than us both,' Raven said as he gathered everything and added they had to get going again.

Zyron – she finally got a name out of him. The name of the bird that both startled and captivated Lia, just like his master. From the outside it looked like a common raven, yet it must be the stranger's Wish creature. How fitting.

Lia caught herself thinking they could help her find Grandfather and save him from the Order. But why would they? How silly of her, again. Stranger things had happened that day, though, and it was not over yet.

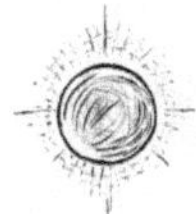

WE KNOW LITTLE ABOUT the original inhabitants of Maar, the sparse tribes that populated these lands before the great migration from the East. It is still uncertain, for instance, if they also had Wishes to make or if they lived a very different life. All we know is that they followed many gods, used a simple alphabet, and worshiped sacred places like the 'spirited woods' of Evergreen.

(from the *Chronicles of Maar* by Alfred from Ostrova)

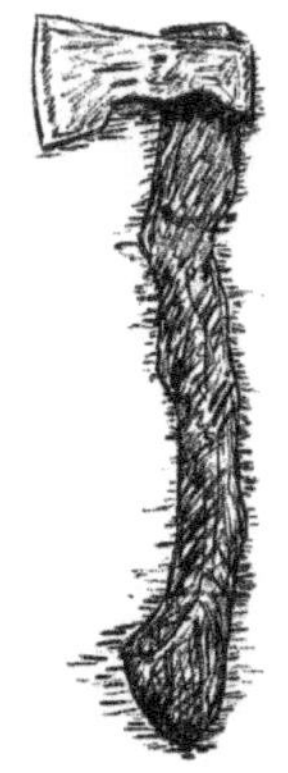

Chapter 13. At the Edge

'What exactly are Vaarians?' Lia asked Raven as they walked, side by side, on what looked like a path in the forest.

'They are one among the many spirits of this place,' he replied.

'How many are there? And what do they do?'

Raven didn't seem in any mood to answer more questions. She was used to it. After a long silence, he said:

'They are the spirits of trees and they are as many as there are trees in Evergreen. And since nobody ever counted them all, it's basically impossible to answer your question.'

Ignoring his crankiness, Lia asked what other spirits lived in the forest.

'These are those you can easily see as they are not afraid of humans, especially when they're young. The others stay hidden but, don't worry, they are usually the ones you wouldn't want to meet anyway.'

'Why?' Lia said, pushing her luck.

'Because it would mean we did something wrong,' Raven replied shortly.

Lia wasn't sure if he was trying to scare her but decided not to probe any further. They walked in silence again. The road was getting steep and the forest thicker. Little light was piercing through the branches above and Zyron, who had been flying beside them, was nowhere in sight.

'How come Lady Laurnic managed to live in this forest?' she said after a while, not really expecting an answer.

'Because the forest accepted her Wish,' Raven replied softly.

'I thought her Wish was to have a mirror, trap people inside it and steal their Orbs,' Lia said pensively. 'And she hid in Evergreen because she had made this forbidden Wish.'

'It is more than that,' Raven told her. 'Laurnic wanted eternal youth and used her Great Wish to set up the perfect trap for people like you.'

'But why would the guardian spirits of the forest allow this?' Lia wondered.

'It is because she gave her Wish to the forest. Or rather, she gave her life to the forest the moment she made her Wish. This is why we need to get out of here as fast as possible,' Raven answered. 'We took something from Evergreen and this is not a forgiving place.'

Without saying another word, he hastened his pace, forcing Lia to catch up with him.

Walking in silence for more than an hour, they ended up near a field of marshes. Lia looked around in disbelief. She took out her map and started searching for the forest's edge. Around the place she thought they would exit Evergreen there were no fields, but high hills. The hills of Seabor, the only ones standing between her, the Wish Order, and her grandfather. She hoped.

Confused, she asked Raven about it. He didn't look at the map but told her they hadn't reached the end of Evergreen yet. Zyron's powerful voice broke the silence as he flew high above and started circling the swamps.

'We can go,' Raven said. 'But with care.'

He turned towards Lia and held her hand. She was surprised by this gesture. His touch felt surprisingly warm.

'The Evergreen swamps might not look like much, but they are very dangerous. So dangerous not even Vaarians dare crossing them. Yet we must if we are to leave this place before the sun sets.'

'What makes them so dangerous?' Lia asked, almost with disbelief. To her, the field in front of them looked just like any other and the only danger she could foresee was getting all muddy and wet.

'I'll show you,' Raven replied. And, as he said it, he took a fallen tree branch and threw it in the closest water hole. It dropped with a splash and, to Lia's bewilderment, it sank completely. The water looked shallow and yet it was deep enough to swallow the branch whole.

'That could be you,' Raven said looking back at her as if to check that she got the message.

A little irritated by the whole demonstration, Lia replied that she understood she had to avoid stepping in the water.

'Is it also burning like the stream in the forest?'

'No,' Raven answered. 'This water is not burning, but it is treacherous. Not every puddle can swallow you, sometimes the land itself is shifting so you are well advised to follow exactly in my footsteps.'

'But Raven, how would you possibly know every bit of safe land here?' Lia asked with scepticism.

'I don't. Still, I have a better chance than you to get us across,' he answered and made Lia the sign to follow.

As she stepped into the open field, she could sense the air was cooler despite the fact that they were walking under the sun. The land they were crossing was made up of water, mud, stone and low grass. Zyron was gliding just above their heads, in complete silence, looking as focussed as his master.

Raven walked carefully, testing the ground with his bow. At times, he took them through shallow waters, populated mainly by frogs and crustaceans. In the grass, Lia could see snails and small, colourful lizards.

Despite the coolness, and the fact that they were walking slowly, it was a nice change of scenery. Lia remembered how much she liked the house of Lady Laurnic the first day she was there… how easily she could be fooled by appearances. All this time, she had suspected the Cardinal, yet her fear of him drove her exactly into the hands of the Wish Thief.

But, even if he was innocent, the Cardinal surely had something to do with her grandfather's disappearance. The Order's riders were chasing her, after all, and she had seen her grandfather held in the Order's prison. She needed a way into that prison without being recognised or caught.

Looking in front of her, Lia saw Raven. He was one of the lone travellers she heard about in her village, roaming the lands of Maar and trying, like herself, not to get caught. Her grandfather warned her against talking to such nomads. But perhaps he was wrong and Raven could help him, just like he was helping her.

Lia's thoughts were interrupted by a sudden move in the puddle near her. She saw a bright yellow fish jump out of the water. She gasped and then, realising what it was, started laughing. Raven didn't see the fun in it. He told her once more not to stray behind him.

'What kind of creatures live here?' Lia asked, trying to make small talk.

'There are plenty, but most of them live deep under the surface,' he replied in his usual, brisk manner.

Zyron let out a shrill call that made Raven look to the sky. The bird suddenly took a dive and started flying close to the surface of the water. Raven told Lia to stand still as he walked in Zyron's direction.

She decided to sit down. She reasoned that, if the stone near her didn't sink yet, it was probably safe to rest on. The sun was setting. It was getting cold. It had been chilly during the whole day.

The marshes around emitted a thin layer of blue-green vapour. It was a beautiful sight to see. In the water beside her, she noticed again tiny yellow fish either swimming lazily or chasing each other. The water looked shallow and she was tempted to put her feet in. They were so swollen they barely fit in her old boots after a long day of walking. Imagining Raven's reaction to her doing that was enough to amuse her.

Lia closed her eyes. Bright wave lines and the tiny fish remained vivid in her mind. Lines and circles started moving around, merging and splitting playfully. They made up a strange image.

With her eyes shut, Lia started to see a shape made of light and shadows. A familiar face, a face she had been desperately longing to see. As she opened her eyes, the face reappeared on the surface of the water.

Lia instinctively looked up. There was nobody there. In the water, the image was moving, coming closer and closer. She could see her grandfather, in his brown coat, wearing his big, heavy glasses. He was looking at her with such deep sadness that Lia felt tears welling at the corner of her eyes.

She fell to her knees at the edge of the water and, without thinking, reached out to touch his face and bring it closer to her. She couldn't.

Something pulled her back. Lia tried violently to free herself from Raven as he turned her towards him. She shouted and kicked him in order to break loose from his grip. Raven caught both her hands and held her close, so close she felt his heart beating fast, next to hers.

Raven was as scared as she was. For a brief moment, she felt she finally understood him.

'I saw him. Just now,' Lia said with sorrow in her voice.

'Who?' he asked and looked down at the water.

'My grandfather, right here.' As she turned to show him, the image had vanished. In its place, two yellow fish were slowly swimming under the surface. It was gone. All gone.

Lia asked Raven to believe her and, for the first time, he said yes.

'It is because I believe you that we have to cross at once.'

'But why? Why should I see him now and here?'

'What did Laurnic's mirror show you?' Raven asked. And then she remembered: it was her grandfather, yes.

'Laurnic learnt from you what you wanted to see the most and used her mirror to make it appear. The forest knows that too and it will continue to use the image of your grandfather in order to keep you here. You must be strong…' He seemed to want to say her name but didn't know it.

'Lia,' she told him.

'Lia,' he echoed.

For a fleeting moment, she saw him smile.

'I need to find him, Raven. My grandfather is being held by the Order and I need to get there and save him,' Lia felt relieved after telling him.

'You will do no such thing,' he replied calmly. 'If you go to the Order you will never come back.'

'I thought that too,' she continued. 'But now I know I was mistaken, I know the Cardinal is not the Wish Thief, it had been Lady Laurnic all along. She made Wishes disappear, I saw the last one fading away in her necklace. If only I could reach the Order, perhaps I could talk to the Cardinal and tell him I found the Thief and we are all safe now and–'

'You are wrong,' Raven interrupted her, 'Laurnic has been known to the Order for a long time. They tried to catch her in Evergreen but in vain. Few came back from that quest. But this… you cannot win this battle, Lia, trust me,' he said pleadingly. 'You need to go into hiding, I can help.'

Lia refused categorically. 'I have to try, Raven. I have to find my grandfather. I don't care about their Wish Thief. Grandfather and I will both go into hiding when we are together. You can help us then.'

'If there is anyone left to help,' he replied and looked up to the sky. Zyron was nowhere to be seen and the sun was setting. 'We are not far from the edge of the forest, come, walk behind me and we'll soon be out.'

Lia followed swiftly, this time trying to avoid looking at the water. She was thinking about everything Raven had told her. If he was right and Laurnic was not the Wish Thief everyone was looking for, then it must be the Cardinal. And he, indeed, was one person she could not fight. Not alone at least.

Lia remembered how it was when her Wish had been stolen. How powerless she felt, how unfair it was. She shook just thinking of it. And she was the one who couldn't care less about her Wish Orb. How must others feel? How would it be for Afilon if he couldn't get his flute? What would his family do?

And then she remembered how relieved she was to get her Orb back. How happy – yes, she was happy, she had to admit it– to know it was safely with her. The victims of the Thief would never experience that joy. He had to be stopped. Had to. This was much bigger than her and her grandfather.

She could try to expose the Cardinal, but to whom? The Wish Order had so much power that even the King himself was unlikely to go against it. They represented the highest Order in the Eastern Kingdom. They were the guardians of morality for all the Wish-Makers in the Kingdom. And now, they were the ones who had to be defeated.

As Lia decided that she had to find solid proof of the Cardinal's wrongdoings, a sight caught her eye. Through the fine mist covering the marshes, she saw the tall and dark trees of Evergreen again.

Raven took her hand as they hurried through the last part of their journey across the wetlands. Zyron landed on his shoulder and, in the mild light of the sunset, Lia looked at the two together. The only companions she had.

She held Raven's hand tighter as they went back into the forest. The air was warmer and darkness was starting to creep in through the trees.

In front of them lay many paths, some partially hidden by thick bushes. She had the impression she had seen that place the first night she got lost in Evergreen. But it couldn't be. The only similarity, strangely, was that Raven was close to her.

He hurried them through the trees, trying to quickly find the way out. And then, all of a sudden, he stopped.

Lia looked up. The forest had ended. The only thing standing between them and the empty fields ahead was a river with rapid waters.

'Come on!' Lia said, excited, as she tried to pull him towards the river. Raven didn't let her go of her.

'Damn this forest,' she heard him say. 'This river was not here before. It is not supposed to be here. The wretched forest doesn't want you to leave, Lia,' he said ominously. 'These waters would burn us, we cannot cross them, at least not like this,' he continued.

'But why? What could the forest possibly want from me?' she asked all frightened.

'I don't know… maybe you are supposed to replace Laurnic, I don't know…,' Raven said, deep in thought.

'Why, how… I don't understand,' Lia replied. 'You have to tell me what you know Raven, please. Maybe there is a way I can help, so tell me,' she demanded.

Raven turned towards her. Lia felt once more that she was being evaluated and that he still did not trust her. She tried to calm down and asked him again what he meant by her replacing Laurnic.

'You remember I told you Laurnic gave her life to the forest, right?' he started explaining. 'Well, her Great Wish was not used to create the mirror you saw in her house. That mirror had always been part of Evergreen, just like the shiny surface of the marshes and this river right before us. The water here has magic properties and Laurnic simply used them to lure her victims in and make them vanish.'

That's why the inside of the mirror felt so much like burning, Lia thought, but didn't want to interrupt. He probably knew this already.

'In fact,' Raven went on, 'she gave her Wish to the forest and, in return, she asked to receive other Wishes from it. The Wishes of people lost through Evergreen. You were one of these people, Lia. And since she is gone, the forest lost her Great Wish as well. You, on the other hand, have another Great Wish to make…'

'Then I'll give it!' Lia said suddenly. 'I will give my Wish Orb to the forest, Raven, if that's what it wants from us. If this will help us escape.'

He looked at her in surprise, as if seeing her for the first time. Then Raven smiled. Not a scornful, superior smile, but a friendly one. Lia found herself smiling back.

'You cannot just give your Wish to the forest. It doesn't work that way. You would need to stay here for your Wish to keep shining,' he told her.

Then he took a deep breath, put down the bag he had been carrying, and started looking through it. He found what he wanted. It was a small axe.

'This river was not here before. Well, if we can't cross it directly, then we'll have to make a bridge,' he said with a new sense of determination and started looking at the trees around.

'No, Raven, you said we shouldn't harm anything here,' Lia said, startled. He did not listen to her but continued to touch different trees and assess their width and length.

'Listen, I can help,' she continued. 'I can make my Wish and you can be my Witness. I can give myself a pair of wings and help us fly over this. I know I can, I had a friend who…' Raven stopped her.

'You will do no such thing. First, you won't be able to carry us both and, second, you are not going to waste your Wish for this.'

'But-'

'Listen to me!' he shouted. His voice echoed through the trees.

'You have to promise me that whatever happens, you will not use your Wish to save me.' Lia kept quiet. Raven put her hands on her shoulders and looked into her eyes. 'Promise me you will never do this.'

'OK, I promise,' Lia finally agreed.

He had chosen a tree and told her to run across it as soon as it was lying down. Bang! The axe was a bit too small for the job and Raven was in a hurry. Every blow echoed deep into the forest and made Lia shook. Bang! In the eerie silence around, she knew the forest was watching them.

Then it happened. From up the tree, a beast covered in dark, grey scales came down fast, rushing towards Raven. It resembled a full-grown bear but its front legs were much wider, equipped with a set of massive blue claws.

It was a Vaarian, Lia realised, a full grown one. It had none of the cubs' playfulness. Raven was ready to face it.

With one swing of the axe, he hit the beast as it jumped down at him. Lia expected Raven to be crushed but he moved away fast and the Vaarian fell at his feet. For a moment, there was silence again.

Then, from behind her, she heard heavy footsteps. Two more adult Vaarians charged towards Raven, growling as they passed by her.

The first fell under one of Raven's arrows, the second had time to reach him and hit hard with his enormous paws. Raven tried to avoid the blow but he wasn't quick enough. His right arm was bleeding and, taking the axe in his left hand, Raven hit the beast's head as hard as he could.

He didn't lose any time checking if the spirit was still alive but turned back to the tree he was cutting, hitting it again and again. Bang, bang, bang! With a loud crack, Lia saw it move for the first time.

But, before she could come to Raven's help, two other Vaarians appeared from the bushes opposite her. It was getting dark and Lia couldn't see how many others were around, waiting to attack.

Zyron charged towards one of them, trying to peck its eyes. The other was already by Raven's side. He struggled to keep it away with his axe. The beast, bigger than all the ones she had seen until then, was not giving in. Raven managed to hit it once but the thick scales around its neck protected the creature well.

Standing on its hind legs, the Vaarian kicked the axe from Raven's hand. He tried to reach for his bow, but it was too late. The Vaarian was over him. Raven managed to use the animal's weight to give the tree a final blow.

As the beast overpowered him, the tree finally fell down with a loud crack, creating a natural bridge over the river.

'Now Lia, run!' Raven shouted from underneath the Vaarian whose claws were ready to pierce his neck and chest.

'No!' Lia yelled back and hurried towards the river.

She took the water bottle, shaking, and filled it up. Quick, quick! A few drops touched her hands, but she didn't have time to feel them. All she did was hear, behind her, the terrible roar of the Vaarians, Zyron's cries, and Raven's struggle. She was breathing fast, feeling she was ready to faint.

She ran back towards Raven as fast as her legs could carry her, careful not to spill the water.

Lia hit the big Vaarian standing on top of Raven with her fist at first. As it turned around, she threw the water from her bottle directly into its face. She had no idea if these waters hurt Vaarians as much as they hurt her but, on the spot, it was the only thing she could think of.

It worked! Thank the Wish-Maker. The Vaarian let out a mighty growl and took a few steps back.

It was all they needed. Lia helped Raven stand up. His shirt was soaked in blood and both of them hurried towards the fallen tree.

Zyron was flying around, trying to deter two other Vaarians that were fast approaching. They were not going to manage to pass in time, Lia realised.

Quick, argh, if only…

She pushed Raven on the tree trunk and turned around to face the attackers. Despite everything, she was not worried for herself. She only feared Raven was too hurt to cross on his own and would fall in the burning waters of the river.

She looked back and saw him get to the other side. He was safe. She could breathe again.

The Vaarians had reached her, their enormous paws extended, ready to grab. Lia did not move. She stood still and closed her eyes. When she opened them, a strong light was piercing through the dimness around.

Wish Orb in her hands the Vaarians stood still, mesmerised by it.

'Let me go,' she said. They did not move.

'Forgive me, please, and let me go,' she asked louder.

The Vaarians looked at the Orb, then at her, and slowly moved away. Holding her Wish Orb, Lia turned around and, still shaking, carefully crossed the makeshift bridge to the world outside Evergreen.

Bravery is the greatest quality of a Northerner. Cunning is the character of those in the South. Honesty is the virtue of Westerners. Hospitality is second nature for the people in the East.

(*Book of Wishes*, 'The four kingdoms', appendix added in the 5th century)

Chapter 14. The Fox and Badger

TUDOR WALKED THE DIMLY lit corridor slowly, trying to make as little noise as possible. When he reached the last door on the right, he knocked gently two times and waited. The door opened and he swiftly went in.

Matei and Clara welcomed him to a dinner table with two candles, half burnt, and a plate with a loaf of bread and three green apples. It was the only meal they could afford.

The room was small, with two beds, one slightly bigger than the other, and an enormous wardrobe whose doors refused to close properly. However, it did have a large window overseeing the Inn's garden – a long stretch of muddy grass with no flowers and a few wild bushes.

The place was cold yet the air inside was stale, as the window had been blocked shut by the owner.

'These were all I could find,' Tudor said as he laid down a bunch of street posters on the bigger bed. They all bore the Wish Order's emblem.

In the candle light, the two cousins recognised Lia's face alongside the faces of four other people under the heading *Wanted by His Majesty's Highest Order*. Similar announcements had been placed throughout the Eastern Kingdom, as far as they could see on their journey.

Every time they took down as many as they could without being caught. They knew very well what the punishment for this crime would be – as none of them had come of age, they wouldn't go to prison but pass directly into the custody of the Order. Correcting the moral flaws of its wards was a special task of the Wish Order, one conducted by its most brutal servants.

'At least we know they didn't find her,' Tudor said, trying to see the bright side of things as he sat down at the table and started eating some bread.

Clara picked up the posters and lay on the bed, looking at the pictures.

'We need to burn them before anyone finds them here with us,' Matei decided and tried to take the papers from Clara. She didn't want to let go.

'These are beautiful drawings,' she explained before handing them over to her brother who placed the posters inside his shoulder bag.

'Oh, Clara,' Matei said jokingly, trying to mask his annoyance. 'I really hope you won't waste your Wish on becoming one of the Order's portraitists.' The thought never crossed her mind, but she did appreciate good artwork when she saw it.

Since Lia had disappeared that night in the forest, they had only been on the road, trying to find her. After some discussion, the three of them agreed that, if she had not been abducted by the Order (and most probably she hadn't, given that all her clothes and the map were gone), Lia must have continued her journey alone to the Order's seat. She had been adamant that the Cardinal was the one who took her grandfather. Besides, even if she had been caught on the way, they would again find her at the Wish Order. Only one place to go then.

'I wonder who the other people in the posters are,' Clara said.

'Wishfulls maybe?' Matei answered, while Tudor kept quiet, swallowing big bites of bread at once. 'I mean, they cannot be criminals and they certainly have nothing to do with the famous Wish Thief everyone is talking about, at least if Lia is among them.'

'No, they are not criminals,' Tudor agreed. 'On the contrary. The Cardinal pretends to gather all these people in order to protect them. At least that's what I heard in town and this is why soldiers are looking for them everywhere. They have no idea they would be sending them directly to-' He stopped.

'Do you really believe it, Tudor? Do you think the Cardinal is responsible?' Matei asked with the tone of someone who had been thinking about this question for a long time. Tudor didn't reply.

'Responsible for what exactly?' Clara asked her brother.

'For this whole thing. For pretending to protect Lia and the others while all along wanting to take their Wishes. For claiming to look for the Wish Thief when he *is* the Wish Thief!' Matei said passionately.

'Be quiet,' Tudor interrupted him and pointed to the door. 'We don't know who might be listening here. The innkeeper gave me a strange look when I went out this evening,' he said softly.

Matei walked to the door and listened for noises on the corridor. He couldn't hear any.

'Listen,' Tudor whispered. 'We have no evidence that the Cardinal is the Thief or that he kidnapped Lia's grandfather. But we don't have any evidence to the contrary either. What we are certain of is that we want to find her. So, our best chance is to get close to the Cardinal, as close as we can, without being caught ourselves. Especially with these posters in our bag.'

'Let's see who finds who in the end,' Matei said, visibly excited about the "mission," as he called it, while at the same time trying to lower his loud voice.

The cousins went over their travel plan once more and talked about the best way to enter the Order's prison without being seen. If Lia was right, her grandfather was imprisoned there. And, if she had gone against the Cardinal as they suspected, she might be there as well.

Matei defended his idea of capturing two soldiers and stealing their outfits. Tudor insisted they should try instead to join the kitchen staff of the prison. Clara supported Tudor's idea and, as usual, this made Matei threaten to split from them once they reached the Eastern Fortress. All three knew he was bluffing.

Looking at a detailed map of the Eastern Kingdom (they had bought one on the way with the money Tudor received from cleaning an entire stable), they saw there were at least three ways to get to Samor, the Order's Seat and the King's Castle.

The shortest and the most travelled way followed the river Vifar and the main commercial route of the Kingdom. This was the most direct but the least safe of all their options. The Cardinal and his soldiers were probably aware that the three of them disappeared from Ostrova at the same time as Lia and her grandfather did and, although they weren't yet on any public poster, that didn't mean nobody was looking for them. Besides, Lia was almost sure to avoid taking that road herself.

The second involved a long detour through the high hills of Samirod, a safer path, but also a considerably longer one.

The third, certainly the most hazardous, had them follow the edge of Evergreen until the northernmost tip of the forest. From there, in two days' time, they could reach Samor and the Order's prison.

'We should aim for the hills of Samirod,' Tudor concluded. 'It takes a while but it's much safer than any of the other options.' He looked for his cousins' approval. Clara nodded but Matei was determined to challenge the plan.

'We can reach Evergreen and continue along its edge. We would save more than a week of hard climbing. Remember how much of a hurry Lia was in? She probably didn't make any stops along the way and we are lagging too far behind. If she needs our help in Samor, we won't be there for her,' Matei pleaded. Tudor and Clara stayed silent.

'Besides, this way we are sure to meet few soldiers along the way,' he tried to persuade them.

'Don't be so sure about this, Mat,' Tudor replied holding the map in his hands. 'The Oder is looking for more than Lia and, as we know, many of the fugitives might have found shelter in Evergreen.'

'Who's mad enough for that?' Matei asked.

'Let's take the longer road, as Tudor said,' Clara intervened. She had been sitting on the bed in silence, contemplating one of the posters she had taken from the travel bag. 'The important thing is to leave as soon as we can,' she added, looking at her brother. Matei reluctantly agreed.

'And we will leave,' Tudor replied. 'But not tomorrow, as we have no more money. I have found Matei and I a job helping one of the wealthy villagers move. I bargained for a good price.'

'I can help as well,' Clara begged, but the others insisted she should stay back at the Inn, with their few belongings, and get rid of the posters.

'I can do that tonight and still join you early morning. I am stronger than you think,' she insisted.

'This is not about strength, Clara,' Tudor explained. 'We need you here to listen to the talk at the Inn and see if, by chance, anyone met Lia on the road.' It was true, Clara had helped them before by eavesdropping on two soldiers of the Order who were talking about the "girl from Ostrova".

The information she learnt had brought them to where they were, in Xarios, and to spending the night at The Fox and Badger, the cheapest Inn outside town.

Clara finally agreed to stay put and they went on talking about what else was needed for the road and how to spend the money the two would get the next day. There weren't many villages on the hills of Samirod, as far as the map showed, and that meant they had to carry enough food for at least a week.

Matei also needed a new pair of shoes. The ones he had were more than two years old and terribly worn out by the journey. He insisted that was not the case but both Clara and Tudor were adamant about it.

'We should keep a few silver coins for when we reach Samor,' Matei tried to convince them otherwise. 'We will probably need them to find another delightful Inn like this one until we can enter the Order.'

'Yes, probably, but without new shoes you won't reach Samor at all. And it would be a shame to leave you behind, barefoot,' Clara said and smiled.

'There we will have to find a day job anyway, even for a short while,' Tudor added, then suddenly fell silent.

He moved quickly, opened the door and pulled someone in from the corridor. Matei and Clara gasped in surprise.

'Who are you? What were you doing by the door?' Tudor asked with a menacing tone, pushing the stranger against the wall. Matei jumped to help his cousin and brought one of the candles from the table to see the stranger's face better. Clara quickly hid the poster under the bed.

'Don't hit, don't hit!' he shouted when both Tudor and Matei got near him.

'Tell us who you are' Matei said, trying to figure out who they were dealing with. The stranger had a long, bony face with two small blue eyes that examined them with a mix of fear and anger. One of his cheeks had a long, deep scar, most probably made with a blade.

'Wait a second, aren't you the innkeeper?' Matei asked. Tudor let go of the visitor and closed the door to the room without losing sight of him.

The innkeeper looked around suspiciously. He didn't know what to expect from the three of them. With a scornful tone, he asked Tudor why the violent welcome.

'You tell us,' Tudor replied. 'Are you so used to listening at closed doors that you forgot what happens to those who do?' he asked pointing towards a staff they have been travelling with, resting at the head of the bed.

'By the King's beard,' the innkeeper cried. 'If I have known you were so ill tempered, I wouldn't have let you in! Here at the Fox and Badger we run a most respectable business–'

'Everyone knows how respectable your business is, sir, so let's stop polishing a broken Orb,' Matei cut him off. 'Tell us what you were doing listening behind the door or else you won't be seeing the back of it any time soon,' he threatened, embolden by the presence of his older cousin.

The innkeeper gave Matei a long look, from head to toe, as if trying to make sure he was the one who had spoken. 'Lad, you have some nerve talking to me this way. You are many springs away from your Rite and many more springs to be my age, you rascal!'

Before Matei or Tudor could reply, Clara stepped in. She touched Matei's shoulder and, turning towards the stranger, asked him for his name in a quiet tone. Caught off guard, the innkeeper mumbled an answer and told the girl she'd better temper her fellow travellers.

'Good, mister Favoc, nobody here wishes you ill, rest assured,' she said calmly and looked at her brother and cousin. 'What we want to know is what exactly brings you to our room.'

'Ha, that's a good question,' Favoc replied, faking amusement. 'Well, your friend here dragged me from the door. I was minding my own business, just trying to see if anyone needed me before going to bed, when I was literally assaulted by this guy here,' he said, pointing to Tudor who was eager to say something.

Clara stopped him with a hand gesture.

'There is nothing to attend to here, Sir, we are also ready to rest for the night and thank you for your concern.' And, as she finished talking, Clara opened the door of the room and wished Favoc goodnight.

Puzzled by this unexpected turn of events, he looked around one more time, his big scar visible in the light of the candle. Reluctantly, he wished them good night and closed the door behind him.

Once the innkeeper was out and they heard his footsteps moving down the stairs, Matei and Tudor turned to Clara.

'I did it because we need to stay here one more night,' she anticipated their question. 'Because you and Matei have work to do in town tomorrow while I try not to *stand out* from the other travellers at the Inn, remember?'

'But Clara, this crook might have heard our conversation. He might know that we are trying to help a fugitive,' Matei said quietly. 'He could sell us to the Order for a good ransom,' he whispered. Clara lowed her eyes.

'You are probably right,' Tudor stepped in. 'We do need to work tomorrow, we need the money to travel. And it is best if we don't attract too much attention. Favoc might remember you tomorrow, Clara, but at least you were the one who got him out of trouble.'

Turning towards Matei, he added: 'At the same time, we know the innkeeper cannot be trusted and we should take all the necessary precautions while we are here.' He bowed. 'I am sorry I brought us here, I heard about the reputation of this place, but…' His cousins were quick to reassure him.

Before going to bed, the three of them agreed on what each had do the following day. After they'd put out the lights and wished each other goodnight, Tudor kept listening for any noises outside.

He thought, as he often did, about Lia. She had to be out there somewhere, perhaps in need of help, perhaps having found it. He couldn't stay mad at her for leaving them. She probably felt she had to; she would never have done it otherwise. And he would find her, even if he had to use his Wish to do so. They were going to escape the Cardinal, save her grandfather, and leave this wrenched Kingdom behind. All together.

As he fell asleep, Tudor dreamt that the two of them, Lia's grandfather and his younger cousins were on a big boat, sailing into the Sea at the Edge, leaving the Eastern Kingdom for good. In his dream, the Fox and Badger was placed on the shore, and Favoc cheerfully weaved at them from the front door. They couldn't help but wave back at him.

YOU HAVEN'T HAD A friend until you meet an Easterner.

(Saying in the Eastern Kingdom)

Chapter 15. Maxim's House

THE GOLDEN EYES OF the furry and cuddly animal were half closed as it licked Lia's face. It looked like a big fox, but a highly unusual one, with enormous ears and giant paws. It was Maxim's Wish and his only companion in the underground house she and Raven found shelter in for the last two days.

The fox-like animal was much more than a pet in the house. It also had healing powers, as Lia realised when she saw how fast Raven's wounds cured after Simon – that was the creature's name – licked them. At first, she feared Raven's deep cuts might get infected because of it. She had been so worried for him, so extremely worried.

In just a couple of days though, Raven recovered almost fully with the help of his friend and his Wish beast. And Maxim, as Lia soon discovered, was not only a great host but also a skilled cook with a matching sense of humour.

Seeing the two friends together there couldn't be any two people in Maar more different from each other. Tall, thin and gloomy Raven was in the company of one of the most talkative fellows Lia had ever met, and that was counting Matei. Maxim was a short, round, red-haired, endlessly cheerful woodcarver who lived close to the edge of Evergreen.

If there was one thing they had in common, it was their preference for eccentric pets. But, even in this regard, Simon was much more sociable than Zyron would ever be (or allow himself to be, she suspected).

'So, tell me again, Lia, how did this skinny little twig fight two, three, or how many Vaarians?' Maxim asked laughingly but did not wait for her answer. He knew the story by heart, having heard it for the first time the night Raven, with his last ounce of strength and supported by Lia, guided them both to the home beneath the ground.

'Old buddy, you should have known better than taking on more than one at a time, especially without me,' he added joyfully. Raven responded with a vague smile.

'This reminds me of the battle of Zima, when we fought four guards before entering the vault, do you recall?' Maxim went on undisturbed, this time addressing Lia as if she had been there. 'Oh, that was a good day, wasn't it? Two of the guards saw us enter through the South gates – I told him to go through the West gate, but he wouldn't listen – and, before we could take them on, two more appeared from nowhere in front of us...'

'Maxim, that's enough,' Raven said softly. 'You know I still need rest and you've filled Lia's head with enough stories already.'

'What?' Maxim turned around in surprise, looking as if he had heard his friend speak for the first time.

'You probably don't want me to tell her why we were there but it's fine to admit it, why not? We went to rob the town hall, it's true,' he went on making the confession no one requested. 'But, Lia, you should have seen their ruler. He was a special kind of bastard, you know. He made the people in Zima fight only to be able to sell weapons to everyone. Trust me.'

Lia didn't know what else to do but nod. Meanwhile, Simon had fallen asleep with its head in her lap and with his big paws resting on her knees.

'But our friend is quite the warrior, you probably know by now that there's more than meets the eye with him,' Maxim continued, talking again about Raven as if he was absent.

'I have never seen anyone as skilled with the bow and arrow and he's not bad with the sword or whip either. If it weren't for him, I must admit, that worthless ruler of Zima would have gotten his way.'

Maxim fell silent while he lit his pipe meticulously, lost in his memories.

'Well Maxim, it seems to me you are quite special yourself,' Lia said after a while, trying to add something to the conversation. 'I can see that from how well you took care of us.' Raven gave a slight nod while Maxim smiled and continued smoking his pipe.

'He helped me a lot as well,' he said, pointing to Raven. 'In fact, Simon and I wouldn't have this hideout if it wasn't for him, but that's another story. I am just happy I was close by when you came out of Evergreen. What were you two doing there in the first place?'

'Just having a little stroll,' Raven said, trying to avoid opening a new conversation, but Lia was keen to retell the story.

The night they arrived at Maxim's, Raven could barely lead the way and needed Lia's support to walk. It was then that Lia learnt about Maxim's Wish and how Simon in fact had more virtues besides healing and keeping company – his big paws helped dig the hiding place he and his master called home. Maxim, in turn, learnt that Lia was running away from the Wish Order and, without asking for details, pledged to host her for as long as she needed.

'So, we are both in your debt, Maxim,' Lia concluded, partially to annoy Raven and partially because she had become very fond of his friend.

'Don't mention it, Lia,' Maxim replied with a wink. 'And, remember what I told you. You and this guy lying in bed all day like a real sloth,' he pointed towards his friend, 'can count on Simon and me anytime.'

Lia knew she could not stay there for long if she was ever to find her grandfather. But that also meant being alone again, on the road, without her friends and without Raven and Maxim. The thought of leaving them made her sad.

During the past two days she had studied her map carefully and saw that she needed to travel for a few more days. But what if she asked Raven and Maxim to join her?

That would be selfish of her. Maxim had been kind to put himself at risk by hosting a fugitive, perhaps two... And Raven, he still wanted her to go into hiding but this meant letting go of Grandfather.

She could never do that.

***

After dinner, the three of them wished each other goodnight and went to bed in three separate rooms. It still surprised Lia that a house whose entrance could barely be seen from the outside had so many rooms and all of them spacious and cosy.

Maxim had certainly taken good care of this home and, as a talented carpenter, furnished it with tasteful furniture made of oak, pine and birch. There was a smell of freshness, of wood and grass, coming in through the narrow, horizontal windows of the living room. The shelves were full of tools and wooden figures depicting people, animals, and far-away places.

In Lia's room, on her bedside table, there was a small sculpture of a child sitting on the shoulders of an adult. All Lia could see in it was her and her grandfather. Another reminder that she had to leave. And soon.

Lia took the small figurine in her hands, looked at it for some time and headed outside for a walk. On the way out, she saw Simon's big yellow eyes glowing in the dark. She petted the Wish creature gently and closed the door behind her without a noise.

It was an unusually cold night, the first one that year that truly announced the winter ahead. Lia felt the cold but, at the same time, welcomed it. It was a good distraction from her own thoughts. The moon was hidden by the clouds and everything around was drenched in darkness.

Luckily, she got to know the surroundings quite well over the past days. She knew how to get to a fallen tree nearby and, as soon as she reached it, she sat down, closed her eyes and took a deep breath.

The freshness of the air and the sound of insects singing their end of autumn songs were both calming and painful to her. They reminded Lia of a time long, long ago – in another life, it seemed – when she would sit outside, on cold nights like this, wrapped in a blanket on the rooftop of her home.

She needed a plan to reach the Order. Crossing Evergreen and everything that happened there delayed her considerably, but she was grateful for getting out of the cursed forest at all.

However, she was still not where she expected to be. She thought they had exited Evergreen very close to Samor but, after talking to Maxim, she realised they were still far from the capital. More than this, there weren't many safe options for travel. She had to return to the edge of Evergreen and follow it north, a thought that was anything but comforting.

Lia sighed and, just then, noticed someone was approaching her with a small lantern. It was Raven. He walked slowly and, when he reached the fallen tree, asked if he could sit down. Lia nodded.

'When are you planning to leave?' he said after a moment of silence.

'Well, it depends on when you are going to be finally cured,' Lia replied, surprised by the question. 'I mean… you did save my life back there, it's the least I can do to—'

'You don't owe me anything,' Raven interrupted in his usual tone.

There was silence again. Lia didn't want to say anything anymore. For the past days she had been nothing but nice to him, helping whenever he needed something or had to move around. And, in exchange, Raven continued being cold if not outright scornful. Just like the day they met.

For a moment, in the forest, she thought they had become friends, silly her! But, except for Maxim perhaps, she had no more friends. She lost them when she left Ostrova without an explanation or a goodbye.

Lia didn't want to give Raven the satisfaction of noticing her sorrow, even in the dim light beside them.

'What you could do, if you wanted, is to listen to my advice and follow me out of the Kingdom,' Raven said suddenly.

Lia didn't need to look him in the eyes to see that he was serious. Raven was just as serious as ever.

'How do you imagine I can leave the Kingdom without my grandfather and without-' she wanted to say "friends" but stopped.

'Without whom?' Raven asked.

Lia started telling him about Tudor and his cousins. About the fact that they were ready to sacrifice everything for her and become fugitives. But she couldn't allow that and had left them behind near Ostrova. She couldn't imagine leaving the Kingdom without seeing them one more time.

'They probably tried to follow you,' Raven said after thinking for a moment.

'I don't think so,' Lia replied. 'Or, at least, I hope not. That would be foolish of them and they have nothing to do with this.'

'And yet they are part of it,' Raven said without any malice. 'Lia, don't you realise your friends were ready to follow you into Samor and stand up to the Order with you? Why do you think that is?' He didn't wait for her answer. 'From what you told me, it's because they care for you and if that's so, they probably didn't just go back to the village. If you are indeed determined to go through with your journey, your best chance is to have them help you.'

Lia was surprised by his logic. Not only that it made perfect sense and that she missed her friends dearly and needed them, but the fact that Raven could understand it before she did.

But, surely, it was too late to find them. How, when? Anticipating these questions, Raven started asking her about Tudor, Matei and Clara. What they looked like, what they had with them and what their travel plans were. Lia responded diligently and didn't dare question the reason for his newfound interest in her friends. She found comfort just in talking about them.

'Raven, do you think I will find them again?' Lia asked in the end, fearing his answer.

'It is possible,' he replied to her surprise. 'The world becomes a small place when you know what you are looking for.'

'I am looking for them, and I am also looking for Alfred, my grandfather,' Lia continued.

Raven fell silent. He reached for something inside his pocket. When he brought it to light, Lia realised it was the small wooden figurine from her nightstand. He gave it to her with a rare, sad smile. Lia's eyes started tearing up as she took it.

'Can you help me find him?' Lia asked, her voice shaking with emotion. Raven looked her in the eyes, then stood up. He didn't answer but told her she should go to bed because they will have a busy day tomorrow.

He started walking slowly towards the house, leaving her alone with the lamp and the figurine. Lia stood still, trying to understand what he meant by this. As always, Raven's behaviour was a mystery to her.

Was he going to help her? Did he care at all about her grandfather and her friends?

She was suddenly too tired to even think about these questions. All she could do was decide that, whatever happened the next day, she needed to be on her way soon enough.

***

The following morning, as Lia opened her eyes, she saw Simon at the head of the bed. He watched her intently, as if waiting for her to wake up. Lia chuckled and ran her hands through his reddish fur. Simon purred like a cat, to her delight. Just then, Maxim entered the room wishing them both a good morning and pulling the curtains.

Despite being early morning, Lia felt well rested and used her regained energy to help Maxim prepare breakfast. She was told it was only the two of them and Simon that morning because Raven had left earlier.

Lia was startled by this news. Noticing her reaction, Maxim assured her he was feeling much better and left with Zyron.

'That bird won't let anything bad to happen to him, you know it. And they will be back probably for lunch,' he said and winked. 'I know those two, they wouldn't miss the chance to get a hot plate for free!'

Lia spent the rest of the day helping around the house in order to distract herself from thinking about Raven's return and, most of all, about where he went. She knew very well he was capable of doing anything – including not coming back.

It was late in the afternoon when Zyron flew in through the window, making Simon playfully try to chase him out again. Lia's heart started beating faster.

When Raven walked in, he looked indeed much better than the day before, no more signs of weakness or limping. He seemed though to be in a hurry as he asked Lia and Maxim to join him right away.

'Where are we going and will there be trouble?' said Maxim, excited about the prospect.

'The usual amount,' Raven answered before he turned towards Lia and gave her a short sword to carry with her. She took it without thinking what that meant or what it was for.

From the living room, Lia could hear the two talking. Maxim was asking Raven whether he should take his pipe as well, a question that received a rather impolite answer.

'If things go well, Lia and I will be moving out of here old buddy,' Raven added.

'And, if they go wrong?' Maxim asked.

'Then I'm afraid you will be moving out with us.' Maxim's roaring laughter shook the house and Lia couldn't help but join in.

The second greatest duty of all, after the duty to one's community expressed through wise Wish-making, is the one to family and friends, expressed through the loving use of one's Wish.

(*The Book of Wishes*, On Wish-Making)

Chapter 16. Swords are Drawn

CLARA COULD SEE THE sun set from the dirty window of the room. The Inn's yard was deserted, no sign of either Tudor or Matei anywhere.

After she and her brother got rid of the Order's posters before sunrise, she returned to the Inn and spent the day mostly downstairs, trying to be as inconspicuous as possible. Nothing much happened that day. Travellers came in and out of the Inn and Favoc, the nosy innkeeper, was mostly out.

His absence didn't reassure Clara much. A man had asked to talk to him in private and Favoc left soon after. She couldn't tell if the two knew each other from before, but it was clear the visitor made the innkeeper nervous.

Clara hoped Favoc didn't go looking for the Order's soldiers who – from what she got from overhearing other conversations – had arrived in town the night before. There was talk of men and winged beasts sent to track down fugitives and those helping them. One of the Inn's guests, a visibly drunk old man with a missing leg, even told of a six-headed dragon brought to town but everyone laughed at him. A dragon, maybe, but one with six heads?

More trustworthy sources mentioned the presence of a Captain, one harsh-looking man called Karos, sent to bring back a girl in particular. And, although Clara's heart jumped hearing this news, the girl's description didn't fit Lia at all.

Meanwhile, Tudor and Matei were still missing. They were supposed to have finished work after lunch. Clara was increasingly worried at the prospect of them meeting Karos or Favoc on the way back.

When it was close to dinnertime, she decided she had waited long enough and her best chance of knowing if anything had happened was to go into town. She wrote a quick note, left it on the table and went out.

Except for one of the maids, there was nobody in the main hall of the Inn. That was strange considering that, from what she had seen the day before, many visitors had dinner there. Something must be going on, she thought, hoping it didn't involve Tudor and Matei.

As Clara stepped outside, she couldn't find any of the usual carriages or horses either. An eerie silence had descended upon the Inn and its regular inhabitants. The road to town was equally empty but Clara decided to travel by its side, just in case.

A few minutes later, she was reassured to discover that it was the right thing to do. In the distance, a group of people was approaching the Inn. Clara stopped and hid behind a tree, waiting for them to pass.

There were three people, and they were walking side by side without talking to each other.

The one Clara saw first was a gigantic man, both tall and rotund, with half of his face covered by a thick, red beard. He was carrying two blocks of metal on his back, an act of strength that could only be explained by Wish-Making.

The traveller walking on the other side was just as strange, if not more. Almost as tall, this man was shockingly thin and… elastic. His head, hands and feet moved loosely, and Clara could swear they extended and contracted slightly with every step. This made the stranger appear both tall and short at the same time and helped him walk slowly yet keep up with the others.

Between the two curious men, Clara recognised Favoc, his face and movements displaying the usual combination of cowardice and shrewdness.

As the unlikely trio disappeared from sight, it was a great relief to see Tudor and Matei coming her way.

They were also walking to the side of the road and, by the look of it, they were alright and equally in a hurry to get back to the Inn.

'We are sorry to be so late, Clara,' Tudor said after giving her a hug. 'We finished work after lunch, as we knew we would, but it was simply impossible to get out of town sooner.'

'Was it because of Karos and the Order's soldiers?' Clara asked them.

'Always up to date, little sister,' Matei replied cheerfully. 'Yes, he and his men blocked all the roads out and kept checking everyone at the gates. Luckily, they gave up an hour ago and this is how both us and Favoc and his buddies were able to leave,' he added pointing ahead.

'So, you saw them as well,' Clara said pensively. 'I wonder what they are up to.'

'Nothing good, you can be sure,' Tudor answered. 'This is why we must leave the Inn quickly. Matei and I did a good job today and even received some extra coins for it. You have a new pair of shoes coming,' he told Matei, who pretended he didn't hear.

Instead, Matei asked Clara if anything else had happened during the day. She told them about the strange visitor and how Favoc was out most of the time, but they knew that part already.

'We need to be very careful,' Tudor said as they started walking back. 'I don't know why the innkeeper needs these people and I sure hope it has nothing to do with us. I saw one was carrying things on his back.' Clara nodded.

Tudor proposed they enter the Inn through the side door, the one leading to the kitchen, and then leave the same way.

The room was already paid for, so there was really no need to bother Favoc with anything related to their departure. Clara had started packing earlier while waiting for the two of them. Matei suggested going for their stuff by himself, but the others wouldn't hear of it.

'You just want to have all the fun, don't you?' Clara joked, happy to have found her brother and cousin alive and well.

The Inn yard was as empty and quiet as before. As the sky turned darker, only the kitchen window and one of the guestrooms had lights on. And yet, the three friends knew the place was not deserted. Favoc and his two companions must have arrived there already.

As planned, Clara, Tudor and Matei entered through the small back door and looked carefully towards the Inn's kitchen. Nobody in sight. The four candles on the table had been burning for some time.

'This is strange. Let's hurry, get our things and get out of here,' Tudor whispered.

The three of them walked up the staircase trying to make no noise. When they entered their room, they started gathering the last things still lying around and, talking softly to each other, decided on what else was needed for the road. Clara remembered her pencil box was still on the windowsill and reached for it.

What she saw outside made her jump back in horror. There was somebody out there, in the growing darkness, looking inside the room. And that somebody was hanging upside down!

With a loud bang, the stranger smashed the window, making Tudor and his cousins instinctively cover their heads. When they looked up again, he had entered their room and was moving fast on all fours, on the ceiling, as if some magic glue held him upside down.

As his hands reached towards Clara, expanding beyond their normal size, she recognised the thin man that had been walking beside Favoc earlier that evening. She fought back as the stranger tried to take her by the neck, while Matei grabbed the only knife they had and stabbed the stranger's right hand. The man let out a terrible scream.

Just then, the door to their room was blasted open and through it came Favoc's other companion, the gigantic, bearded man. Tudor tried to push him out but, with a simple move of the hand, he threw him back to the wall. Matei let out a shout and charged at him with the knife only to be pushed back just as violently.

'Remember we want them alive,' somebody said from the corridor and the giant stopped. As Clara hurried to check on her brother and her cousin, the bearded guy made room for the person who spoke to come in. Favoc wore a big grin as he entered.

'Good evening, my dear guests,' he said ceremoniously. 'Why, you weren't thinking about leaving us on this splendid night, were you?' He pointed to the bag on the floor while picking up the knife from Matei.

'We paid what we owed you, innkeeper,' Clara said angrily.

'Oh, child, but this is not about what you owe me,' Favoc replied. 'This is about how much more I can get if I hand you over to the Order. They will be interested to meet you, it seems,' he continued with a big smile.

'But we haven't done anything wrong,' Clara protested. Favoc informed her that he was not the one to judge them.

'There are others who will. Just remember a certain fugitive called, what was it... Lia?' he pretended to check with his two friends, despite the fact that the big one did not utter a word and the thin one could only shriek from pain, sitting by the windowsill.

'Look what you did to poor Mikoi, is that how you treat fellow guests?' Favoc continued, uninterrupted. 'I think that, beside the Order's Seat, you will also see the insides of the King's dungeons, as you should!'

For a moment, Tudor, Matei and Clara wondered if Favoc had heard them talking the night before. No, Clara thought, it was probably the visitor who alerted him about them. She had no idea who he was.

As if invoking his presence, the next thing Clara saw was another man outside the broken window, with a stretched bow in his hands. It was him! In an instant, she and her friends heard Favoc's mighty scream – his knee had been pierced by an arrow.

'You!' he shouted in anger, pointing towards the armed stranger who had now entered the room the same way as Mikoi before him.

'Andros, get him!' he ordered the giant standing in the middle of the room in a visible state of mental confusion. Before he could act, though, the stranger made a jump and punched him hard. The blow led to Andros budging a little.

Tudor and Matei, however, seized the occasion and grabbed the giant's feet, making him stumble towards the window. Andros was close to falling over Mikoi but, at the last moment, recovered his equilibrium and attacked the stranger with a mighty roar. His fist missed him and pierced through the wall behind as if it was made of paper.

Andros's anger didn't only reveal his strength, it also made him catch fire! Clara had guessed his Wish incorrectly earlier – he could easily turn himself into a living torch.

The window was by now used as a door. Another man entered through it, stepping over Mikoi who was, by that time, lying on the floor. This man carried a blanket in his arms and was accompanied by a large animal that looked like a dog (or was it a fox?) but was able to climb well using its front paws.

The newcomer wasted no time and threw the blanket over Andros.

'You promised to wait for me!' he shouted at the man with a bow while he started to hit Andros enthusiastically over the head with the club from his waist.

It was a great opportunity to flee. That meant, however, passing Favoc who was still at the door, holding his knee, as surprised as they were by the sudden turn of events.

When the three rushed towards him, Favoc vanished on the spot, leaving a pile of clothes behind and a blooded arrow. From the clothes, a scruffy looking badger emerged and ran out of the room first.

The three of them followed it and rushed to the stairs. The sounds of the violent fight taking place in their former room made it clear they escaped in the nick of time.

And, as the three friends were descending the dark staircase, they saw someone else waiting downstairs. It was a young woman, her sword shining in the dim candlelight. They stopped at first, then rushed down towards her.

Shouts of joy temporarily overcame the noises of smashed furniture coming from upstairs. Lia and her friends had met, at last, in the most unlikely place – Favoc's Fox and Badger – at a most unlikely time.

What would Favoc and his friends do to Lia if they found her standing there, they worried. Lia made them a sign to be silent and pointed to the main entrance.

When she opened the door, the four realised there was more company waiting for them outside than inside. A Captain of the Wish Order, two soldiers and two winged dogs, smaller than the Cardinal's but equally ugly, were right there, looking to get in.

When the two groups met, everybody stood still. Karos, the Captain, recognised Lia on the spot.

'Step outside, all of you, this instant,' he said in a commanding voice.

'Do you really think I will make things easy for you, servant of the Thief?' Lia replied in anger and held up the short sword, leaving her three friends speechless.

The soldiers did not expect that either, as both of them instinctively took a step back. Karos, however, slowly took out his own sword and smiled, visibly enjoying the challenge. The Order's dogs started growling.

His mighty pose was disturbed, however, by a raven flying low over his head. The Captain waved his sword in annoyance. It was Lia's turn to enjoy the scene and, to everyone's astonishment, materialise her Wish Orb.

'This is what you are after, isn't it?' she asked Kavos provocatively. 'Well, you'll just have to chase after it.'

And, as she said that, Lia threw her Wish Orb high in the air, making the soldiers and her friends gasp and the Captain instinctively lift his hands.

But there was no use for that. Zyron held the orb firmly between his claws and, croaking loudly, started flying higher and higher.

'You fool!' the Captain shouted and ordered his soldiers to follow the raven at once. The two dogs were quick to fly after Zyron while the men ran on the ground, cutting the air with their swords hopelessly.

Left alone, Karos turned to Lia and her friends in anger.

'Not only you are running from the Order, but you have disobeyed one of the most basic rules of our land. Giving your Wish away is a serious crime, young girl, I thought even you know that,' he said, threatening Lia with his sword. 'When we catch that wretched bird and get your Wish back, you'll have many things to answer for!'

Tudor, although carrying no weapon, placed himself between Lia and Karos. 'You will have to pass through me first,' he said. 'And me,' Matei added, stepping forward, as did Clara.

Lia felt her eyes filling up with tears and her heart swelling. Sliding between them, she touched the Captain's sword with her own.

'You have the four of us to fight, Karos,' she said defiantly.

And, just as she finished her sentence, the stranger with the bow landed on top of the Captain from above, making him fall down and drop his weapon. Tudor picked the sword up quickly as Raven used the surprise attack to tie the Captain's hands behind his back.

'There you have him, all wrapped and ready,' he said promptly and stepped aside. Karos, still numb from the blow, tried and failed to stand up. Pushing him back down, Lia took his face into her hands and, looking him in the eyes, asked: 'Where is he?'

The Captain, blood running down his nose, was in no mood for riddles.

'What are you talking about, you lunatic?' he shouted. 'You, who prefers the company of outlaws instead of the Order's protection, you dare ask me questions?' he shouted back at her.

Before Lia could answer, a loud noise coming from inside the Inn made everyone aware of the fact that the building had been burning for a while. Thick, dark smoke was rising towards the sky, but the small explosion was followed only by an eerie silence.

And then, coming out of the main entrance, was Maxim and his Wish beast, Simon.

'Your visit at the Inn needs to be cut short, my friends,' he told Tudor and his cousins as he passed by. Stopping in front of Lia and Kavos, he complemented Raven on a job well done.

'It is a fine catch you have here,' he told his friend before bowing to the Captain's level in a mocking manner. 'I am afraid we won't be able to enjoy your company for much longer,' he addressed Karos. 'The hour is late and we need to start preparing dinner. Speaking of which,' he said, turning to the rest of the group, 'Simon and I have to run quickly to pay a last visit to the Inn's kitchen before it closes.'

'Time to go, Lia,' Raven agreed and gently tried to move her away from Kavos.

'But,' she protested, 'I need to know.'

'This is not the time nor the person to ask your questions to,' Raven said. 'It is time to be with your friends though,' he added, turning towards Tudor, Matei and Clara.

And so Kavos was left alone, on his knees, accompanied only by his thoughts of revenge and the sight of the burning Inn.

THE BEST TEACHERS DON'T call themselves that.

(Popular saying in the Eastern Kingdom)

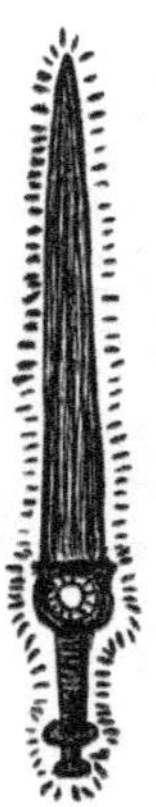

Chapter 17. In Training

R ARELY HAVE THERE BEEN dinners as merry as the one at Maxim's that night. The group of six, joined by Simon and Zyron, arrived at the underground house just before midnight. It had been a long day but none of them were ready for sleep.

After installing Clara in Lia's room and Tudor and Matei in the one next door, they started making dinner with the food stolen by Maxim (or "borrowed," as he repeatedly said) from the Inn's kitchen.

'It would have been burnt anyway,' he said half-joking, half-apologetic, making them all laugh.

Clara and Matei washed vegetables, Raven and Tudor roasted meat, and Maxim collected fruits from trees outside known only to him. Lia couldn't find her place. She was running around, from one person to the next, restless and excited as she hadn't been in a long while.

When Raven had asked her about her friends the night before, she certainly didn't imagine he would find them the very next day. And neither did he, as he later told everyone over dinner. In fact, they had all been extremely lucky to find each other. And this was because he managed to get a good lead about where the three of them were from the morning, when he passed by The Fox and Badger.

'I actually thought you were the one who told Favoc the Order was looking for us,' Clara said timidly. 'I remember seeing you at the Inn asking to talk to Favoc in private. After that, he left and we only saw him, well, you know when,' she added.

'I did talk to him in private, that's right,' Raven said in a friendlier tone than Lia was used to. 'I tried to find out who was at the Inn and pretended I was a spy working for the Order. Fortunately, I managed to find out about the three of you. Sadly, I also made Favoc suspicious, eager to see if there was any profit in it for him. Sorry for that,' he concluded.

'But we are all safe and together now, and it wasn't your intention for us to be harmed anyway,' Clara said quickly, turning a bright shade of red.

'If anything, the four of us are in your and Maxim's debt and we will always be,' Lia added with a big smile as the others nodded vigorously.

'How did you know what to bring for the fight?' Matei turned to ask Maxim who was busy devouring a whole chicken with nothing but his bare hands. 'I mean, you brought a blanket to put out the fire and all,' he continued, allowing Maxim the time to swallow a particularly big bite. After he meticulously wiped his fingers and mouth with the tablecloth, Maxim answered that he had known Favoc and his group for some time.

'You are actually lucky he didn't bring Manot as well, that guy is a born killer! He can guide swords directly into your heart with the power of his mind, the evil bastard,' Maxim continued. 'Luckily, it was only the other two and, for as impressive as they look, they are easy to handle.'

'What happened to them, actually?' Tudor asked from the other end of the dinner table.

'They ran off in the end, the big one carrying the skinny one on his shoulders like a scarf. Now that was something you don't get to see every day!' Maxim laughed. 'At least the two have some kind of affection for each other, like brothers should, even criminals like them. But Favoc, the eldest, was the first to abandon ship, the rat.' He emphatically punched the table, making the food shake, before starting to eat again.

'Technically, the badger,' Matei corrected him, causing Maxim to almost choke on his next bite.

'Well, if Simon had managed to get him, the Inn would have been called the Fox only, isn't it so, Sim?' he asked affectionately, looked under the table and threw another bone to his pet Wish. 'By the way things were when we left, there might not be any Inn to talk about after all,' he pondered.

'Don't you think Favoc will come after you with his brothers though?' Clara couldn't help but ask. 'I mean, he must have seen both of you.'

'Don't you worry, little miss, this is not the first nor the last time we have crossed paths. In fact, my buddy here and I had a debt to settle with this scoundrel.' He wanted to go on but looked at Raven and remained quiet.

'In any case, the four of you have nothing to worry about as long as you stay here with Simon and me. We'll take good care of you and, when it's time to go, we will make sure you are well prepared for the trip. I hear you are looking for trouble harder than we are.' He turned towards Lia. 'The Wish Order is tough to get into and even tougher to get out of, my friends.'

There was a moment of silence at the table. In the end, Tudor spoke, trying to sound uplifting:

'But if there are people who can do it, it must be the four of us!' he said, extending his hands towards Clara and Lia, who were sitting beside him. 'And these two in particular have been so brave in the past few days. Clara knew how to deal with Favoc better than Matei and I did and Lia, well, let's say I've never seen her raise a sword at someone, little less a Captain.'

'Or throw her Wish Orb, that was amazing,' Matei intervened. 'It fooled me as well, I was about to go after the raven myself,' he said and pointed towards Zyron who had finished its meal and was resting on the table near his master, his eyes half closed.

'Actually, that wasn't the first time it happened,' Lia said petting Zyron who, surprisingly, accepted her signs of affection. 'But that is another story for after dinner.' She looked at Raven with a smile.

Tudor in particular was curious to know more about the tall, dark-haired stranger at the table. It was clear that a bond had formed between Lia and Raven, someone he and his cousins knew nothing about. But it was not the right time to ask questions.

The merry dinner went on until the early hours of the morning. The group eat, drank, sang songs and played games through the night. Maxim was regularly accused of cheating at cards but was never caught, Tudor and Raven had an intense match of juggling bottles (with quite a few casualties), while Lia and Clara formed a team that decisively won at mime.

When dawn came, Maxim made the beds for everyone and the travellers finally broke off into different rooms to rest for the remainder of the day.

Despite feeling tired, Lia couldn't sleep for another hour as she laid in bed. She was overwhelmed by emotions, from the joy of finding Tudor, Matei and Clara, to the concern for whether they had really forgiven her. And also, the feeling of deep gratitude towards Maxim and Raven, especially Raven, who was not only helpful but so kind to her friends.

Maybe he liked them from the start? Or maybe he liked her enough to like her friends as well? She fell asleep before she could figure out the answer.

***

The sun was up high when Lia woke up. She looked around her room, saw she was alone and, for a moment, wondered if she didn't imagine it all. But the bed beside hers was unmade, so Clara must have slept there.

Lia changed quickly and passed into the living room. Everyone was up already, talking in low voices. They stopped and cheered when they saw her.

'Good morning, sleepy!' Matei laughed while Clara asked her if she disturbed her when she got out of the room.

'Oh no, actually I didn't hear a thing,' Lia reassured her. 'Did you all sleep well?' As she looked around, she noticed Raven was not there.

'He's out with his bird,' Maxim said, reading her mind. 'You know how he is, he needs time alone and I think we might have pushed him well beyond what he can handle yesterday.' He gave Lia a wink.

She smiled but remained silent. Her eyes met Tudor's and she noticed he was looking at her intensely.

He asked Lia if she would take a walk with him, Clara and Matei. 'It's been so long and we have a lot of catching up to do,' he explained. No convincing was necessary, Lia was more than ready to join them.

The four friends followed the road going from Maxim's house towards the edge of Evergreen. At first, they walked in silence, enjoying the feeling of being together on a beautiful, unusually warm autumn day.

'This reminds me of our afternoon walks in the forest back home,' Matei said after a while.

'The trees seem so much taller here, though, their leaves are darker but also softer,' Clara commented, looking up. Lia found it was a good opportunity to tell them what she learnt about those trees from Maxim, the masterful woodcarver.

But, as she started talking about types of wood, she knew her friends had other questions to ask her. And, all of the sudden, she decided to change the subject and talk about her grandfather instead. It was her chance to make them understand why she left them behind. And, also, why she was so grateful to find them again.

Tudor and his cousins listened without interrupting. Lia told them about the dream she had – she couldn't explain the cave in any other way that would make sense – and what she then saw in Lady Laurnic's mirror. Her grandfather was imprisoned, she saw it with her own eyes. But trying to save him would be very dangerous.

'Not something I can ask anyone to help with. Not even my friends,' Lia said, unable to look at them.

'But there is no need to ask this of friends, Lia, this is what friends do,' Tudor answered, taking her hands in his.

'When we left Ostrova, we knew what kind of journey lay in front of us,' he went on. 'And we continued on it because we care for you and your grandfather.'

'And because we love a good adventure!' Matei added enthusiastically.

'Yes, please don't rob us of any of it, especially my brother,' Clara joked.

'Now, the question is, where do we go from here and what is our plan?' Tudor said. He explained what he and his cousins were thinking about, including the idea of becoming cooks for the Order. 'And we should be the ones doing it, Lia, because they know who you are, your picture is in town squares all over the Kingdom,' Matei added. 'I am pretty sure there are quite a few posters with your face on them around the Castle.'

But Lia wouldn't have any of that. She thought instead about capturing a group of soldiers and entering the Order disguised as them. Matei cheered.

'That would be quite a sight,' they heard a voice from behind the trees. Tudor jumped to defend his friends but it was Raven who came out and greeted them with a smile.

'I am afraid that the Order's guards shouldn't all be judged by the same standard as Kavos and his laughable group. They are well-trained and have made Wishes that will help them capture folk like the four of you,' he continued.

'Some can see perfectly in the dark, others can immobilize people simply by touching them. Others are capable of commanding the wind and sea. You need more than strength to beat them, you need real skill.' He fell silent.

Tudor was the first to react. 'So… what are you proposing?'

'I already made my proposal to Lia,' he replied, not looking at Tudor but at her. 'The smartest thing you could do is make yourselves disappear, cross the Southern border and join my buddies and me there. We don't have much, Lia knows, but what we are missing, we know how to get and from whom.

'But,' Raven continued, anticipating an interruption, 'if I learnt anything about Lia is that she doesn't listen to reason. However, I am ready to try one last time.'

'Don't bother,' Lia said determinedly.

'Let me finish, please. You and your friends *will* go to the Order, you will try to enter its prison and find your grandfather. But you will be prepared for it,' Raven said, surprising all of them.

'How?' Clara asked.

'By knowing how to fight your enemy,' Raven told her. And he added to the rest of them: 'For this to happen, you need to trust me and give me one month.'

'What?' Lia cried, 'but it will be too late by then!'

Raven came close and placed his hands on her shoulders.

'Lia, for all we know it might be too late already.' He could feel her becoming tense.

'Yet, if it's not too late, this month will make the difference between victory and defeat. Remember,' he said, turning to the others, 'you are dealing with the most powerful Order in the entire Kingdom.'

'And the one ruling it, the Wish Thief,' Lia said, bitterly.

'Let's not worry about the Thief and focus instead on getting you ready,' Raven tried to persuade them.

'Will you come with us?' Matei asked, in a state of visible awe.

'Let's not worry about that either,' was his answer.

When Lia and her friends returned to Maxim's house, dinner was almost ready. Zyron was fighting Simon for a bone with Maxim breaking them apart while stirring the stew. Lia and Tudor offered to help Maxim but he refused, claiming his guests were never required to do housework.

'Well, you might live to regret this rule as we will camp here for quite a while,' she answered back. When he heard the news, Maxim was so excited that he started going to each one of them, shaking hands, giving hugs and even trying (and almost succeeding) to kiss Raven.

It wasn't until the food was burning that they remembered the meal and sat at the table. A second merry evening followed, this time focused on how best to prepare Lia and her friends for the journey ahead of them.

Raven was of the opinion that, due to the short time they had, each one should focus on mastering one weapon. This was exciting news, especially for Matei, who stood up so fast he almost tossed his plate.

'I want to learn sword fighting!' he said emphatically.

Tudor, because of his skills as a fisherman, decided to improve his use of nets and spears. Clara, to their surprise, was passionate about the bow.

'This is Raven's speciality, isn't it?' her brother started teasing her.

'If you continue talking, Matei, I think her first arrow will find its way to your behind,' Maxim said laughing.

And Lia, well, Lia didn't know what to choose. Maxim was quick to propose the hammer – his favourite – but quickly changed his mind after taking a second look at the girl.

'How about the short sword?' Raven suggested. 'You would have a better chance at hiding it when you enter the Order. Plus, I heard you did a good job the other day with the one I gave you. You can keep it if you want.'

'You are ready to part with Solia?' Maxim asked in disbelief. He didn't wait for Raven's answer and started telling everyone the story of how the two took it from the treasury of the Northern Stronghold. It was the only object they managed to escape with, chased by a flock of angry ice birds.

Eager to change the subject, Raven insisted on arranging a training schedule but Maxim went on about the intricate designs on the blade.

'The small sun inscribed on it, Lia, is the emblem of the Stronghold, which is quite ironic considering how bloody cold and dark it gets up there.'

The dinner continued deep into the night. By the end of it, the group had decided Lia and Clara would be taught by Raven and Tudor and Matei by Maxim. Everyone was happy with their choice of teachers and students. Matei proposed a contest midway through, and the girls agreed enthusiastically. Tudor, on the other hand, was concerned with learning fast and practicing as much as possible.

'Maybe we should find Kavos and his men again? I am sure he is up for a re-match!' Matei suggested.

'He is probably busy gathering people with strong Wish Orbs from this part of the Kingdom,' Maxim replied with a tinge of anger in his voice.

'We will free all of them when we get to the Order,' Matei said, trying to animate everyone. But none of the others joined in. The sheer difficulty of their task was clear to all of them.

'I want to find my grandfather first of all,' Lia said. 'But if I… if we can help stop the Order from stealing Wishes, I think we have a duty to do so.'

She was interrupted by Raven who was finishing his drink by the window.

'You have no duty to anyone. And the sooner you understand that, the better it will be for you and your friends,' he said in his usual, harsh tone.

'The four of you cannot fight the injustices of this realm,' he continued, looking directly at Lia. 'And if you think you and your friends can defeat the Order, you are more foolish than I thought and Maxim and I are wasting our time.'

Maxim made a sign to intervene but remained quiet.

'Let this be your first lesson: beyond the friendship that binds you, you are alone. And free. If you get to Lia's grandfather and save him, your only duty is to keep your freedom.' After saying that, Raven looked out the small window again.

'But this freedom means nothing if it is not shared with others, Raven,' Lia said as she moved towards him.

'You of all people should know how precious this is. You risked everything, your life and your freedom, to save me. And now it is my turn, together with my friends, to help others.'

She expected him to tell her off again. He didn't. Instead, Raven smiled a sad smile and wished them goodnight.

'We start tomorrow at dawn.'

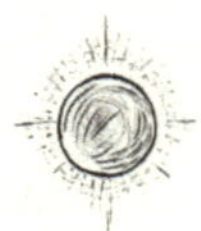

THE KING OF THE Eastern Kingdom's birth right is to rule over the whole of Maar. This right is bestowed upon him by the Wish Order, the keeper of the Book of Wishes, and its Cardinal, the guardian of Wish-Making in the realm. The Cardinal shall be the King's main advisor and first servant, and the wisest of Kings takes the council of the Order and works with its Cardinal to ensure peace and prosperity in the East and across all the lands of Maar.

(*Book of Wishes*, 'The right to rule', appendix added in the 4th century)

Chapter 18. The Secret Chamber

'How is it possible for them to be missing?' the King asked once more, growing visibly impatient.

Opposite the long, rectangular table in the Council room was the Cardinal. His grey robes took an even darker shade in the faint light of the half-lit chandelier. He was seated in his chair, ornamented with the Order's emblem. At his feet, tense like his master, was the winged dog.

'Your Highness, I am conducting the most thorough investigation, I can assure you,' the Cardinal replied meekly. 'And we have a lead, a good one this time.' He sounded nervous, unconvincing.

'I don't want any more leads, Cardinal, I want you to hand me the culprits without delay,' the King shouted. 'I have never seen the

Order in such disarray, people at the Court are starting to talk, do you know? Soon, everyone in the Kingdom will. How can you justify gathering young people to protect them and then have some disappear without a trace? And from under your very nose!' He pointed accusingly at the Cardinal who seemed to be deep in thought.

After a moment of silence, he replied:

'My King, I know the reputation of the Order is at stake. I know my own reputation is at stake. But I will not rest until I find the missing Wish bearers, the Wishfulls, and the Wish Thief.' The dog at his feet started growling upon hearing the last name. The Cardinal made a quick sign to stop it.

'Meanwhile, all the others are locked up in the West Tower, just like you ordered, well taken care of. They are guarded night and day by some of our most loyal servants, the best soldiers in the whole realm,' he said, looking for the King's approval.

Instead, the King shook his head and dismissed his arguments with a move of the hand.

'The best, you say? Only last night another Wish bearer disappeared before their eyes. How can you trust them? How can I trust any of you?'

The Cardinal stood up as if burnt by the question. He turned around, ready to leave, then faced the King again. With a trembling voice, he said 'Alexandru…' but could not continue.

'I think you fully realise the seriousness of the situation. I am not accusing you of anything, Aron. But I won't be able to stop others from laying this at your feet,' the King said, this time more softly.

He continued. 'I will give you a chance to find the missing Wish bearers. I put at your disposal my own Guard, soldiers who excel in their skills beyond everyone else. If, by the end of this moon cycle, you are not able to bring me the missing ones, the culprit, or both, I will have no choice but to dismiss you and take charge of the Order myself.'

The Cardinal didn't reply but seemed to have registered the decision. He bowed before the King and started walking towards the door, followed by his dog. Before opening it, he felt a touch on his shoulder. King Alexandru stopped him from leaving.

'Aron, you have been a father to me when I had none. And there is nothing, *nothing*, that pains me more than to see you in this situation. I will do everything in my power to help you, please know this,' he said and hugged the old man.

The Cardinal did not resist, nor did he respond to the King's affectionate gesture. He avoided his gaze.

'But you have to tell me everything you know, Aron,' the King continued, not letting go of him. 'Tell me what is happening. Tell me, for as difficult as it may be…'

'I have nothing to say,' the Cardinal finally replied, setting himself free from the King's hold. 'I will gladly accept your Majesty's offer and use the Royal Guard to trace the missing ones and catch the Thief. This is my duty. Towards the Order, the Kingdom, and towards you, Alexandru,' he said, as tears started gathering in his eyes.

The King kissed the Cardinal's cheek and opened the door for him.

Left alone, the King stood still for a while, by the door, as if expecting it would open again. Then he moved to the table and took a long look at the embroidered tapestry of Maar. The Eastern Kingdom was still there, the largest of all others.

Knocks at the small door to the side of the Council room interrupted his thoughts. It was a servant from his own cambers. He bowed to the ground and told the King that dinner was being prepared at the Castle, asking him how many of the Kingdom's Generals would be attending.

King Alexandru had forgotten about the dinner he had arranged the week before. Distracted, he told the servant to prepare a meal for twenty people and to let everyone know he might be late. The servant bowed again and left. A few moments later, the King left through the same door.

He walked down a set of stairs, passed another meeting chamber, much smaller and more austere than the Council's, and stopped before another wall tapestry. It depicted the four seasons, in the shape of four mythical beasts. A yellow bird with four wings for spring, an iron bull for summer, a two-tailed fox for autumn and a giant white cat for winter. The King pressed on the cat's blue eyes and a noise came from behind the tapestry. He looked around to check if he was being watched then moved the tapestry and went through the door that had opened.

The King then climbed a circular staircase and walked through a long, faintly lit tunnel for a good while until he reached the end. There was no exit in sight. He stopped at the last torch and pushed it up. The wall moved with the same rusty noise as before. He stepped through into the Castle's library.

Checking he was alone, Alexandru walked to the first aisle of books and picked the one with green and gold covers. This time the shelf moved, revealing a small door in the wall. He looked around again before opening it, bending down, and passing through.

The room he entered was unexpectedly large. Displaying the riches of the Royal chambers, it had a massive table made from a single block of wood and a carpet weaved in Coros, the famous city of craftsmen. Two small paintings hung on the walls, well-lit by three torches, and a large chest of drawers was placed between them. A map of the Eastern Kingdom, made in old leather and semi-precious stones, was laying open on a small table, close to the door.

On the only chair beside the small table sat Lady Aril, watching him come in. As the King entered, she stood up and bowed gently.

'Your Excellency,' she said, lowering her gaze. In the yellow reflection of the torches, her hair looked golden, falling over her shoulders and covering her crimson robes.

The Kind walked towards her and raised her head. He remembered someone else's eyes. Lady Aril's were a dark shade of blue, so dark they seemed black, piercing through him. The King smiled and stood back.

'Thank you for coming on such a short notice,' he said courteously.

'I am always at your Majesty's disposal,' Lady Aril replied softly. 'Especially in these hard times…'

'What have you heard?' the King asked.

'I am afraid the news will not please you, my Lord,' Aril said. 'Four Wish bearers disappeared from the tower over the last week. The most recent one vanished just the night before.'

'Four?' the King asked in disbelief. 'Are there no guards placed at the door, no locks?'

'There are always six guards, your Majesty, and two sets of locks made by the best blacksmiths of this Kingdom. But what it seems, my Lord, is that the Thief doesn't use the doors.'

'How so?'

Lady Aril stepped closer, as if ready to whisper a secret.

'I studied the room myself, Sire, and saw scratch marks on the windowsill. The windows themselves were locked from the inside but I suspect the Thief used them rather than the door. That is why the guards never saw or heard anything.'

'So, the Wish Thief can fly,' the King concluded, speaking more to himself than her.

'More than this, your Majesty, it is someone who can open and lock windows from outside. Perhaps the Thief uses something or someone else, a weapon or beast, to perform this kind of deeds?'

She paused for a moment, letting the King reflect on what he just heard.

'Or it is someone who used his or her Wish to travel in ways yet unknown to us,' she continued.

'That is not possible,' the Kings said curtly. 'The Great Wishes have all been accounted for and none broke the law of the land. I had inquired into this myself. The answer is clear. It can only be someone who uses the window and can either fly or is helped to fly out of the tower. We need to place guards outside the West Tower as well. Bring our best archers.'

'Yes, your Excellency, this is a good plan,' Lady Aril nodded. But then she stopped, looking as if she wanted to add something else without daring to. The King noticed and encouraged her to go on.

'I think having more guards is a wise decision, Sire, but I wonder if they should belong to the Order,' she said, moving back to the table.

'Why wouldn't they? The Order has some of the best soldiers. I personally asked our Generals to participate in their selection and will ask them again about it tonight.'

Lady Aril remained silent. 'Unless…' the King started cautiously. 'Are you suggesting we cannot trust the Order itself?'

'My Lord,' Lady Aril turned back to face the King. 'Each time the Thief has struck they seem to have known where the Wish bearers were, how to reach them, and most of all, where the guards stood. And, as your Majesty knows, we have tried many things so far, including disguising soldiers. The fact that nothing worked makes me suspect – and forgive me, Sire, for daring – that the Thief might be closer to us than we think.'

The King's face darkened. He turned away, moved towards the big table and set on a chair. After a brief silence, he asked Lady Aril if she thought the Cardinal knew about any of this.

'It is not my intention to make any accusations, my Lord,' Lady Aril replied calmly. 'Nor to imply guilt when I have no evidence of it. But…'

'Continue,' the King ordered.

'Members of the Wish Council are talking about how, over the past months, our Cardinal seems to have changed. He looks more tired but also worried, as if something is weighing on his shoulders. Of course, this situation is difficult for all of us. And it is increasingly harder not to tell the families of those we have under our protection what has happened. But the Cardinal opposes this vehemently. He wants us to cover things up, to buy time, but… time for what?' she asked without expecting an answer.

She continued. 'Your Majesty knows that he didn't even inform you when the first incident occurred. I have been thinking for a long time why that was.'

'He is ashamed, afraid… Perhaps he wants to solve things himself, as he usually does?' the King suggested. He was visibly displeased with the conversation, yet Lady Aril continued undisturbed.

'The Cardinal is all of these, Sire, but he is also troubled by what is going on in a way different to any of us. And… with your Majesty's permission, I could look into this as well,' she volunteered.

The King remained silent. He stood up and started walking around the room, went back to the small table and stood over the map, as if looking for an answer. Lady Aril waited quietly in a corner, watching him closely.

'Yes,' he conceded. 'You have my permission, Lady Aril. And you will respond only to me on this matter. But be warned that I do not accept treachery or falsehood,' he said in a menacing tone.

Lady Aril bowed in reply. She didn't say anything else, feeling the King was in no mood to explore the Cardinal's possible guilt any further. She waited for the King to dismiss her.

But he didn't. Instead, King Alexandru called her to the table and asked where the soldiers were placed in their search for the two Wishfulls. Lady Aril explained her plans and what she knew from the Generals on the ground. She told him that about a month ago, they managed to find some of the fugitives but none of them could be brought in.

'You remember, my Lord, the incident at the Fox and Badger Inn. Kavos and his soldiers were defeated by accomplices travelling with the girl they were after. Our men paid for their incompetence, I can assure you. Kavos has been demoted and the two soldiers accompanying him have been dismissed.'

The King seemed lost in thought. 'Who exactly defeated them? Were they outnumbered?' he finally asked.

'Not really… It seems that the girl was with friends from her village of Ostrova, but it was someone else who intervened, one of the nomadic criminals who plague our Kingdom.'

'Who?' the King insisted.

'I am looking into this, Sire, as it is a warrior the Order dealt with before. A man who always seems to be accompanied by his raven. All I could find out until now was that he is a mercenary from the South.'

The King frowned as if he remembered something unpleasant but he remained silent.

'Your Majesty, the girl we are looking for is one of the Wishfulls. She goes by the name of Lia,' Lady Aril continued, eager to demonstrate her knowledge and effectiveness.

'This man,' the King interrupted. 'We need to find him. Because wherever he is, this girl Lia probably is as well. And as long as she is in the hands of someone like him, she might disappear forever.'

All of a sudden, a flash of determination passed through the King's eyes. He looked back at the map on the table and asked Lady Aril to continue.

'As well as Lia from Ostrova,' she said reluctantly, 'we are looking for Daria from Farios. Both girls are-'

'The brightest Wishes in our land,' the King finished her sentence. 'The two girls the Order was supposed to be monitoring at all times and educating for the good of our Kingdom. How is it possible that such girls are missing?'

'My Lord, they were being monitored. Lia was living with her grandfather, a person well known by the Cardinal, someone you knew as well… And Daria, well, she escaped two times from the Order's school and returned to Farios to be with her brother. After an incident, the Cardinal decided it was best for her to live in her village together with her brother. But when the Order's soldiers came for them, they were already gone. Fortunately, we know for sure they didn't lose their Wishes, Excellency. At least, not yet.' Lady Aril's voice had dropped to a whisper.

'Kavos saw Lia's Wish just a few weeks ago,' she continued in a more uplifting tone. 'And we found Daria's brother around the same time. She was with him but somehow managed to escape our soldiers. He, on the other hand, is now in the Order's dungeon.'

'Good, good,' the King replied, absentmindedly. 'As long as you and your men are doing everything you can to find and bring these girls here. Their Wishes are vital for the Kingdom, they *cannot* be wasted or stolen, do you understand Aril?'

'Yes, Sire, of course,' Lady Aril was quick to reply. 'I assure you, no effort is spared in trying to find them. Our spies told us they are not far from the capital. My suspicion is that they might pay us a visit soon. Daria will surely try to find her brother and Lia-'

'Lia is being accompanied by the man with the raven,' the King muttered.

'Yes, probably,' Lady Aril conceded. 'In any case, as soon as we find them, they will be placed under our watchful eye in the Tower and-'

'No!' the King interrupted. 'Have you learnt nothing from what just happened?! That is the last place we should bring them. Clearly the Wish Thief has infiltrated the Order and the tower is not safe anymore. The only reason we are still keeping the rest of the Wish bearers there is to hopefully attract the Thief again and, this time around, get hold of him.' Lady Aril bowed but said nothing.

'The moment you find any of them, you bring them directly to me,' the King ordered.

'Yes, my Lord, it will be as you command,' Lady Aril said, still not raising her eyes. 'But this means not informing the Cardinal and I-'

'Your allegiance is to *me*, Lady Aril,' the King replied, looking at her as if to check if he could trust her. 'And, through me, with the Kingdom. Aron is aging fast, I'm afraid. He failed to protect the Wishfulls and he might have even put them in more danger for all we know.

'I need you to keep an eye on him. Report to me and only to me. We cannot afford a scandal that would shake people's trust in the Order. Not at this time.'

'Yes, your Majesty,' she replied and, in her eyes, the King saw the same determination as his. 'I shall not let you down, Sire,' she added, bowing once more as she left the room.

The King went back to the table, folded the map, placed it in his pocket, and made his way back to meet the Generals for dinner.

One never says goodbye to a friend.

(Saying in the Eastern Kingdom)

Chapter 19. Farewell

LIA AND HER FRIENDS woke up before sunrise. They started packing in silence, taking as many useful things as possible without using too much space. Most of all, they needed to keep the bags light.

From the kitchen came the appetising smell of fresh bread. Maxim was making a final breakfast for everyone and shouting once in a while to remind them what to take.

'Make sure you don't forget the rope!'

'And the extra spear and arrow tips I made for you!'

'Oh, you'll need candles too, you can take the thick ones from the top shelf in your bedroom, Tudor.'

'Also, the hand drawn map of the Order's prison, you can take that too. But you better come and give it back one day! You can correct what's wrong in it, it's been given to me by Gheorghe, and he did like his liquor, that fellow.'

On any other day, his friends would have replied joyfully, ready to tease him. On that particular morning though, they were all focused on packing and trying hard to avoid acknowledging that it was time to leave.

Maxim continued to do most of the talking at breakfast, followed by Lia and Matei. They went over the plan for their journey one more time and asked Raven questions, sometimes the same one more than once. Characteristically, he answered mainly by either nodding or shaking his head.

'You will be fine,' Maxim said, the first rays of morning sun dancing on his face. 'You were, after all, the best pupils I ever had! Isn't that so, our silent friend?' Raven nodded in response.

'Matei, you are really talented at sword fighting, as we all discovered. If you ever need a job in the future, let me know – there are plenty of things to do out here for a fine swordsman such as yourself.' Maxim looked towards Matei who was so touched by the compliment he almost choked on the milk.

'Clara,' Maxim continued. 'You are ready to give Raven some serious competition in an archery contest. If I didn't know better, I would have said you practiced before, young lady.' Clara blushed instantly.

'And Tudor, your skills as a fisherman serve you well with the spear. I have no doubt you will be the best fisherman on the Great Lake or whatever waters you choose to sail on.'

Tudor, Clara and Matei all thanked Maxim for all his help.

'And what about me, Maxim, did you forget me already?' Lia said half-hurt, half-amused by the omission.

'My dear, I chose to speak of you last for a reason,' Maxim answered affectionately. 'This is because I met you first and, even if it has been only a few weeks, I feel I know you best, Lia. You became, in this short time, something of a daughter to me.'

'Or a younger sister,' Raven intervened in jest.

Maxim ignored his friend. 'And this makes me so proud to see you become a skilled warrior, ready to face the Order and the Thief. Whichever comes first.'

Maxim's voice was trembling with emotion while Lia's eyes became wet. She gave him as strong a hug as she could.

'This won't be the last one today,' she warned him, trying to hold back her tears. 'We wouldn't have been able to do much without you and Raven, the best teachers we could have ever hoped for.' Tudor and his cousins cheered.

'I in particular, Maxim, am grateful to you for training me to be better than Lia,' Matei declared at his own peril, continuing the friendly argument born the day Clara and Lia challenged him and Tudor.

It was only after Matei and Lia agreed they needed a re-match that the group of friends started thinking about what they would do when they reached the Order. The discussion sounded light-hearted but everyone was worried about the journey ahead. Lia was trying hard not to think about the possibility of losing her friends again, this time for good… She had seen them chased by soldiers in the dream world, but they were now better able to defend themselves. She had to believe that.

Raven, who agreed the week before to be the informal head of the expedition, told them it will take three days to reach the capital but only if they walk during the night as well. They all agreed, Matei enthusiastically so. When they arrived, they would be hosted by a friend of Raven's, a merchant who lived in the old part of town, close to the Order's Seat.

'Sabim, yes, he is not a great cook but at least he can be trusted,' Maxim said while collecting the empty plates after breakfast.

Sabim was involved in delivering vegetables to the Order every other day and thus could help them get in. Once inside, they would split into two groups. Matei and Tudor's job would be to distract the guards and lead them to the inner yard. Raven showed everyone its place on the map.

While Matei and Tudor were luring the guards away, Raven and the girls would enter the prison, look for Alfred, and free him.

'And then we will get out through the tunnel they use to deliver food and meet Matei and Tudor outside the gates,' Raven concluded. They had listened carefully, and dared to imagine how good it would feel to be done with it all. The morning sun helped them feel optimistic about this plan and ignore the danger.

'What if we don't find him, though?' Lia couldn't help asking. There was silence at first. Tudor said that they would simply have to try again and perhaps look in other parts of the Castle.

'Your grandfather could not have disappeared without a trace and if there is anyone who can help you find him, that person is Raven,' he said. Tudor looked at Raven for a word of encouragement but he remained silent.

'Well, at the end of the day,' Maxim intervened. 'You know where to come back with or without your grandfather, Lia. Simon and I will be waiting for you all. And remember, we will never forgive you if you forget us.'

'How could we?' said Clara. 'You make some of the best bread we have ever tasted.'

'Not to mention the best wood sculptures,' added Tudor.

'And you made the best Wish in the whole universe!' Matei concluded, petting Simon who was snoozing in his lap.

'Oh, good you reminded me,' Maxim was quick to reply. 'I have some gifts for you.' And, as he said that, he quickly left for his bedroom and came back with a bag full of presents to everyone's delight.

Matei received a new pair of shoes which made him very happy, and his friends very relieved. He would certainly have been stubborn about replacing the old ones. Clara was given a carved flower made of four different types of wood. For Tudor, Maxim handed over copies of his best recipes, a gift that was cheered by the whole group since Tudor had proven himself to be a promising cook. Lia received a sword belt and holder made of silver and leather. She was glad to have Solia ready at hand.

'And for you, my old friend, what could I ever give you?' Maxim asked Raven theatrically.

'Well, perhaps you could return all the treasures we lost because of your impatience?' Raven replied sarcastically. 'And, if not, I will simply do with continuing to count you among my friends.'

Maxim was visibly touched by this answer and almost dropped from his hands the box he had prepared for Raven. When he opened it, Raven discovered a Royal emblem with its three Orbs, made of solid gold.

'It is the last one I stole,' Maxim said with a smile. 'And this one was for you.' Raven took the emblem, looked at it, then placed it in his pocket.

The two friends shook hands and Raven promised to be back soon. The others seconded his promise. They took their bags, their weapons and maps. After looking around one more time – mostly to remember the place rather than check if anything was missing – they walked out followed by Maxim and Simon.

The two of them agreed to accompany the group to the edge of the forest. Around noon they had reached it and, visibly sad to part company, they said their final goodbyes. Simon followed them a bit longer along the road before returning to his master and going home.

Despite leaving Maxim and Simon behind, Lia and her friends remained cheerful as they continued to climb the steep hills towards the north. Raven in particular seemed to be in a good mood, willing to share stories from his many journeys around Maar.

It was one of the rare moments since leaving Ostrova when Lia really believed she would find Grandfather and they would rebuild their lives with Tudor and his cousins. And maybe, just maybe, Raven would agree to join them and leave behind his endless wandering. Then it would all be perfect.

***

The night came fast that late autumn day and, with it, a thick mist descended over the forest. Raven had planned to walk two more hours, but it was so dark and misty they risked missing the right path.

In the end, they started a small fire and took out the dried meat and crusty bread Maxim had prepared for them. Wrapped in blankets, the five started humming old songs and telling jokes, accompanied now and then by Zyron's guttural calls.

As the light diminished and the cold started to bite, Raven told the others to rest while he went to gather more wood. 'You will need all your strength as we have to continue our journey later tonight,' he added.

Lia said she didn't feel tired at all and wanted to keep him company. At first Raven refused but she insisted. 'You don't want me to keep the rest awake with my chatter, do you?' And so, the two of them, shadowed by Zyron, headed into the milky darkness carrying only their swords and a small hand torch.

'This forest is not far away from Evergreen. So why aren't there any guardian spirits in these trees?' she asked.

'Because we are lucky tonight,' Raven replied as he gathered broken branches from beneath an old pine tree and passed them to her.

'We have been pretty lucky, haven't we?' she said, upon reflection. 'Or, at least, I have. I started this journey alone and now I have four friends by my side. And that's not even counting Maxim and Simon,' she said cheerfully. 'I can't wait for you to meet my grandfather, Raven, I think you'll like him.'

'Do you think he will like me?' Raven asked with a smile.

'I am sure he will, and you two will have a lot to talk about,' Lia confirmed. 'You see, my grandfather has read a lot of books and told us many things about the places you've been to. I can see you staying up late by the fire and talking about the world beyond the Eastern Kingdom. I've done it so many times as a child. I loved listening to his stories about the Southern lands, where my parents disappeared.'

'I know those lands well, Lia. I could take you one day and try to find out what happened to them. I am sure in less than a week we could meet someone who can tell us their story,' Raven said confidently.

Lia didn't reply. She was thinking about the possibility of visiting that part of Maar, the fallen Kingdom that had captured her fantasy as a child. Her grandfather would never agree, of course. He would surely tell her he had already lost family there. And that it is better to read than to travel.

Perhaps, after all, Grandfather wouldn't like Raven that much. But he would certainly respect him.

Meanwhile, Raven told her how they could reach the Southern lands most easily and what kind of landscapes and people they would find there. It didn't sound very appealing, but Raven sounded so enthusiastic that she kept nodding eagerly.

'Raven, do you think we will be able to escape the Order and live our lives in peace elsewhere?' she suddenly asked him.

It was a question that had been weighing heavily on her mind over the last month. She and her friends might have learnt some fighting skills, but they were no match for the Cardinal and his mighty guard. That was certainly the case in Ostrova, where nothing happened without the Order's blessing.

'The Order and the King are not all-powerful,' Raven answered after a while. 'Maar is much bigger than they could ever conquer, despite their greed and malice.'

Lia was surprised to hear Raven say this and could sense the bitterness in his voice. Did he know the Cardinal or the King personally?

'But you know this already,' he continued. 'You have seen how even inside the Kingdom there are places they cannot reach.'

'Like Evergreen,' Lia said softly. 'Yes, but only witches and spirits live there, Raven. That could never be a life for me or my friends.'

Her voice grew more confident. 'What we need is to stay here and fight. For ourselves and all those harmed by the Cardinal.'

Raven said nothing. Instead, he let fall the piece of wood he had in his hands and turned away from her, trying to find his balance.

'What's wrong?' Lia asked, startled. He did not answer.

'If I said something that upset you, tell me. I know you don't want to stay and help others, you told me that. But you… I can't keep running forever. Don't you agree, Raven?'

When he turned around, Lia gasped. His face had changed. Not his physical features, but his gaze. He seemed at once to be looking at her, mesmerised, and beyond her, aimlessly, into the darkness of the forest.

'Raven! Raven!' she called, dropping the wood they had gathered and starting to shake him. Nothing changed.

Then, all of a sudden, he grabbed her hand and twisted it behind Lia's back, immobilising her.

'Raven, what's happening to you?' she asked, struggling to set herself free.

'Your Wish,' she heard him say softly. 'Show it to me.'

Her heart sank.

'No. And if you don't stop this right now, I will draw my sword. This is not funny,' Lia said as she managed to escape his grip and moved away from him.

She didn't know what exactly was happening, but she knew she had been in the same situation before.

'Give me your Wish,' Raven said in a tone that was not his own.

It had happened before, yes, in her grandfather's house. On the day she fled. Raven was acting and looking just like the robbers back then. They, too, were after her Wish Orb.

'Raven, I don't know what is happening to you, but you need to wake up,' Lia said with resolve, grabbing the torch in one hand and Solia, her sword, in the other, its blade gleaming in the light. She tried to control her breathing.

Then she remembered what else happened that night. The thieves had many Wish Orbs and started using them. Lia instinctively looked at Raven's hands. No light there. Relief. Then someone grabbed her ankle. Lia looked down and, with horror, saw a moving root. The root was growing around her ankle, like a human hand, pinning her to the ground.

She swiftly used her sword to set herself free. She was surprised at how easy it was to sever it, amazed by her own strength. Control your breathing, in, out, in, out, that's it!

When she looked up towards Raven, Lia saw two creatures coming out of the ground behind him. They had a human shape but were made of rocks, branches, roots and mud. And they were moving towards her.

She had been here before. She knew what she had to do. In, out, in, out.

Lia quickly pierced one of them with her sword. It went through and got stuck within. She looked at Raven for help, but he was not there to help her. Instead, he extended his hand and asked again for her Wish.

Lia used the torch to set the monster beside her on fire. The fire spread quickly, melting the branches and dead leaves inside which allowed her to free her sword.

Then the second creature came near, hands reaching, ready to grasp her. With a mighty swing, she cut its arms off. They twitched on the ground. Before she could sever its head, her sword was stopped by another.

It was Raven's.

Without looking directly at her, he started to fight her, advancing bit by bit. He had a huge advantage as he knew all the moves that he taught her. But Lia walked back, defending well, looking around to see if other monsters appeared or if her friends heard the noises. They didn't. The sounds of the fight drowned in the thick, white mist.

As her back touched the old trunk of a fir tree, she was forced to stop. Raven sensed the opportunity and disarmed her. She held her breathe.

'Your Wish,' he repeated in that unfamiliar voice. And then, just as he raised the sword against her, he himself was attacked.

Another memory had awakened. Zyron was flying in to save her just like before, this time from his master.

Lia took the chance to escape, picked up her sword and struck the armless creature approaching her. She looked back only to see Raven hit Zyron. The bird fell to the ground. Blood rushed to her head.

She roared and started the fight again, Solia shining in her hands. Raven was now on the defensive but could not focus. He looked at Zyron who was struggling to stand. For a moment, Lia had found her friend.

In that brief moment, Raven looked at her and shouted: 'Go away!' And as he said that, he buried his sword in the ground and collapsed near it, screaming in agony. 'Go away, go away, go… away.'

She wanted to stay and help, how she wanted that! But how? All she could see was that her presence was prolonging his suffering. If she left, maybe the real Raven would return, take care of Zyron and get rid of those creatures. If she stayed, they would keep coming back and his torment would go on.

And so, she went. She ran through the trees and fog, her heart beating faster than before. All the while, Lia looked for her friends. She found them fast asleep and woke them all up. They jumped to their feet, not knowing what had happened. They all asked where Raven was.

Lia told them there was no time to lose and that she would explain everything later. They packed swiftly and, barely knowing where to go, made their way into the forest and the wailing noises of the night.

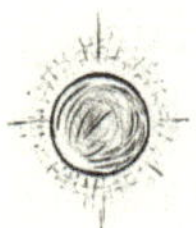

A SMALL NUMBER OF Wishes never become reality. This is either because the Wish-Maker did not properly focus on formulating the Wish, or because the Wish itself was too big to be granted.

(*The Metaphysics of Wish Orbs*, school textbook)

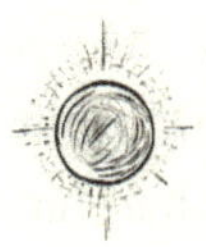

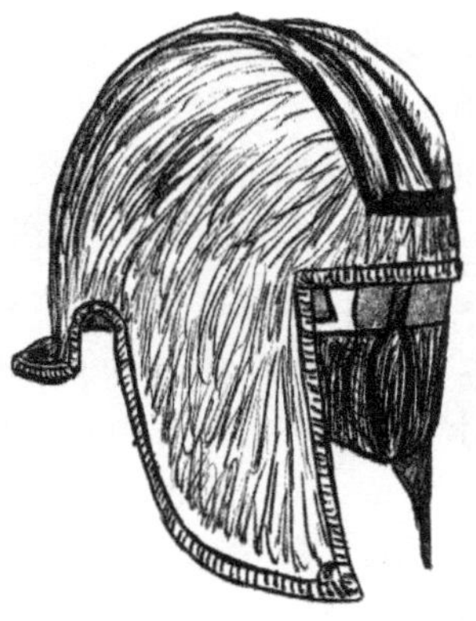

Chapter 20. Daylight

IT WAS DAWN AGAIN when Lia and her friends decided to take a break. They had been walking all through the night after finding the path they were supposed to follow.

It was the path marked by Raven the day before on the map. Although they didn't talk much, Lia knew Tudor and his cousins were full of questions, even after she told them what had happened. It was Clara who asked first if they should wait for Raven to join them.

'I don't think he is coming. It is no longer safe for us to travel with him and Raven knows it,' Lia said with sadness in her voice. 'He was not himself when he attacked me, I know that,' she added quickly. 'I have seen it before, in Grandfather's house, the night we left Ostrova. I think the Cardinal is more powerful than we think, he can control the minds of people and somehow got to control Raven's as well.'

'But do you think he is alright?' Matei asked. 'Shouldn't we go and try to save him from the Cardinal?'

'Moving on and getting to the bottom of all of this is the best thing we can do for Raven. I am certain that we will meet again,' Lia tried to put on a smile. 'He wouldn't abandon us, not like this. And when he thinks it is safe to meet again, he will come to us.'

'That's right,' Tudor said, wanting to encourage the others. 'I mean, he found the three of us before when he didn't even know us, he can surely do it now!'

'Yes, and this is why we need to keep to the path,' Clara agreed. 'But do you think we can still talk to his friend Sabim and ask for his help once we reach the Order's Seat?'

'I am sure we can,' Lia said, trying more to reassure herself. 'We should go on according to plan. If Raven and Maxim trusted Sabim, so will we. Let's rest here for a while and then be on our way.'

They unpacked their blankets and prepared a quick meal. The ground was frozen early in the morning so the four had to sit close together to keep each other warm. Matei and Tudor made a small fire and Tudor offered to watch over them all while they slept. Matei vehemently argued he should be staying on guard but, in the end, was the first one to fall asleep.

Lia, on the other hand, kept awake, thinking about what had happened and whether she made the right decision to leave Raven.

What if he was hurt? What if the creatures that attacked her turned against him? What on Maar were those monsters anyway? These questions chased away her sleep, despite her fatigue.

It was all inexplicable. Was it poison, like the one Lady Laurnic used? No, even when poisoned, Raven would have never hit Zyron that way. And he would never have attacked her either. He had her life in his hands several times before and he even held her Wish Orb once. He was not the Wish Thief. Instead, Raven and the robbers she met previously were possessed by something. Or someone. Someone who was trying to get to her.

The Wish Order must be behind it all, who else? The Cardinal was powerful, she knew this well, and his power went much beyond commanding the Order's soldiers. She could see that now.

Above all, Lia had the certainty that everything would become clear once she reached the Order and met the Cardinal again. But how she would challenge the Cardinal's power, save her grandfather, and free the other Wish bearers imprisoned with him, she did not know yet.

***

It was close to noon when Matei and Clara woke up. Lia and Tudor didn't have the heart to disturb their sleep; they had proven themselves tougher and braver than anyone imagined.

The four of them had another quick meal with the last leftovers from Maxim and went back on their way, this time going downhill towards Samor, the mighty Eastern Fortress.

'You should have woken us up,' Matei complained. 'When the night comes, we will have to take another break anyway, otherwise we might miss our way…'

'Oh, don't you worry, Matei, I am sure you will be able to carry us on your back after resting so well,' Lia said jokingly, inviting similar remarks from Clara. Matei started teasing them back, saying they should use their Wishes to make him stronger if they harboured such high hopes.

Tudor, on the other hand, was more concerned with keeping to the path and making sure nobody was following them. They were escaping the Order. Should it find them, Lia would be taken away for good.

Tudor swore that he would not leave Lia alone again. Even letting her walk with Raven in the forest was a mistake, he thought. If he had been there, or at least awake, he could have heard Lia's calls for help. He could have defended her from Raven.

This came to show they should trust nobody but themselves, they all agreed on that. And, even in Samor, they had to be careful in dealing with Raven's contact. Whether Raven was a friend or a foe was not certain, but one thing was clear: they couldn't take any more chances with strangers.

***

In the afternoon, the group reached one of the main roads marked on the map.

'We made good progress,' Tudor said looking at it. 'If we keep it up, and walk all night, we will be very close. All we need to do is take the small road to the left here.' He showed the map to Lia.

Once on their way, the group started talking in low voices. Not about Raven, the one on everyone's mind, but about Ostrova and their childhoods.

Matei reminisced about his favourite place in the woods. It was a small fortress made up of bricks and roots, built and defended by many generations of children from the village. That place was the witness of several "wars" between groups of friends, each trying to plant their made-up flags on top. He got very close to doing that once, if it had not been for the butcher's boy, Lazar, who blocked him at the last moment.

'That cost him a broken arm,' Matei said proudly.

Clara reminded them of when Professor Filip summoned all the students in the schoolyard because he had found a dead mouse in one of his drawers and suspected – and who could blame him? – that Lia put it there.

'But you know it wasn't me, right?' Lia argued. 'I still think it was Eduard, that boy was shy but clearly braver than all of us.'

They wondered where Eduard ended up. And what happened to Professor Filip back in Ostrova?

'I am sure he is still tormenting students as we speak,' Lia said thoughtfully. Tudor thought things must have changed at the school and in the village after they left.

'Our neighbours saw we all disappeared. And maybe some others too. The Cardinal was determined to straighten things up and I can only hope he didn't harm anyone we know,' he continued.

'Well, I would be fine if he made Filip spend a few nights in the dungeon, thinking about everything he had done over the years,' Lia replied while Matei and Clara cheered.

'Quiet,' Tudor said all of the sudden.

There was something behind the bushes in front of them. They could hear movement. Raven, Lia thought.

The group crept closer to the noise. What they saw sent a chill down her spine. It was a Royal lieutenant.

They could tell that from the white helmet and the dark red orb and crown emblazoned on the back of his silver armour. The soldier was looking inside a small bag and taking out its contents. His sword was on the ground, between him and the bushes in which Lia and her friends found cover.

Lia signalled for them to go back silently but Matei thought differently. He pointed energetically to the lieutenant's armour. The man was dark-skinned, tall, and well-built, but his armour could fit Tudor well, even Matei.

Clara made desperate efforts to stop her brother, but he got more and more excited about the idea. Lia and Tudor shook their heads urgently in disapproval but it was too late.

Matei had already rushed out and, to everyone's surprise, including the soldier's, he got hold of the man's sword.

'Aha!' Matei exclaimed, amazed by his own daring. 'Be kind, sir, and give us the armour you are wearing.' He pointed the sword at the stranger.

Oddly, the soldier stood up slowly and extended his hand calmly, telling Matei to give the sword back. Seeing there was no other choice, Tudor and the others came out of the bushes and stood by Matei.

Encouraged by this, Matei took a few steps forward but was cut short by his opponent, who made a quick jump. The man grabbed

Matei's hand, the one holding the sword, and threw a punch that hit him right in the stomach. The blow was so violent that Matei dropped the sword and flew back, ending up in the Lia and Clara's arms.

'Listen here, we don't want trouble,' Tudor intervened. 'But we need your armour and helmet, now be good and give them to us.'

The stranger said nothing so Tudor continued. 'You can see you are outnumbered,' he said. To drive home the point, Clara took out her bow and placed an arrow in it. Lia drew her sword, as did Matei.

The soldier remained undisturbed and picked up his own sword, took out a whip from his belt and invited them to come get the armour. Once more, Matei led the offensive.

And, once again, he was thrown back, this time by a whip blow. With a swift move, the soldier caught his legs and sent Matei face down to the ground, his sword flying high in the air.

Before any of them could react, a second whip blow came and, this time, Clara was swiftly disarmed.

Tudor tried to throw his net and tangle the stranger, but he was too fast for him. The net missed and Tudor had the tip of his spear severed by the soldier's sword.

Meanwhile, he turned towards Lia. She defended well. The two started a sword fight so violent that every blow seemed to send sparks flying. Lia could tell that her opponent was stronger than her and had a better technique. If only Raven was there with them…

Before Lia could surrender, Solia flew from her hands and the four friends found themselves tightly wrapped together by another blow of the whip. The soldier made a thick knot and slowly proceeded to collecting all their fallen weapons. He had a good, long look at Solia, as if appreciating the craftsmanship.

'OK, you got us,' Lia broke the silence. 'Take the weapons if you want but leave us alone, we are just four travellers and we will be on our way as soon as you set us free.'

'I see,' the lieutenant muttered. His voice was soft. 'And what did the four travellers need my armour for?' he said coming close to them and looking Lia in the eyes.

From up close she could see his face had smooth features and piercing, inquisitive green-brown eyes. But there was no sign of hostility in them, and this reassured Lia. Perhaps they could get themselves out of a messy situation after all. Matei tried to talk but she stepped on his foot to make him stay quiet.

'Listen, we are sorry, really, for causing you this trouble. We are not thieves, we… wanted to use your armour to enter the Order because I need to find my grandfather there. He was taken prisoner,' she said in the end, deciding honesty would be best in those circumstances.

Indeed, the soldier looked at her for a few moments in silence and then took the helmet off. The four friends gasped as they realised they had fought a girl around the same age as Lia. Her black hair was long but braided at the back.

'Unfortunately, I need this armour myself, as I have a brother to find in the same prison,' the girl said softly.

'I know you!' Clara shouted all of the sudden. 'You are on the Wish Order's posters, aren't you? You are Daria, one of the Wishfulls they are looking for.'

Daria was not at all upset to have been recognised. On the contrary, she smiled and, returning to the bag she was unpacking, took out one of the posters and unrolled it.

'Yes, that is correct. And let's see, who else do we have here,' she said, looking carefully at the poster and comparing it to each of their faces. 'Lia, I believe?' she asked after a quick inspection.

'Yes,' Lia said and smiled as well. 'And these are my friends, Tudor, Matei and Clara,' she added pointing to each one of them with her head.

'I could introduce them better if we were not wrapped like this.'
With a swift gesture, Daria set them free.

Still rubbing his belly, Matei came forward. Unable to look her in the eyes, he apologised to Daria and said the whole thing was his idea and he forced the others to join him on the spur of the moment.

'Apology accepted,' the girl replied curtly and advised him, in the future, not to judge his opponents based on appearances.

Then she gave them back their weapons and told Tudor the spear could probably be fixed if he had another metal tip. He had many more, indeed, as Maxim had been cautious to pack plenty for them.

'Well, it was a pleasure of sorts,' Daria said, as she started putting back things in the bag. 'And I wish you good luck, Lia, in finding your grandfather.'

'Wait,' Lia said. 'If we are both looking for someone in the Order's prison, why don't we look for them together?'

It had been a short and brutal encounter, but Lia knew that if she could befriend Daria, together they stood a much better chance against the Cardinal and his men.

'No offence,' Daria answered, 'but what good would it do me to travel with four other people? It is hard enough to keep a low profile as it is.

'Besides, we would have a better chance if we travelled separately. At least only one of us would get caught in case the trip is cut short.' And, as she said it, she closed the bag and was ready to go.

'What if I told you I know the Cardinal?' Lia asked quickly. It worked. Daria stopped but did not look back.

'And, if we join forces, we might have a chance of stopping him,' she pleaded.

Daria turned and said she was listening. Lia told her story quickly, everything she knew about the Cardinal. Daria was visibly interested so Lia went on. She didn't say anything about Raven or Maxim, but she did tell of her adventures in Evergreen.

'That is close to my village of Farios,' Daria said. Lia was excited to hear that and asked Daria if she knew Madam Mariana. Daria said she did, of course, as she and her brother lived only two houses away.

And then they discovered they had something else in common: Madam Mariana had tried to marry both of them to Afilon! Tudor didn't know this part of the story and suddenly became curious, but the girls were too amused by the coincidence to describe Afilon to him. When Matei and Clara began teasing their cousin about it, he became red. Lia held his hand and told him she would never marry anyone without asking him first.

'So, Daria, what do you say? Together we can find your brother and my grandfather and teach the Cardinal a lesson,' Lia asked one more time, hoping for a different answer. Daria considered it.

'Alright, but I get to keep the armour,' she joked.

They happily agreed and a new group of five started heading towards the Royal city of Samor.

THE CARDINAL OF THE Wish Order is chosen by the Council of the Elders, a body that historically included two of the wisest men or women from each one of the four Kingdoms of Maar. After the betrayal of the South and the Wars of the Three and of the Two, the Council had been reduced to four people from the Eastern Kingdom. These are usually former Cardinals and advisers of the King. By tradition, the King himself is not part of the Council of the Elders.

(*History of Maar*, school textbook)

Chapter 21. The Way In

THE ROAD AHEAD WAS easier to travel despite the biting cold. Daria, meanwhile, proved more talkative than she seemed at first. She spent most of the journey telling Lia and her friends about Farios, the life she and her brother had there, and how she got to know the Cardinal.

Just like Lia, they had lost their parents early on but, unlike her, Daria and Dragomir didn't have a loving grandparent to look after them. So, they looked after each other. Right up until their lives were interrupted by the Order's attempts to take control of Daria's fate.

Lia was very interested in these stories and the insights they gave into the Cardinal's thinking. But although Daria certainly disliked him, she was not convinced that he was the Wish Thief.

'I don't know, Lia. Yes, he's a harsh and rigid old man, but a criminal?' Daria said, after being told about how the Cardinal treated Lia and her grandfather during his visit to Ostrova.

'If anything, he is likely to do something wrong while trying to do what he thinks is right. And what he thinks is right is based on the Book of Wishes, not his own views.'

'I agree he is inflexible,' Lia replied. 'I could see this from the only time I met him, but what if he thinks that what is best for him is also best for the whole Order?

'How else can you explain the fact that he wanted to gather all the Wishfulls in the Kingdom? Isn't it too much of a coincidence that, at the same time, Wish bearers started disappearing without a trace?' Lia insisted.

'Well, precisely! He thinks he is defending Wish bearers from the Wish Thief, whoever that might be. I saw him many times as a child and he was obsessed with keeping me safe. And that, for him, meant me living my life inside the Order. At least until my Rite. The Cardinal could not imagine my brother and I could take care of ourselves but, in the end, he had to let me go.'

'What made him change his mind?' Matei was curious to know.

'Well, let's just say that the Order's guards had a hard time keeping an eye on me. And then I managed to set the Council room on fire. They had been warned. Anyway, that was the last straw,' Daria said proudly.

'I thought they would throw me in the dungeon on the spot but, to my surprise, the Cardinal just sent me home. He seemed rather sad to see me go but I'm not foolish enough to assume it was because he was going to miss me. Rather, he was upset that he couldn't have his way,' she ended pensively.

Matei had just found his new idol. Tudor, on the other hand, was mostly silent, trying to assess whether this new road companion was trustworthy. Lia suspected her friend was determined not to have what had happened with Raven happen again.

Lia accepted Daria's reservations about the Cardinal's guilt. They each had a different experience of interacting with him. Besides, Daria didn't know Lia's grandfather and could not understand how significant it was that he argued with the Cardinal about her before he disappeared.

She didn't mention Raven though. At some point, she even wondered if that was all it took to forget him, but the sadness of this thought alone proved her wrong.

'How do you know your brother is held by the Cardinal?' Clara suddenly asked Daria.

'Well, Dragomir and I left our village because we didn't want the Order to separate us again, but we were caught in an ambush on the road to the Endless Sea. We fought hard but we were outnumbered. Dragomir was captured by the Cardinal's dog. That stupid beast lifted him up in the air and took him away,' she said angrily.

Lia shivered remembering her own encounter with the winged dog.

'He must have been taken to the Order's Seat and interrogated. But we planned what Dragomir could tell them anyway. I only hope he is not hurt,' Daria continued. Lia comforted her while thinking about her grandfather – she also didn't know if he was hurt or even alive.

'This is why I know for sure the Cardinal is waiting for me to come,' Daria continued and then fell silent.

'Couldn't he just assume you continued your journey to the sea?' Tudor broke the silence.

'No, he knows me better than that. The Cardinal knows I will do everything in my power to find Dragomir. He is the only family I have,' she said with a trembling voice. 'And I showed my brother in the past what I was capable of doing for him. This is how I also know the Order will not harm Dragomir. They need him as bait, those bastards,' Daria added.

Lia tried to share her optimism. Maybe her grandfather was being kept safe knowing she would try to find him as well?

'But this means I am a step ahead of them,' Daria went on. 'The Cardinal probably expects me to do something foolish like forcing my way in through the front door. I did warn him he would regret the day he gets to see me again. But I have a better plan and, since we are travelling together, I will share it with you.'

Daria made them a sign to stop and, under a big oak tree, Lia and her friends gathered tightly around her.

Lowering her voice, as if someone was about to overhear precisely that part of the conversation, Daria told them about the existence of a secret underground entrance into the Order. Lia wondered why Raven and Maxim didn't know about that.

'Is the Cardinal aware of it?' was Tudor's first question.

'I don't think so,' Daria replied with a smile. 'This passage was built long before the Order. It actually belongs to the fortress that was there since the Eastern Kingdom was founded by the Kings of old. Legend has it that the Order's Seat was built on the sacred ground of the people who lived in Samor before the great migration began.'

Lia and her friends knew, from the little they listened to Professor Filip in class, that the four Kingdoms of Maar had been created by invaders coming from the east long, long ago. Little was known about the people living on those lands before the Easterners' arrival, except that they had a different alphabet and followed their own calendar. They also worshipped many Gods, a system of beliefs that was eradicated by the first Wish Council and replaced by the Book of Wishes.

'Then how do *you* know about this passage?' Tudor insisted while trying not to sound rude.

'Glad you asked!' Daria said, not bothered by his question. 'My friend Lucas is a monk in the Northern Stronghold. He's one of the keepers of the Old Library. He was captured by the Order once and, in exchange for helping him escape from the Order's prison, he told me about the passage that goes from the prison to a military post outside the Order. In fact, he himself got out by travelling it.'

'Can we trust him?' Lia asked.

'You can always trust the word of a Northerner,' Daria replied decisively. Lia thought it was best to give this plan a chance since Raven's connection, Sabim, was probably hard to find.

'There are a few drawbacks to this idea though,' Daria admitted. 'For one, the entrance to the secret passage is hidden inside a garrison outside Samor. Luckily, this post usually has less than ten soldiers defending it, so it shouldn't be hard to get in.'

At this point, Matei was jumping up and down with excitement and Lia could see that Tudor was wondering if they had said yes to Daria's proposal too soon.

'This is where having a Lieutenant's armour will come in useful,' Daria said with a smile.

'Second, and more importantly, it's not one tunnel but a system of underground passages and they are quite easy to get lost in it. At least this is what Lucas told me. Fortunately, again, we have some help,' she reassured them.

'There is a small underground stream to guide us, but we need to follow it closely, even if sometimes it will look as if it takes us back. The tunnels had been built precisely to trick intruders and, from what I heard, not many travellers got out, so we need to be very careful. And we will be,' she concluded enthusiastically, trying to animate her companions.

Matei, as expected, was fully on board with the plan. Clara and Lia added that they would do whatever was necessary to get in and help Daria find the right route.

Tudor, however, was not convinced. He wanted to know if Lucas managed to get out safely or if another person had entered the tunnels since. Daria admitted she did not know the answer to either question. Afterwards, still doubtful, Tudor asked her where exactly they would exit.

'This I know quite well,' Daria said happily. 'We get out in the main corridor of the Order's prison, so really the best place to be if we are looking for Dragomir and Lia's grandfather.'

'But won't this corridor be full of guards?' Tudor insisted.

'It would be during the day, but not late at night, when the guards change. And this is why we need to enter the tunnel before midnight, today. Lucas told me it only takes a couple of hours to reach the exit but I think we should add an extra hour in case we get lost.'

'Great plan!' Matei applauded, while Lia and Clara declared themselves satisfied with the details. Tudor said he still had reservations but that, in the end, Daria's plan was better than having no plan at all.

Daria was pleased to see them on board but pointed to the setting sun and told them they needed to speed up if they were to arrive in time at the garrison. 'Otherwise, we would need to wait one more day and I don't know about you, Lia, but I sure miss my family.'

And that was something they could all agree with.

***

It had started snowing as the group descended the steep hill towards the military post. At first the snowflakes came down slowly, dancing in the light evening wind. But, as the evening grew into night, snow began to fall heavily and they all had to watch their steps much more carefully.

The lively chatter faded and the group turned silent, each thinking about the big task ahead of them. Unlike the past few days, Lia had the distinct feeling she would not find Alfred in the Order's prison. That she might, in fact, never see him again. These new thoughts made her sad, but she didn't want to share them with the others. Especially with Daria, who was so certain of their success.

It was perhaps because Daria had been at the Order before and knew the Cardinal better than Lia did? But then, why did she find it hard to believe he was the Thief or, at least, that he was involved in the whole thing?

It was dark when Daria lit a torch and told the others to follow her closely in a straight line, as they were getting close to the garrison. She asked them for a rope and Tudor quickly took one from their bag.

'I am sorry,' Daria said, 'but I have to tie you up, loosely, and have you follow me like this. And I also need to carry most of your weapons. Any small knives can stay with you, but hidden.' She then explained that, if they were to meet any soldiers patrolling the grounds, they all had to pretend they were her prisoners.

'I will be the Lieutenant who brings in the famous Lia and her rebel friends! All the while, you be ready to set yourselves free and pick up your weapons.'

'How can we be sure they will let you in with all of us? What if they already know a Lieutenant is missing?' Tudor asked.

'This is highly unlikely,' Daria assured him. 'This garrison is a post of the Order and I am wearing a Royal soldier's outfit. Despite the proximity between the Order and the Crown, they don't communicate so well with each other, at least when it comes to soldiers and garrisons.'

'And how will we know when exactly to break free and start fighting?' Matei wanted to know.

'I think it will be quite clear when that happens,' Daria said with a wink, boosting Matei's admiration for her, if that was even possible.

***

The garrison was now in sight. It was a small building but, as Daria told them, most of it lay underground, under the thick layer of snow. There were two soldiers at the gate yet nobody could say how many more waited inside. Daria hoped for no more than five, but these were special times for the Order.

The two soldiers asked the approaching Lieutenant to identify himself. 'Finon,' Daria answered, keeping her voice low. Lia had no clue whether that was the Lieutenant's actual name or it was made up on the spot. Daria added "he" brought important prisoners who needed a break from the road before reaching the Order.

To their relief, this information seemed to satisfy the two guards. The main door opened, revealing bright lights, warmth, and the sound of voices.

Once their eyes adjusted to the light, the five newcomers saw three more people. Fewer than they feared. However, they also saw an enormous creature standing in the corner, a Wish beast that resembled a bear but carried two sets of horns on its head. His look reminded Lia of the Cardinal's dog. It was not a pleasant memory.

It was probably the Wish of one of the soldiers, but also a dangerous foe to come against in battle. They were already in though, there was no way back.

Daria had reverted fully to the behaviour of the Royal Lieutenant they met in the forest earlier. Her answers were short, monosyllabic even, and her tone was sombre, making it hard to guess she was a woman.

The three soldiers in the room were curious about the prisoners and started asking Daria plenty of questions. Her reply was that "he" had been given orders not to discuss them with anyone. Lia was impressed by her acting.

Her answer left the three soldiers visibly frustrated. One of them stood up fast and made a few determined steps in Lia's direction.

'It's you!' he shouted and made her heart jumped. It was Kavos, the Captain they last saw in front of the Fox and Badger Inn, or whatever was left of it after the fire. It came as no surprise to Lia that he harboured resentment towards her and her friends.

'I knew you wouldn't get away for long, you brat!' he continued, animated by both rage and a good dose of alcohol.

'Do you see what you've done to me? I've became a garrison soldier! *Me*, one of the best Captains in the Kingdom,' he said while doing his best to keep his balance. In the process, he surveyed the people surrounding Lia and got even more animated as he recognised them all.

'Step aside, soldier,' Daria said as she intervened between Kavos and the captives. 'These prisoners are none of your concern.' She was determined not to engage him just yet.

A violent push from Kavos changed her mind and she knocked him unconscious with a punch, then threw the weapons she had to her friends. That was the sign, they all knew it.

The giant bear and the other two soldiers in the room were all equally surprised to see the prisoners both free *and* armed. Daria didn't lose any time and blocked the door from the inside.

The beast was the first one to charge, making the five friends take a step back at once. As it ran towards him, Tudor threw his net over the creature, making it roar angrily and almost crash into them. Taking his chance, he used his spear and tried to aim for the neck. He failed.

Daria saw this and jumped on the creature's back. She lifted her sword and planted it right between the two pairs of horns. With a mighty noise, the beast collapsed on the floor. She and Tudor quickly joined Lia and Matei who were clashing swords with the two soldiers.

Matei's left hand had been bruised in the exchange but he and Lia managed to corner their opponents. Clara had her arrow pointed at them and this, together with Daria and Tudor's arrival, promoted a quick surrender. Lia almost couldn't believe how lucky they'd been.

It had been an unexpectedly short fight, but the five companions had no time to celebrate. There were strong knocks at the door and shouting from the outside. The garrison had received reinforcements and, if the door got opened, they wouldn't have an easy time fighting everyone off.

Well aware of this, Daria speedily tied up and blindfolded the three soldiers including Kavos, who was only half conscious. She asked her friends to block the door further by using the table and chairs in the room.

Then Daria kneeled by the fireplace and started touching the bricks on the left side one by one, looking for something in particular. Lucas told her everything he knew about the passage, including how to get in. When she felt a loose brick, she grabbed it and, to everyone's surprise, a small passage opened right in the middle of the room. Lucas had been right.

The five friends looked inside. The tunnel was dark and emitted a stale smell. Not particularly inviting.

'Here we go,' Daria said and got in first. She was followed by Lia, Clara, Matei and, lastly, Tudor, who was asked by Daria to move a small lever near the entrance to close it back.

In the tunnel, the light and noise were drowned by silence and darkness. None of them spoke, fearing they would make their presence known to whatever might be lurking around. But they were certainly alone so Daria made her strong Wish Orb appear, illuminating the passage ahead.

Lia soon followed with her Orb. Guided by the two bright lights, the group made its way deeper and deeper into the labyrinth.

'WHERE DO WISH ORBS go when we make them disappear?' asked the apprentice.

'They are always there, but not visible', answered the master.

'How would we know this, if we cannot see them?'

'You can feel the energy of an unmade Wish in your body. It is an energy that doesn't let the mind rest. The thrill of possibility, the terror for what might come. They are both gone when the Wish is made. Life becomes easier to live then, even if not less complicated.'

(A Dialogue; text forbidden by the Wish Order in the 5th century)

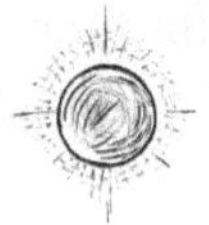

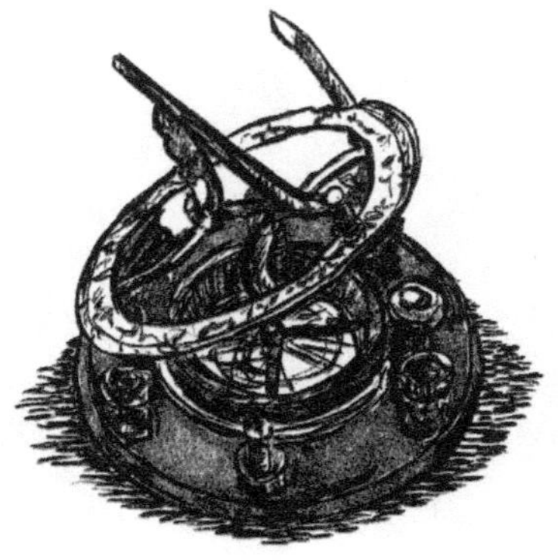

Chapter 22. The Passage

THE DESCENT WAS RAPID at first and the five friends had to hold on to the walls of the narrow corridor that opened in front of them. There seemed to be no proper stairs and, if there ever had been, they were long gone.

There was also no underground stream in sight, but they all waited to reach a split in the corridor before worrying too much about which way to go. Apart from their careful footsteps, a deafening silence surrounded them which none of them dared break. They knew they had to go on and find their way out as soon as possible even if, according to Daria's friend, they were hours away from entering the Order's prison.

Luckily, the light from the two Wish Orbs was so powerful it revealed much of the way ahead. They could not possibly miss the river with that kind of brightness.

The tunnel suddenly became flat, but still no sign of running water. The walls were moist though, and had a slimy and unpleasant feel to them.

The structure of these walls was also curious. Lia wondered why some parts were built from stone while others seemed to be bare, exposing earth, rocks and roots. She also noticed small holes made in the stone sections, perhaps intended to hold torches to light the path. It was strange to think that, long ago, the dark tunnels they found themselves in were probably frequently used. Maybe even inviting to cross. Not anymore, that was certain.

'Where should we go?' Matei asked when the path finally split in two. There was still no sign of an underground river or anything of the kind that could guide them.

Daria said they should stop for a moment and listen carefully for the sound of water. They did, but all they could hear were heavy drops falling from the ceiling.

'Perhaps the river dried out?' Tudor wondered out loud. He proposed taking the tunnel to the right.

'This one seems to be going a bit deeper than the other and, if we are to find any water, it should be down rather than up, right?' The others agreed with his logic and moved on, with Daria and Lia leading the way.

They travelled in silence, more concerned than before about reaching their destination. Daria tried to reassure the others by telling them they could always retrace their steps if needed.

And then the road split again, this time into four different tunnels. One of them was blocked due to a collapsed ceiling. 'Well this eases our choice!' Lia said, trying to lift their spirit.

But the task of choosing the path was becoming harder. Clara suggested leaving pieces of rope behind so that, if they were to come back, they could at least identify which direction they'd come. Her proposal was unanimously accepted.

The group decided to follow the middle tunnel, if anything because it might connect with the others along the way and it seemed the best kept of all of them. The air felt slightly colder inside it, Daria noticed, something that could indicate there was water ahead. The others couldn't really feel the difference but were happy to trust her on that.

If anything, the air was becoming harder and harder to breathe. The tunnels didn't seem to connect with the outside world.

The group of five moved on assuming – or hoping – that nothing and no one called those underground tunnels home. So it was all the more surprising to find parts of a travelling bag. The piece of cloth was old, half rotten, so its owner must have either escaped or died. And yet, this trace did give them new hope: the tunnel they have chosen had at least been travelled. Perhaps it belonged to the monk who told Daria about the path? She could not tell what had happened to him, but if he came this far from the Order's prison, he probably made it to the end.

A grimmer discovery a few metres on subdued their enthusiasm. They found two bones, possibly human, half buried in dirt. None of them was eager to inspect them further.

'This doesn't mean Lucas didn't manage to get out,' Daria said.

'Yes, but it shows someone else didn't,' Tudor replied, asking them to hurry. The air was even harder to breathe and they all started to feel slightly dizzy because of it.

It was with a collective cheer that they finally found flowing water. Down the tunnel, springing from the ground, a small stream made its way forward. They didn't know for sure if that was the stream the monk had referred to but, even if it wasn't, it could still lead them out.

'It must be reaching somewhere outside,' Lia said, with new hope in her voice. 'And, if we are lucky, this outside will be closer to the dungeon than to the garrison.' Daria shared her excitement. Tudor was cautious as usual and suggested they continue leaving marks behind, just in case.

Soon the opportunity to do this presented itself, when the tunnel split once more in two. The intersection was different from the previous ones as it started from a small, circular room with an ornamented stone ceiling. There seemed to be writing on the walls but none of them knew how to read it. The five of them tried to make sense of the symbols. Some looked like houses, others like waves and Wish Orbs. The air was thick with dust and they had no time to imagine the stories this writing could tell.

'It must be the old alphabet,' Clara said, before laying a piece of rope along the path they came from, just in case. They went on following the water.

The path was now easier to travel and the five friends were able to speed up, despite the air growing increasingly stale. Hoping not to find any other bones on the way, they stayed focused for any signs that would point them towards the exit.

'How much longer, do you think, until we reach the Order?' Lia asked Daria.

'No more than an hour I would say,' she replied. 'It seems that we didn't lose our way after all. Even if I've never travelled these tunnels before, I feel we're on the right path, no?' she asked the others. They all nodded, even Tudor, who kept his worries to himself.

'You have a bright Wish, Daria,' Matei said, trying to help the time pass. 'You and Lia don't have to Wish for light, wherever you are. Well, not that Lia wants to Wish for anything in particular but-' he stopped, sensing his last remark was out of place.

Daria, ready as usual to make conversation, was curious to know more. Lia, on the other hand, wanted to avoid the discussion altogether.

'I don't really know what Wish I would make, that's all,' she replied. 'Did you and your brother talk about this?' she asked, genuinely curious.

'Of course we did!' Daria replied eagerly. 'Dragomir wants to create a cure for burns. You see, our parents died in a fire soon after we were born. Dragomir and I are twins, I don't know if I mentioned this. But it is good to know for when we arrive at our destination as you will know who to look for.'

'And you, Daria?' Lia wanted to find out. Since Daria was also a Wishfull and had lived part of her life at the Order, she must have heard the Cardinal talk about the "proper" ways of Wish-making many times before. She must have come to resent him and his stupid rules. Or did she?

'I didn't tell this to anyone, except Dragomir, of course,' Daria replied. She hesitated before continuing. 'But I guess we are all in this together,' she said and laughed, looking around.

'Well, it probably sounds strange, but I actually want to give those people who need it a second Wish.' Her companions did not expect to hear this. Matei asked if that was possible and Daria replied that a Great Wish should be able to accomplish it.

'And even if it is not possible, it is still worth a try,' she said, passionately. 'Think about it, how many people do you know who regretted their Wishes? How many of them were forced into making a Wish they did not want in the first place? And how many were punished for disobeying?

'Our only relative, a cousin living in Farios, was actually condemned for Wishing he could breathe under water. He wanted to leave his village for the open sea. It was selfish of him, they said, and took him away from us.'

'We have a similar story,' Matei said. 'Eduard, a boy from Ostrova, Wished himself a pair of wings. Luckily, the Order was too slow to get him so he just flew away and we never saw him again.'

'Well, it is precisely these kinds of stories that make me mad,' Daria said with conviction. 'Why were Eduard and my cousin supposed to make one Wish that defines their lives and to have this Wish imposed by the Order? Why didn't anyone defend them and their choices?'

Lia thought about her grandfather. He would certainly have tried to help.

'Daria, I can see why you want to use your Wish to help others,' she interrupted. 'But all of us know that what you propose goes completely against the directions set by the Wish Council. You would not be allowed to make such a Wish or would become a criminal for making it.'

'This might or might not be so,' Daria replied. 'The Council talks about the single Wish we make. They would have to rethink their laws if some people are able to get a second Wish, wouldn't they? As for myself, I couldn't care less what the Cardinal or the Order think of my Wish,' she said casually. 'If they were really concerned for others, and not only themselves, they would have thought of it long ago.'

Lia could not agree more. She felt nothing but admiration for her new friend. Daria was not only a fearless fighter, but someone ready to help others by putting herself at risk.

Lia never thought about her own Wish that way. She had seen it more like a burden, the living proof that her life was controlled by others. But, making her Wish wasn't meant to be a sign of sub-mission, nor an act of empty rebellion. It could improve the lives of people, with or without the consent of the Order.

Lia was thinking about this when she heard Daria ask about her Wish. She felt she needed more time to think before answering. Just then, their attention was distracted by a terrible sight. The stream had disappeared.

'It went underground again,' Tudor said, pointing to a small hole next to them. Assuming it might re-emerge somewhere down the path, the group hurried along only to find another intersection, this time with three potential ways forward.

They had no way of knowing the right path, so they decided to each cast a vote. The middle tunnel was again preferred by all, except Tudor. He insisted they should go back instead of going further and becoming trapped. The air was almost impossible to breathe.

Daria and Lia both argued that they were already too far inside the tunnels to waste time and air going back. 'Besides,' Matei said, holding his bruised hand. 'There must be even more soldiers and beasts inside the garrison now.' It was the first time he had ever tried to avoid a fight.

Tudor conceded. He and Matei offered to carry Clara since she looked close to fainting from the lack of air. The group was moving slower and slower until, guided by the light of the two Orbs, they found themselves in a small room with two other paths in front of them.

'Haven't we been here before?' Lia asked, frightened. She could recognise the strange writing on the ornamented ceiling.

'Yes, we have,' Daria agreed. 'And this means we moved in a circle,' she said angrily. 'But why is there no water to guide us? And why can't we find the rope left behind by Clara?' she asked, this time with panic in her voice.

'We are lost!' Matei said and fell to his knees, Clara collapsing near him. Tudor tried to catch both but had little strength left.

There was almost no air left to breathe. Lia found each breathe she took dry and painful. The five of them were slowly suffocating underground. Daria sat down with her head in her hands.

'This is all my fault,' she muttered. 'I should have never risked our lives like this, based on a story I was told,' she lamented. Lia sat next to her, intending to comfort her friend. But her mouth was too dry to utter any words.

As the two of them looked up, they saw a third light shining in the darkness of the small chamber.

It was Tudor's Wish Orb. He was holding it in his hands and, even if it was less bright than the other two, the light inside it was twinkling fast, as if its energy was awake and moving. Tudor's eyes were closed.

'Tudor?' Lia said, anticipating what was about to happen.

She had seen it happen several times before, but never imagined that Tudor would go through his Rite of Passage that day. At least not like that. His cousins stood up and touched Tudor's shoulders. They were giving him the support required by tradition ("through the bonds that united them"). Lia couldn't be a Witness. Not when he was wasting his Wish for them.

'Tudor, no, not now! Not like this!' she insisted.

It was too late. Tudor lifted the Orb and said: 'I take you all as Witnesses.' His voice was solemn, and Lia saw the determination on his face. It was time.

'*I Wish*,' he said, and his voice began to tremble. '*I Wish for a Compass that would guide those using it wherever they want to travel, away from harm's way and towards the refuge they seek.*'

As he finished making his Wish, Tudor threw the Orb to the ground, breaking its shell and setting its light free. In a moment, it was gone. In the place it fell, a Compass appeared. It was small, made of carved wood, silver and dark green leather. Its magnetic needle was spinning in circles.

Tudor gently picked it up and the needle suddenly became stable. It pointed to the tunnel on the right. Taking the lead, he told the others to follow him.

With new strength, the group advanced, guided safely by Tudor's Wish. He had completed his Rite, the first among them, just a couple of months before it was time.

Lia had imagined her best friend's Wish back when she lived in Ostrova. She had expected it to be a memorable event, attended by Tudor's friends, his cousins, and by her and her grandfather. Tudor was supposed to use his Orb to become a better fisherman. Instead, he had a Compass, and he was saving them all with its help.

Perhaps when Daria made her own Wish, Tudor could be given a second chance? Lia found comfort in this thought.

They walked as fast as they could and eventually found the stream again, moving faster than before. It turned into a small underground river and the feel of water refreshed them. They could almost breathe normally again.

Lia and the others became excited thinking their journey underground was close to its end. After they passed two more chambers like the one Tudor had made his Wish in, the Compass pointed them for the first time to a tunnel going upwards.

'This is it!' Daria said enthusiastically. 'I know it. Thank you, Tudor, for making such an inspired Wish. Without you, we would have been lost down here.' The others agreed wholeheartedly. Tudor advised them all to save their breath for when they were out.

And, indeed, after a few more steps, they came to another door. The lever to open it was on the side but nobody went to touch it. They suddenly realised that the door was all that separated them from the Wish Order.

'We don't know what's through there so I will get out first and warn you if there is any danger,' Tudor said in a tone that allowed no argument.

'Hold this, Lia' he added, passing her the Compass. She refused to take it. What did he think was going to happen to him? She won't allow it.

'If there are soldiers around and I am caught, you can find the way to safety by using it. Remember my Wish, this can serve any of us,' he said with a reassuring smile. Maybe his was not a wasted Wish after all. Lia agreed to take the Compass.

Even before seeing the light, they smelled the fresh air coming in and started breathing eagerly. It was ironic, Lia thought later, that it was precisely the air from a dungeon they found so refreshing.

It was still night time, the moment they had hoped to enter the prison. And, to their relief, there was silence. Nobody seemed to be around. Tudor made the sign that it was safe to get out.

They found themselves in a hallway surrounded by a series of empty cells. Why are they empty? Lia thought.

Before she could ask the others, she screamed. Someone pulled her violently by the hair. The shock made her forget the pain. From the ends of the corridor, soldiers kept pouring in, disarming her friends one by one. Lia instinctively reached for her sword but she was hit in the face and dropped it on the floor.

With what little strength she had left, Daria managed to set herself free but a tall woman with white hair stepped in front of her. Daria tried to take out her whip but the woman swiftly grabbed her hand and threw lights in her eyes. Blinded, Daria aimed at her opponent with her sword. She missed.

Lady Aril caught her firmly by the neck and pushed her head against a wall. Daria sank to the floor. The fight was over.

'You are all coming with me,' Lia heard the woman say as she became light-headed and passed out.

THE KING IS THE Kingdom's sword, the Cardinal its shield.

(*The Book of Wishes*, On the order of the realm)

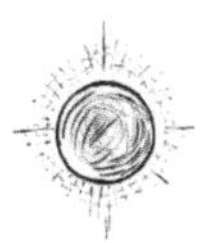

Chapter 23. Dinner Time

WHEN LIA CAME BACK to her senses, she was being dragged up a staircase with her hands tied behind her back. Lady Aril led the way and two soldiers from the Order pushed everyone from behind. Daria was the only one struggling and several times the procession had to stop because of her.

'Do you think you are not in enough trouble for running away from us? Or breaking into a military fort and killing one of the Order's Wish beasts?' she heard Lady Aril tell Daria. 'You and your friends are criminals and will be treated as such if you continue to disobey me.'

Her voice betrayed an increased level of irritation. She did not hit Daria again but instead held her head firmly, as if to impress her words directly into it. Matei and Tudor tried to intervene but were held back by the soldiers.

There was nothing they could do, Lia thought. They were the Order's prisoners but at least she would be reunited with her grandfather soon. If he was still alive… Before that, though, she would probably see the Cardinal and his horrid dog. Why couldn't they just send her to prison directly?

Soon enough, after passing through long corridors with nothing but torches on the walls and going up another long flight of stairs, they found themselves inside a small chamber. Although the decoration was stern, it did display two portraits – one of them was the Cardinal and the other was a man Lia had never met, yet reminded her of someone else.

The soldiers were ordered to stop as Lady Aril knocked gently on the door that displayed the Order's symbol. She waited to be called in, then led the group into the Council room.

The first thing Lia noticed was the massive, rectangular table in the middle and the eight ornamented chairs placed around it. There was nobody else there. The thick, purple curtains were drawn, keeping the darkness at bay. The room was lit by the biggest chandelier she had ever seen.

All the chairs were empty, as far as she could see. And yet somebody had invited Lady Aril in. Where was he?

'Finally,' she heard a voice say from the other end of the table. The Cardinal must be sitting in the tall chair, turned away from them. When the chair moved, she felt the urge to run and shout in his face everything she thought about him and his wretched Order.

She was stropped in her tracks by what she saw. Instead of the Cardinal, another man stood up. She recognised him from the other portrait hanging in the waiting room. It was a bearded man, wearing simple, dark clothes, which made his golden belt stand out all the more.

When she saw Lady Aril bow and noticed the white crown on his head, Lia knew they were standing in front of the Eastern King.

'I don't think this was necessary, was it?' he asked Lady Aril in a serene and surprisingly warm voice as he pointed to the ropes tied around their hands. Aril was visibly caught off guard. She mumbled something about intruders and resistance but was interrupted by the King. This time, he addressed Lia and her friends.

'You will have to forgive the Wish Council, they are not used to receiving guests,' he said with a smile.

Lia looked around her and saw that Daria and the others were equally confused. The King asked politely for Lady Aril to release the prisoners and the soldiers did so on the spot.

'I want my weapons back,' Daria told Aril, visibly resenting the treatment to which they had been subjected. The King said they would all get their weapons back as soon as they left the room, implying they would be there for a while.

But not Lady Aril. King Alexandru courteously dismissed her. Having recovered her poise, Aril bowed to the King, gave Lia and her friends a distinctly cold look and left the room.

The King asked them if they were hungry. None of them answered, but the question did make Lia realise she could barely remember when they had last eaten.

'I am surprised,' the King said. 'I was told you walked for hours in underground tunnels and, before that, caused quite a stir at a military post.' He didn't sound upset about this but half-amused. Did he find it funny that they fought his soldiers and broke into the Order?

As if anticipating the question, the King continued:

'Not that this is something I approve of, you understand. But as far as I know, Daria… is that you?' he asked and Daria nodded. 'You come looking for your brother while you, Lia,' he looked towards Lia and she nodded as well. 'You are visiting us with your friends because?'

'I am here to find my grandfather, Alfred,' she answered.

'Your grandfather?' the King asked, raising his eyebrows. 'I wasn't aware he was here. Alfred from Ostrova is someone I hold in great esteem and I would be very upset not to have been informed about his visit.'

'He didn't come willingly,' Lia said boldly. The King frowned and whispered with a low voice, as if to himself. 'Many didn't.' Then he asked the others for their names. Tudor, Matei and Clara answered nervously, trying to be as courteous as they knew how.

'You are true friends for joining Lia on her perilous journey,' the King said after a moment of reflection. 'And I owe you all an apology.' His last remark caught the group by surprise.

The King paused and turned towards the ornamented tapestry on the wall, depicting the lands of Maar. He seemed lost in thought and nobody dared ask him anything. In the end, he took a deep breath, faced his guests again and started talking in a grave tone.

'The Cardinal is in prison and his trial will be tomorrow. He was arrested yesterday night, after Lady Aril discovered a coffer full of stolen Wishes hidden under the wooden floor of his chamber.' He made a brief pause, as if to study their reactions. The five friends stood still, waiting to learn more.

'As you probably know, the Order has been gathering Wish bearers from across the Kingdom and brought them in for their protection. We had guards at the door and outside the tower where they were held day and night. And yet, people kept disappearing one by one. We suspected it was the Wish Thief, of course. Two nights ago, one of our soldiers managed to plant an arrow into the Thief's right shoulder. He had been spotted trying to get in through the window, riding a flying creature that looked a lot like a big, winged dog.'

Lia shuddered and the King continued sternly. 'Yesterday, the Cardinal had a wound in the exact same place... The evidence is clear. It is impossible to ignore it any longer.'

He walked to the table and sat down again in his chair, breathing heavily.

'I take responsibility for this. You had been chased for months to be brought here, to safety. But, in fact, we were sending you right into the hands of the Wish Thief...' He fell quiet.

'No, this isn't true!' Daria broke the silence first. 'This cannot be true. It is all made up, probably by Aril. She looks like someone who would have a lot to gain from all of this. I know her. I remember her. She wants nothing more than to be named Cardinal, believe me!' she pleaded with the King.

Her friends were surprised by her intervention, but the King didn't seem to be. He stood up again, walked to her and gently placed his hands around Daria's shoulders.

'You want to protect him, I know. I would do anything to... I *have* done everything in my power.' His voice started trembling. 'Aaron took care of you, Daria. He took care of me also. But we need to face the facts, we are not helping anyone by denying them.' Daria shook her head but didn't respond.

'I believe he is guilty,' they all heard, and turned towards the one who had spoken. It was Lia. She couldn't look Daria or the King in the eyes, yet continued.

'He is the one who took Grandfather. He also tried to catch me but I ran away. My friends know this and can testify. Clara and Matei saw the Cardinal arguing with my grandfather the day he disappeared. Then, after I was attacked and managed to escape, they found the sign of the Order scrawled on the table in our living room.' She felt a knot in her throat.

'I am sorry, Daria. I know you have your doubts and you have known the Cardinal for much longer than I have. But I cannot stay silent while my grandfather is missing,' she said with tears in her eyes.

'And you shouldn't,' the King replied, turning towards her. 'You can offer your testimony tomorrow at the trial. It will be a fair one,' he added looking at Daria.

'And I promise you, Lia, to do everything in my power to find your grandfather. You have my word. But it will have to wait until after tomorrow. For now, there is something I can do for you though,' he said and rang a silver bell.

The door opened and Lady Aril came back. The King asked her to bring Daria's brother, Dragomir, from the Royal chambers. She bowed and left without even looking at Lia or her friends.

Daria's excitement was palpable. She started telling the others about her brother and how he was going to be so happy to meet them.

'Dragomir won't believe I didn't cause havoc this time around,' she said. 'And he'll be even more shocked that I found worthy companions on the way,' she said with a smile.

Just as she finished, the doors opened and in came Lady Aril accompanied by a young man who looked exactly like Daria, except for having a frailer constitution. It was as if she had inherited the strength of both. At the same time, her twin brother, Dragomir, emanated a peacefulness his sister often lacked.

After a long hug, Daria asked him if he was alright and if he had been treated well. Dragomir said that, at first, he had been taken to the dungeons but, the day before, he got moved to a Castle room and treated very well.

Daria proceeded to introduce her new friends. She told Dragomir it was thanks to their bravery that she managed to find him. And, of course, the King also helped. Daria thanked him as politely as she could.

King Alexandru gave a slight nod and told the group it was time they all had dinner. He asked Lady Aril to arrange it with his servants. If she resented being asked to cater for the group, she hid it well.

As they moved to one of the Castle's small dining rooms, Lia told Dragomir the story of how they all met and got to travel together. She didn't mention Raven but did talk about the time she spent in Evergreen.

When the King heard Lady Crina Laurnic's name, he started paying attention. When he learnt she was gone, he shook Lia's hand and told her she deserved a big reward for it. The Order and the King's army had been trying to reach her for a long time, he said, but the forest was too treacherous. It was Raven who deserved the reward, Lia thought.

Once they were at the table, the King sat down and asked Aril to join them as well. Daria gave her an angry, you-are-not-welcome look but Lady Aril graciously accepted the invitation.

The dinner was lively, peppered with the laughter of Daria, Lia and Matei. King Alexandru and Lady Aril kept a polite smile throughout, although it was clear they both had other things on their mind.

At the end of the meal, the King told them where they would sleep. They had three rooms, one for Lia and Clara, one for Daria and Dragomir, and one for Tudor and Matei.

Then he explained what would happen the next day.

'The Cardinal's trial begins at noon. Four judges of the High Royal Court will be present and, based on their ruling, I will pass the verdict on behalf of the Wish Tribunal.

'The trial will probably last until the evening, as we have over twenty witnesses. As far as we know, most of them will testify against the Cardinal but he will have the chance to defend himself. Unfortunately, the Cardinal has been feeling quite unwell these past days…' he said and glanced at Lady Aril.

'His psychological state especially seems to have deteriorated greatly. If you want to testify, Lia and Daria, you are both welcome.'

'I will,' Daria replied promptly while Lia nodded. Lady Aril took out a scroll and added their names with a feather pen.

'There is one thing I can't fully understand,' Lia said, trying to give the Cardinal the benefit of the doubt for Daria's sake. 'The one thing that doesn't make sense in my story. You see, when I was attacked in my home, and Tudor saw all of this,' she said and looked at him, 'the burglars used Wishes to catch me. Why would someone, especially from the Wish Order, waste Wishes in such manner?'

'This sounds like a violation of the Order's code,' Lady Aril intervened. 'But *if* they were soldiers, this means they also took an oath to obey their commander above all else. It was probably not hard to obey if the commander was the Guardian of the Order himself.'

'I didn't realise the Cardinal had been found guilty already,' Daria said harshly. She was ignored by Lady Aril who continued to tell the King that the culprits should be caught, in any case, and brought to justice.

'That was not the strangest thing, though,' Lia continued, interrupting Aril. 'The man who made a Wish he, well, he made a second one after that.' The King frowned.

'This is not possible. Lia, are you sure that you weren't confused in that moment and it wasn't in fact another attacker making his Wish?' he asked.

'I am sure I remember it correctly,' Lia insisted. 'After all, I had never been attacked before, so I remember everything quite well.'

'You were in a state of shock and it is very easy to imagine things at a time like that,' Lady Aril intervened. Before Daria could argue, Tudor did. 'I was there. I saw the burglar carrying Wish Orbs.'

'Perhaps they had Wish Orbs from the Thief?' the King asked out loud. 'We did discover several of them in the Cardinal's chamber, but this doesn't explain how a person could use more than one. That just doesn't make sense,' he said. Seeing that Lia was not convinced, he added 'This is not to say that what you saw was wrong. But there must be another explanation for it. And until we identify the perpetrators and question them, it will be hard to know exactly what happened.'

'If I may, Sire,' Lady Aril addressed the King. 'It might be that one of the burglars was an illusionist. As you know, we do train some of our soldiers in the magical arts. I could ask the Head Trainer tomorrow if any such trick is possible. It does sound like a cheap deception.'

'I did not imagine things and I wasn't fooled,' Lia said, becoming upset. 'What Tudor and I saw was real, not a magician's trick.'

'Aril, why do you keep trying to explain everything?' Daria asked directly. 'Are you afraid we might conclude the Cardinal had nothing to do with it? That he couldn't possibly have sent men with more than one Wish Orb? That something else might be going on?'

'That's enough for tonight,' the King suddenly ended the conversation. 'We are all tired and tomorrow will be a long day. A very long day indeed.'

'Lia,' he said turning towards her. 'You can give the testimony you want tomorrow, but I agree with Lady Aril that there might be a series of other explanations for what you saw, and it would be best to focus on concrete evidence.

'Daria,' he continued. 'Rest assured that I will not allow anyone to influence the trial. It will be a fair judgement. The Cardinal deserves this and I am certain Lady Aril desires nothing else.' He did not look at Aril but she gave a slight nod nonetheless.

With this, the King excused himself and left using the side entrance. The others stood up and started to walk out.

Daria moved fast so she could be closer to Lady Aril. When they were next to each other, she whispered: 'I am on to you, Aril. And I won't leave this place until I make your mask fall.'

Lady Aril continued walking. Daria thought she heard her mutter 'if you ever leave,' before wishing them all on emphatic good night, sending them off with the soldiers to their rooms and taking the stairs to the upper floor.

A HOUSE STARTS CRUMBLING from the rooftop.

(Popular saying in the Northern Stronghold)

Chapter 24. The Tribunal

THERE WAS A SNOWSTORM that night. Lia could hear the wind smashing against the room's stained-glass windows. Clara was still fast asleep nearby, which reassured her. The room beside theirs was the one of Tudor and Matei. The room opposite held Daria and her brother. Lia wondered if any of them was awake.

She had barely had a chance to talk to them about the events of the evening and, more importantly, the events of the day to come. The Cardinal's trial…

Besides finding her grandfather, the Cardinal being brought to justice was what she had dreamt of ever since she ran away from Ostrova. But now that it was happening, her enthusiasm had waned. Daria seemed to be convinced he wasn't the Thief. Lia, on the other hand, knew differently.

A sudden noise at the window made her shiver. Could it be the Wish Thief trying to get in? If the Cardinal was in prison, and his dog caged, what was she afraid of? …

Lia pulled the blanket over her head, determined to fall asleep.

***

When morning came, the ground was covered in a thick layer of snow. Lia and Clara whispered good morning to each other and went to find the others. Outside the room, in daylight, they could see that the corridor ended with a terrace. Lia opened the door and went out, walking barefoot in the snow. By the lake in Ostrova it always melted fast, but up north they had so much of it!

Her heart was pounding with joy and, for a moment, she forgot where she was and what was about to happen that day.

Her happiness was momentary though. As she looked over the balcony, she saw the spacious inner yard of the Castle. Four high columns were placed at the corners and, in the middle, covering a small fountain, there was a podium. On it, a guillotine had been placed, its blade shining ominously in the morning sun. Lia stepped away and closed the doors behind her.

Clara, Matei and Tudor were waiting for her. The boys had been told breakfast was served and all of them were expected downstairs. Dragomir came out as well but Daria wasn't with him. He told the others that she left the room early morning and asked him to tell everyone she would be back before the trial started.

'What is she up to?' Tudor asked him.

'Knowing her, she is probably looking for evidence to save the Cardinal,' he replied pensively. Lia guessed as much.

The breakfast room was different to the one they had dinner in the day before. Equally spacious, it had old armour and weapons on each wall but only one painting. It must have been very old given that one could barely tell what it depicted. To Lia it looked like a tree carrying heavy Wish Orbs.

They were served a big breakfast with fresh bread, cooked ham, poached eggs, creamy milk, and cake for dessert. Lia couldn't remember when was the last time she had such a feast. The food was as tasty as Maxim's.

Besides the servants coming in and out with plates and glasses, they were alone. The King was absent and so was Lady Aril. There was no sign of Daria either, but her brother didn't seem worried.

Lia and Tudor sat next to each other.

'What will you do, Lia?' he asked quietly.

'I don't know, Tudor. I have been up most of the night thinking about it,' she replied. 'What I know is what I saw, heard, and what I have been told by your cousins. And all of it incriminates the Cardinal.'

'Yes, but will you tell it to the judges?' he asked.

'I will see,' she said hesitantly. 'I will be there in any case and make up my mind. In the end, it's not like I can sentence the Cardinal, right?' she said, remembering the guillotine covered in shiny snow.

'Right. This is out of our hands,' Tudor agreed, trying to reassure his friend. 'It won't be too long now,' he continued, looking at a massive golden clock over the fireplace.

After breakfast, the five of them were told they could walk around the Castle as they pleased so long as they stayed out of closed rooms. Lia couldn't help but think this advice came directly from Lady Aril.

Dragomir offered to show them around. He once spent a summer at the Order and in the Castle with his sister. That was until the Cardinal decided Daria was too distracted by having her twin around.

There were so many great things to see, he announced enthusiastically. The library was one of them. There were actually two libraries, Dragomir explained, but the Order's was the biggest and nicest of them.

'Second biggest in the whole of Maar, after the one in the Northern Stronghold, of course,' he added. Happy to have such an experienced guide, Lia and the other agreed to go on a tour of the library.

The Castle and the Order were connected by one underground passage and one bridge. Placed on a giant rock overseeing the capital, it was impossible to walk from one to the other from the outside. The round dome of the library gave the Order it's characteristically round look, contrasting with the Castle's tall and pointy towers.

Inside the Order's library they found the first document to ever mention Maar. The Book of Wishes they had before their eyes was one of the four made centuries ago, when the kingdoms were first established. They were given to the rulers of each one of the four realms to ensure they abided by the same laws.

Time passed and, after many wars, waged especially by the large Eastern Kingdom, the other realms rejected the primacy of the Wish Order. This "betrayal," as children were taught in school, came from a rebellious ruler from the South. His erratic behaviour doomed not only his realm, but also the union of the four.

'To this day, nobody knows where the Southern copy of the book is,' Dragomir said as the others listened carefully.

Lia thought that Raven and Maxim probably knew, and she should ask them next time they met. If she ever got to see Raven again… He had attacked her against his will, she was sure of it. He had been controlled by the Wish Thief and, if the Thief was indeed the Cardinal, and if he got sentenced, Raven would be free. Free to look for her if he wanted to. Ah, to the Wishless with all these ifs!

'Finally, I find you,' they heard someone address them.

It was Daria. She held something in her hands and was visibly excited. 'I've got her! I found the proof.' Dragomir asked what it was, but Daria replied there was no time to lose. 'The trial is about to start.'

As they hurried along the corridor taking them back to the Castle, Lia noticed other people going in the same direction. Some looked like secretaries, others were high-ranking officials. The most impressive among them wore long robes and Lia wondered if they were the four judges the King had mentioned the night before.

She suddenly felt she didn't want to give her testimony anymore. If only she could see the King first to tell him that. Or even Lady Aril… Was Daria's evidence going to incriminate Aril?

The Wish Tribunal room was as imposing as Lia had imagined. It was not its size that made it so. It wasn't the gold decoration either. They had seen ornamental tapestries and artefacts made of pure gold in many other rooms.

It was the spatial arrangement that set the Tribunal apart. The chamber was organised on three levels, all made of grey stone with round, golden orbs marking the edge of each platform.

In the large ground section, people were standing, waiting for the trial to start and looking towards the elevated centre. The second level had only a small table and a chair. On the chair, although she couldn't see his face, Lia recognised the Cardinal.

On the top level, there was another table. Facing the audience, five people were seated along its length. In the middle, on the highest chair, ornamented with three golden orbs, she saw the King. Two older women dressed in black robes were to his right, and two bearded men wearing the same sombre attire, to his left.

'That's where I need to go,' Daria said looking up. But, from what Lia could see, there was no staircase to reach any of the levels.

Looking behind, she noticed at the back of the room seven balconies, each one occupied by a person, except for the largest one in the middle. In the balcony immediately to the right she could see Lady Aril. She was dressed in black as well, with a dark green shawl covering her shoulders.

The King asked everyone to be quiet. He didn't need to say it twice. In the crowded room everybody stood still.

He told them what the Tribunal had gathered for and what crimes the Cardinal was accused of. The King spoke plainly. His voice trembled slightly but remained grave.

His speech was interrupted once in a while by subdued, wailing noises that came from the far left of the room. Lia tried to see the source of the noise by standing on her toes but there were too many people there. Curious, she moved around. She saw a glimpse of a wing and of metal bars and understood the Cardinal's dog must have been brought in.

Her heart jumped. She hated that beast from the moment she first saw it outside Filip's office. But she couldn't bear the sight of the dog attending his master's trial. The King seemed undisturbed by it.

'I request the right to speak, your Majesty!' she heard Daria say loudly when the King finished presenting the case against the Cardinal.

Everyone's eyes turned towards her. Lia felt out of breath. Her friend was one of the bravest people she had ever met. 'She will save him,' she thought and looked towards the Cardinal's table.

Lia could barely recognise him. The stern face she knew from Ostrova had become much older. His hair was completely white. His once piercing, almond-shaped eyes looked empty and lost, surveying the room.

'Daria of Farios, you will be heard later today,' the King replied calmly. 'You are on the list of witnesses, but there are others to speak before you.'

'Your Majesty,' Daria insisted, 'I have new evidence to bring before you that is relevant. I uncovered it this morning. I beg of you to listen.' She looked around, as if addressing the people next to her. They all kept quiet.

'What is this evidence?' the King asked after a moment of reflection.

'It is a letter, your Majesty. A letter written by Lord Joreas, a member of the Wish Council, and addressed to the Cardinal. In this letter, Joreas warns the Cardinal about a plot. A plot being orchestrated by her!' Daria shouted, turned around and pointed directly at Aril.

There was commotion in the room, but Lady Aril seemed undisturbed. She gave Daria an icy look and nothing else. The King tried to establish order once more. He asked for the letter. At once, one of the royal servants approached Daria, took the letter and sent it flying directly to him.

'What an awesome Wish,' Lia heard Matei whisper.

The King took a few moments to read the contents of the letter, then passed it on to the other members of the Tribunal. He addressed Daria.

'Council Lord Joreas does seem to warn the Cardinal about a plot,' he said, and all the eyes fall on the man in the second balcony from the left. He was not happy at all with the attention and Lia could see him turn left and right, saying he didn't know anything about any letter. Everyone murmured.

'Silence,' the King ordered. 'Whether this letter is authentic or not doesn't matter, it brings no concrete evidence about this assumed plot by Aril to become the new Cardinal.'

'Sire, if I may,' Daria interrupted him. 'The letter states that Aril has been watching over the Cardinal's every step and lied to you about his deeds. She had both the information needed to set him up and the reason to do it. She wanted power.' Daria looked directly at Lady Aril again.

'Daria, there is no evidence in this letter of any of this,' the King said with some sadness in his voice. 'Lady Aril is not on trial here and if Joreas does have material proof I ask him right now to step forward.' Everyone looked towards the man's balcony. Joreas's face became red as a beetroot and he violently shook his head in response.

'Coward!' Daria shouted. 'You will regret not standing up to this snake and her miserable deeds,' she said bitterly. Lady Aril looked down at her with a mix of anger and contempt. 'Aril might be the Thief you are looking for, she-' Daria's voice faded.

The King stepped in again, calling for the trial to start with the first witness. Soldiers from the Order approached Daria, ready to remove her from the room. She refused to leave and said she wanted to hear the witness accounts. Lia saw tears in her eyes.

She moved towards her. 'I believe you,' Lia whispered in Daria's ear.

The trial continued. Soldiers and servants came in front to offer their testimony. They talked about the Cardinal's strange behaviour, the fact that he hid the disappearance of Wish bearers from the Council and the King, that he was seen – not once, but twice – holding something that looked like bright Wish Orbs in his hands.

Three soldiers testified seeing the Wish Thief fly into the West Tower and shooting arrows at him. One of those arrows hit the Thief's shoulder, unmistakably. The next day, the Cardinal had a wound in the exact same place. Lia could see, from the way he stood, that he had been injured.

The murmur in the room turned into chatter and the King intervened once more. The final testimonies included magistrates from the Council. Some spoke highly of the Cardinal, others said they felt betrayed by him and claimed that his crime was aggravated by the fact that he wouldn't return the missing Wish bearers to their families. Lady Aril did not testify.

Lia was finally asked by the King if she wanted to offer her statement. She grabbed Tudor's hand as if to make sure he was by her side. Daria was nowhere in sight. She took a deep breath and said loudly:

'I have nothing to add, your Majesty. You mentioned earlier that evidence is needed to condemn someone. I have no such evidence. My experience with the Cardinal has been brief and I will admit that I suspected him of wrongdoing,' she said, her voice calm but her heart beating fast.

'Yet, listening to the testimonies today, I came to realise I had no more evidence than all these other witnesses.' She could hear people whispering around her.

'The charge brought against the Cardinal is very serious. But it is not matched by proof, in my humble view. The Tribunal is here to judge him, but I have made up my mind. I will not speak against the Cardinal until I can be sure of my accusations.' She felt Tudor's grip become stronger and his hand warmer.

The King thanked Lia and moved to the final part. He asked the Cardinal for his statement. As he did, silence engulfed the room once more.

Lia could see everyone instinctively leaning forward, as if to hear and see better, even though the Cardinal was seated in plain sight. For several moments, the old man did not move. Then, with some difficulty, he attempted to get up, supporting his wounded shoulder.

When he turned around to face the crowded audience, his face was more serene than Lia expected. He looked miserable but composed, his voice hoarse when he spoke.

'Dear colleagues, friends and witnesses, thank you for coming today to see me,' he said courteously, making Lia wonder if he indeed had lost his mind.

'I heard many accounts today about my person and what I might or might not have done, and I have this to say about them-' He momentarily lost his balance. As he stood up again, his gaze had changed. He looked disoriented, staring at a void.

'I am guilty,' he said loudly. 'I am the Thief who stole Wishes from under your noses. The Thief you never suspected but fully deserved for being so trusting and so stupid.' He tried to laugh but could not manage. Alar, his dog, barked.

It was becoming hard to hear him from the protests in the room. The King did not intervene. Lia saw him sinking into his chair, eyes closed, trying hard not to see or hear.

'You will never find the missing Wish bearers!' the Cardinal yelled. His dog started howling, some in the crowd booed, the noise was becoming unbearable.

'And I will continue to catch Wishfulls until there are no Great Wishes left in the whole of Maar,' the Cardinal said. Unexpectedly, he jumped from his platform into lower platform. How could he still be that strong?

The people around him stepped aside fearfully. He moved fast between them and headed towards Lia.

'You thought you got away, you insufferable brat?' he asked her with a hollow voice. Lia felt stuck but, just before the Cardinal could grab her, he was pulled back by Tudor and two of the Royal soldiers.

He was screaming and twisting like a wounded animal, trying to escape. Then, as sudden as he started, the Cardinal stopped and fell to the ground, senseless. Finally, the King's voice was heard.

He was ready to pass judgement.

Lia felt she was out of breath and couldn't stay there one moment longer. As she ran out of the room, she heard the echoes of the verdict from each judge, accompanied by cheers from the crowd and the dog's wailing.

'Guilty,' 'guilty,' 'guilty'… 'sentenced to death by guillotine'… 'in two days' time, at midnight, for all to see and to learn…'

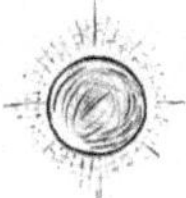

Samor is the oldest city of the Eastern Kingdom, situated at the crossroads between a mountainous north and an arid south, a fertile West and a populous East. In the middle of Samor lies the ancient Rock of the Wise, the place where, according to legend, the first Wish Orb was broken in Maar, after the creation of the land. The exact first Wish is unknown, but the breaking of the Orb is said to have made the rock appear. The rock upon which, centuries later, the seat of the Wish Order and the Royal Castle were build side by side. Stranded on top, they symbolise to this day the close union between Order and Crown.

(from a school history textbook)

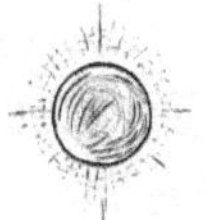

Chapter 25. Clues

LIA DIDN'T LOOK BACK. She heard the shouting, the cries, the applause, but couldn't bear seeing the Cardinal's face. She just wanted to get to her room, close the door behind her and pull the blanket over her head.

In the end, she decided to go the library. The library, however, was harder to find than she initially thought. The Castle had many similar hallways and it was easy to get lost trying to get to the Order's Seat. When she did reach it, everything was silent, just like she wanted. Faint blue lights coming from the ceiling made the room seem detached from the world around.

Only that morning she had been there with her friends. That felt like many moons ago. Back then, she had been wondering whether to testify or not.

A noise behind the nearest bookshelf startled Lia.

'Hey,' she heard Daria say. When she came out into the open, Lia could see her eyes were puffy and red.

'I am sorry I was wrong,' she said quietly. 'I really believed in his innocence, I trusted him. But when I saw him jump down and head towards you.'

Lia raised her eyebrows in surprise.

'Yes, I was there,' said Daria. 'I was at the entrance. I…'

'I am the one who should apologise, Daria,' Lia stopped her. 'I wasn't sure about the Cardinal but now I know he didn't do it. He's not the Wish Thief.'

'But how do you know that? He confessed!' Before Lia could reply, Daria continued. 'If you can prove he didn't do it then please do,' Daria said in a hurry.

'I cannot prove it, not yet. But we have tomorrow to do so,' Lia replied and took her friend's hands in her own. 'I don't have material proof. All I know is how the Cardinal looked at me. I had seen this look before, I-' she hesitated.

'There is something I didn't tell you, Daria. Besides being attacked in my grandfather's house, there was another time someone wanted to take my Wish Orb away. That someone was… *is* a dear friend. He saved my life a number of times and I have complete trust in him,' Lia said keenly.

'How was it then that he tried to take your Wish away?' Daria asked.

'He was possessed somehow. He was not himself. I know it because of the look he gave me at the time. His gaze was… void. Empty. As if it was someone else acting instead of him. That someone is the Wish Thief, I am certain of it! Just as I am certain that the Cardinal was not himself tonight when he made that confession.'

'But, Lia, if you know this, let's tell them, let's go right now,' Daria said loudly. She pulled Lia's hands, trying to get her to the door. Lia resisted.

'We have no proof. It will be my word against every other testimony given today.' Daria realised that and stopped pulling.

'But,' Lia reassured her, 'we will not let the Cardinal die. We know now what we are fighting against. The real Wish Thief is probably very near and what we need to do is find the missing Wish bearers. Maybe my grandfather is with them. Once we find them, we will find the actual culprit.'

Daria's eyes were glowing. 'We need to set a trap. Set a trap for her.'

'So you are convinced Aril is behind all of this?' Lia asked although she knew the answer already.

'Of course! Think about it, Lia, who had anything to gain from such a crime? Who still has the most to gain from it? She does! I am sure she will be named Cardinal very soon, if she hasn't been already,' Daria said bitterly.

Lia thought about Aril. Daria might be right but how could they set a trap? And why would Lady Aril take and hide her grandfather?

'We need to find evidence before going to the King again,' she concluded.

'And we will, once we find your grandfather and the others,' Daria said, maintaining her enthusiasm. 'If you are right, then she is more powerful than I thought, maybe even a witch. But clearly, she is not powerful enough to erase the memories of the people she abducted, otherwise they would have been returned by now.'

'Still, what would she do with the Wishes?' Lia thought out loud.

'We don't know if she actually stole them, maybe she only kidnapped the people to frame the Cardinal?' Daria replied. 'And your grandfather got caught by accident because the soldiers she sent were actually looking for you?'

'There is something that doesn't add up though,' Lia continued. 'Why would the attackers carry more than one Wish with them? Did Aril steal Wishes and give them some? That is not possible, right? Nobody can make a Wish for someone else, someone who is not present.'

'What if the Wishes belonged to the other people, already there, and one person held them for the others?' Daria said, trying to figure things out. The explanation didn't fully satisfy Lia.

She argued they could just as well have kept their own Wishes and, most of all, not wasted them so foolishly.

'But this is exactly what her magic made them do, Lia!' Daria said, in a moment of insight. 'She controlled them to such an extent that they become capable of not only kidnapping your grandfather, but also giving away their Wishes. This only comes to show how dangerous she is,' Daria concluded and muttered a swearword.

'And what do you think happened to these soldiers? How come they didn't wake up from her spell and realise what they had done? What she made them do?' Lia wondered some more.

'Well, they might have, but perhaps they are not alive anymore. Or they are imprisoned together with the Wish bearers?' Daria suggested.

There were many questions they could not answer. But they were determined to find out. They couldn't let the Cardinal pay for a crime he didn't commit.

Lia decided to ask the King the next day to help them find her grandfather. There was little hope he could, if Lady Aril was involved.

'But at least she would know we are not giving up,' Daria reasoned.

'Won't that make her even more dangerous?' Lia asked with a smile, anticipating her friend's answer.

'All the better on my account,' Daria said cheerfully and her laughter echoed inside the Order's library, making the blue lights vibrate.

***

The next morning, Lia and her friends got together for an early breakfast. Although the food was plentiful again, they didn't talk much. It did not feel right to discuss what had happened the day before. As they finished, Daria told the others to meet in her room where they could talk freely.

'After yesterday, people in the Kingdom think they are safe,' she started once they were all behind closed doors. 'But Lia and I know differently.'

Lia nodded, encouraging her friend to go on. 'We believe the real Thief will be caught once we discover the missing Wish bearers. And, with them, Lia's grandfather.'

'I am all in favour of looking for them,' Tudor said first. 'And I am sure the King would agree to this as well. From what I heard yesterday, after the trial, a Royal search is already underway.'

'Well, this search would have been faster had they listened to Lia and me sooner,' Daria said in a low voice.

'In any case, should we go talk to the King about all this?' Tudor continued.

'If we talk to the King, we should also do our own investigation into who tricked the Cardinal,' Matei intervened. 'I believe you already have a suspect in mind, Daria?' he said mischievously.

'Yes, I sure do,' Daria replied, playing with her sword. 'And when I find proof, she better come quietly.'

'We have to be prepared to face her though,' she added in a more serious tone. 'Clearly Aril is a powerful enemy. She is not only good at scheming but she might also be able to control other people's actions.'

'I have seen this before, and I saw it yesterday when the Cardinal came towards me,' Lia said. 'This is why it is important to stay together, I don't think she can control all of us, or at least not all of us at once.'

They decided to speak to the King then and there, but Lia, Tudor and his cousins realised they had no idea where to find him. Daria told the others the Royal Chambers were separated from the rest of the Castle and guarded at all times so all they could do was talk to the guards and ask for an audience. They went at once.

The Royal Secretary greeted them and said the King was indisposed and would not see anyone that day. Daria insisted but they were turned down. Not eager to spend a night in prison, Lia convinced her friend that they could see the King the next day. 'There is still some time. We can organise our own search!'

And so they did. Daria brought them to the reception room they dined in two nights before. She explained that the Castle had five floors and four towers organised in four wings. East, West, North and South. And there was, of course, the Order's Seat. The Order's dungeon was not "open for visits" and they had seen there weren't many prisoners there anyway. If they split, they could search for evidence everywhere else before nightfall.

'It's a very long shot, but at least we won't be staying around doing nothing,' Matei conceded.

Daria asked them to carry their weapons with them, just in case. 'You never know when you might meet the Wish Thief. Given that she is moving about freely.'

Dragomir said that since he and his sister knew most about the Castle, he could cover the East wing and his sister the North and West ones. Matei and Clara could go to the South wing and Tudor and Lia search the Wish Order.

'There won't be much to see because many of the rooms are kept closed, especially in the Order, but at least you can check if there are soldiers, servants or any Magistrates to talk to. I am sure they have been asked before about what they know, but, with a bit of luck, they will open up to a few young people looking for their friend's grandfather,' Daria said smiling. 'Let's all meet back here at sunset.'

Lia took her sword, Tudor his shortest spear and, trying to carry them as discreetly as possible, they went towards the passage to the Wish Order.

On their way, they were surprised not to meet anyone on the corridors. Usually that part of the Castle was buzzing with activity, not least from the guards who travelled between the Castle and the Order regularly.

Lia was deep in thought. If the Thief was responsible for her grandfather's disappearance, and if the Thief was Lady Aril, then surely she wouldn't leave prisoners in the Order, right under the Cardinal's nose. Then again, if she managed to make the Cardinal confess to something he did not do, she was capable of pretty much anything.

As they entered the Wish Order, they noticed again how stern and modest looking the hallways were. There were barely any paintings or decoration to look at.

The library was open but most of the other rooms were not. Inside, they divided the shelves between them and started looking for anything that could help the Cardinal and expose Aril, anything they could read about other than the laws of the Wish Order and the magistrate's duties. No luck with that.

Lia found instead a number of books she remembered from her childhood. Alfred had always been proud of his book collection, and for good reason. He had, for instance, all the five volumes of the geographical treaties of Maar. In contrast, the Order's Library held only three. Lia wondered for a moment what had happened to Alfred's books while they were away. Her grandfather would be so upset to find his collection in disarray…

As she pondered that, Lia heard Tudor calling her from across the room. He had found something.

It was an old book about Evergreen. 'I picked it up because I was curious after hearing about your adventures there. And when I opened it, I saw this,' he said and pointed to the first page.

There was a dedication there for Magda Aril, thanking for her "precious help." It was signed Crina L. 'What did you say the witch you met in the forest was called?'

'Laurnic,' Lia gasped. 'Crina Laurnic!' It had to be her. And Magda Aril could only be Lady Aril. They must have known each other well. And what exactly did Aril do for Laurnic that was important enough to warrant such a dedication?

'It all makes sense,' Tudor said. 'If Laurnic owed her gratitude to Aril, maybe she repaid her with more than one lousy book. Perhaps a little magic as well? Like teaching her how to control minds? Didn't you say, Lia, that she made you hallucinate while there?'

'Yes,' Lia said pensively. 'She did that with the help of a potion. Who knows, maybe Aril has been poisoning the Cardinal for some time? We must take this book and bring it back to the others.'

The only other open room was the Council chamber. They immediately recognised it as the place in which they met the King the night they arrived. Lia and Tudor were once more impressed by the table and its carved chairs. Lia touched the sculpted dog heads on what must have been the Cardinal's seat.

'I never liked his beast,' she said. 'I hated it in fact! But I will never forget the dog's shrieks during the trial. I wonder if he will be executed together with his master?'

'This is the custom, isn't it?' Tudor answered in a low voice. 'This is what Professor Filip told us about the Wishes of condemned criminals. It's how he tried to scare us all into being virtuous, remember?'

'Whatever good that did to him or to any of us,' Lia replied. 'It didn't stop Eduard. It didn't prevent my grandfather being taken away or the Cardinal being sentenced.

'There is no justice, Tudor,' she said angrily.

The fading light outside told them it was close to sunset. Lia and Tudor left the Council room and made their way back to the Castle with only the book from the Order's library in their hands. By the time they reached the meeting room, it was already dark. Matei and Clara were waiting for them. They said they'd had no luck.

'There was nothing interesting to see. Well, except for the big painting of the Queen. She was a very beautiful woman, I can tell you that,' Matei claimed, making his sister blush slightly.

The Queen of the East passed away before any of them were born. Her grandfather always referred to her as a "sad but charming and elegant lady." The King must miss her terribly, Lia thought.

Daria entered the room in a hurry. She had made a discovery of her own. Excited, she told the others she managed to break into Lady Aril's room. The news was met with awe.

'And guess what the Lady hid behind her wardrobe?' she asked the others. They had no idea.

'This!' she said and took out five small bottles with a violet, pasty substance inside of them.

'The potions,' Tudor said out loud and showed the others the book he and Lia discovered in the Order's Library. Daria's excitement grew by the minute.

'Let's drink some of it,' Matei said. He was instantly told that was not a good idea. Then he said they should force Aril to drink some of it herself.

'We will wait to gather more evidence and then confront her,' Daria said. 'We are getting close.'

Time passed and Dragomir didn't show up. It was long after sunset and his sister was becoming worried.

'Perhaps he found something,' Clara said, trying to be optimistic.

'Or maybe he was found by something… or someone,' Daria replied. 'I should have never let him go alone. Especially to the East wing. That tower was closed for many years. The servants believe it's haunted by the Queen and nobody dares go up the stairs anymore. But, if we are to believe in stories, we wouldn't be in this miserable Castle at all,' she said nervously.

'Well, let's go find him then!' Lia proposed and Daria agreed. She wanted to go alone but the others insisted on joining her. As they moved towards the East tower, they noticed the temperature had dropped.

'Perhaps someone left a window open,' Matei said, trying to lighten the mood. It was getting darker as well. Daria lit a torch and used it to show the way. Their calls for Dragomir were left unanswered.

They had reached the circular staircase going up the East tower and still no sign of him. Daria was more and more anxious and so were her friends. Did Dragomir go up the stairs? Probably, Lia thought and looked up.

The spiral created by the stairs made her dizzy. There was light in the room at the top. And, in that light, she saw Lady Aril looking down at them.

Her heart froze. Daria instinctively took out her sword.

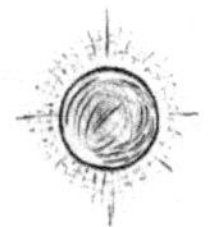

IT IS BECAUSE OF the Order that the Wishfulls of Maar no longer live in fear.

(*The Book of Wishes*, On Wish-Making)

Chapter 26. The Enemy

LIA HURRIED UP THE stairs after Daria. The staircase was circular and narrow, with no handle to hold on to.

The silhouette of Lady Aril cast a long, ominous shadow over them. For a moment, Lia thought she heard Aril laugh but then her stern voice echoed down the tower.

'Not all of you are invited.'

And, as they heard this, Matei and Tudor, who were following Lia closely, suddenly fell back. Matei hit Clara and made her stumble while Tudor lost his balance and almost fell off the staircase. Lia shouted and rushed back down to help them when she hit something invisible and fell back as well.

Tudor, Clara and Matei got up and tried to reach their friends, this time advancing more carefully. It was impossible. Between Daria, Lia and their companions an invisible, yet solid, barrier had been raised.

Tudor told Lia to stand back as he tried to pierce it with his spear but only managed to have it break in two. Matei's sword was of no help either. Daria saw them struggling and came back down. They expected her to find a solution, like always. Instead, she told Tudor and his cousins that she and Lia had to go on and face Aril alone.

'The witch clearly uses magic and the only way to destroy the barrier is to defeat her,' Daria said.

'We have to help you fight her,' Tudor pleaded.

'Don't go without us!' Matei protested, but soon came to realise there was nothing he could do about it. Clara asked how they could help from the other side. Daria told them to go find the King or his guards and alert them.

'If they see what is happening here, they will finally believe us,' Lia added.

'Are you going to waste more of my time?'

The question, coming from upstairs, interrupted their discussion. 'Here I was, thinking you cared about your brother, Daria,' Aril said with a smile.

Daria looked up, enraged. Lia took her hand. 'Let's do it.' Then turned to her friends and asked them again to go to find help. 'We will be fine here,' she said with a smile, and she believed it. Daria nodded and they both ran up, faster than before.

As they approached the room at the end of the staircase, Lia and Daria held out their swords and looked up to check if Lady Aril was waiting for them there. She was not. All they could see was a bright light coming out from the room.

The room itself was circular and had almost no furniture except for a wooden chair and an empty bookshelf. They had both known better days and the whole place looked as if it had been abandoned for a long time. At the other end of the room, they saw a wide balcony, covered in snow. There was no fireplace and, with the doors open, the temperature was close to freezing.

Lady Aril was standing in front of the balcony, with her back to them. To her side, sitting on the floor, was Dragomir. He was unharmed but didn't look at either Lia or Daria as they came in. In fact, he had a blank look on his face. He is under her control, Lia thought.

'So here we are, are you ready for us?' Daria asked defiantly but received no answer. Lady Aril was still contemplating the contrast between the snow and the darkness of the night, or perhaps she was getting ready for battle.

'What have you done to him?' Daria demanded to know, looking at her brother.

'I merely asked him to sit nicely,' Lady Aril said and turned to face them.

She wore a long, dark red dress and a black belt around her waist. Her face betrayed no emotion. Aril held a knife in her hand which she made no effort to hide.

Daria pointed her sword at her and told Aril to step away from her brother.

'You impertinent little girl,' Lady Aril said emphatically, relishing each word. 'Is this how you talk to your new Cardinal, wretch? You forget I have you and your brother's life in my hands,' she said and placed her hand on Dragomir's head.

'You two shall bow to me and present me your Wish Orbs as I command.'

Lia was surprised to hear Daria burst into laughter. 'You want our Wishes, Thief?' she asked mockingly.

'And you want your bother,' Aril replied. 'As Guardian of the Order, I am entitled to ask for your Wishes and you, as miserable little servants, will obey,' she continued with an equal voice.

'And will do it right… now!' she shouted and, as she did, Daria and Lia were hit by a gush of wind so strong it made them fall down and drop their swords. Daria was the first one to pick her weapon up and charge.

The next moment she was immobilised in mid-air. Daria froze before she could reach Aril, who didn't move an inch but simply stood there, impassively looking at her.

'What did you do to her?' Lia asked, coming to her friend's help.

'I just asked for her Wish. And for yours,' Lady Aril answered.

'Why are you doing this? Isn't it enough that you are the Cardinal now? What could you ever do with our Wishes?' Lia pleaded, trying to buy some time and help Daria move again.

'I need your Wishes to keep them safe from their irresponsible owners,' Lady Aril justified her demand. 'It is, after all, my duty now to guard the last two Great Wishes of the Kingdom.'

'How dare you speak of duty?' Lia said angrily and turned towards Aril. 'You imprisoned so many people, including my grandfather. You framed the Cardinal and are leading him to his death. You are at this very moment trying to harm Daria and her brother, who did absolutely nothing wrong.'

'Enough!' Aril shouted, and another gust of wind threw Lia back. She did not fall. Instead, she picked up her own sword from the ground.

'You think you can harm me?' Lady Aril asked with disbelief.

She looked past Lia and out to the staircase. Was she worried someone else was coming? Nobody did. Her friends can't have found anyone yet, otherwise there would have been noises from downstairs. Daria and Lia were on their own. For a brief moment, Lia wished Raven was there, fighting by her side…

'You two have no idea how valuable your Wishes are,' Lady Aril continued. 'And they will be safe with me. You are both careless and ungrateful. You could have had our full protection but decided to fight the Order, to fight the Kingdom itself,' she said, this time with a tinge of anger.

'Why would we give you our Wishes?' Lia asked, circling Aril with the sword in her hand. She was breathing normally, as Raven taught her.

'Because I am the authority here. I make the Law and the Law is not to be questioned,' she replied curtly and took a few steps towards Dragomir.

'If you are the Law then why did you have to take Dragomir prisoner? Why are you keeping him here against his will?' Lia insisted, pointing towards Daria's brother. 'You don't look like someone who has power, you look like someone who wants to steal it.'

Lia could see Lady Aril was no longer amused by her remarks but she went on. 'To steal power from the Cardinal and from the King. Daria was right all along, only I was too blind to see it,' Lia said looking at her friend who remained as immobile as a sculpture.

'If you care about them both, you will do as you are told,' Lady Aril barked back. 'Give me your Wish now or Dragomir will pay the price.' Aril touched his cheek with the knife. Dragomir didn't seem to realise what was happening. Lia told her to stop then took a deep breath. She knew what she had to do.

As she extended her left hand, the Wish Orb began to materialise. Its shine was as bright as the three torches burning on the walls of the tower. Lady Aril's eyes widened, and her mouth revealed a hideous smile.

'Good girl,' she said. Letting go of Dragomir, she came to grab the Orb.

Lia closed her eyes. When she estimated Lady Aril was close enough, she made the Orb disappear and swung the sword as hard as she could. She heard a cry and felt sure she had made a hit.

Lady Aril retreated fast, like a wounded creature. She held her left arm. She had been hit, but not as badly as Lia thought. She must have jumped out of the way at the right time. But, in the commotion, her hold on Daria had weakened and she was able to move again.

Without wasting any time, Daria took the whip from her belt and, with a quick snap, wrapped it around Lady Aril's waist and pulled her forcefully to the ground.

With Aril temporarily immobilised, Daria hurried to check on her brother. She started by shaking him but Dragomir did not react. With his eyes wide open, he was breathing, yet seemed unable to move or speak.

'What did you do to him, witch?' Daria roared and looked towards Lady Aril with fire in her eyes.

Aril had managed to set herself free from Daria's whip and stand up again. She was breathing heavily. A bright patch on her dark red dress showed she had been hurt. Her expression remained icy cold.

'You two will pay for this,' she said as she regained her composure. 'I tried to be reasonable with you. I tried to be nice.'

Daria chuckled but Lia became fearful as Lady Aril added: 'But no more.'

Aril placed herself in front of the open balcony, this time looking towards the room. She closed her eyes and lifted her head up, facing the ceiling.

Lia and Daria took a step back, ready for whatever she might do next. Nothing was happening though. Seeing this, Daria tried to help her brother get up and move towards the stairs.

Then they heard faint noises coming from outside. Something was approaching the tower, fast. They could hear wings flapping. Not one, but many, many more.

The darkness of the night didn't allow them to see what was coming until the first crow flew in, past Lady Aril, straight in their direction. It was followed by another and then another. A whole flock of dark, vicious birds was flying towards and around them, batting them with their wings, scratching them with their claws, biting into them.

Lia started swinging her sword around, cutting through the air and hitting as many crows as she could. Daria did the same, while sheltering her brother's body with her own.

The attacks were relentless though and, soon, both Lia and Daria started to bleed from the cuts on their arms, legs, and faces. In turn, dozens of birds lay around, motionless, after having met their sharp blades.

Through the infernal noise of their battle, Lia could hear Lady Aril's laughter, or at least she thought she did – it resembled too much the terrifying cry of the birds. Daria let go of her brother and tried a few times to reach Aril but the crows kept coming through the open balcony.

They managed to push the two friends back, bit by bit, towards the edge of the staircase. Lia's heart was racing.

'She wants to throw us off,' Lia panicked and doubled her efforts to slay as many birds as possible.

'Have you had enough?' Lady Aril asked. 'Are you ready to obey me?'

'I am ready,' Lia said and materialised her Wish Orb once more. Seeing its glow through the storm of wings, beaks and claws, Lady Aril narrowed her eyes. 'Don't tell me you will do something stupid again,' she said softly.

Lia thought they could be pushed over the edge at any moment. Breathe, just breathe. She started thinking quickly about what Wish to make. Create a wall around them? Immobilise Aril? Or…

She didn't get to finish her thought.

The noise and movement grew faint. The birds started flying inside the tower, one by one, towards the ground, through the circular space of the staircase. As quickly as they entered, they were gone. Even the wounded ones were trying to make it down the staircase as if something irresistible was calling them down there.

Her friends, Lia hoped. She hurried to see but it was dark at the base. The torches had gone off due to the unusual commotion created by the birds. Her Wish could not light up the entire tower and Lia desperately shouted for her friends.

Her shouts were cut short by the hand that covered her mouth. Another hand grabbed her by the throat and Lia was forced to turn and face Lady Aril. The violence of Aril's grip made her drop her sword. She couldn't speak or make her Wish.

Aril uncovered Lia's mouth only so she could slap her forcefully across the face. Lia lost her balance and saw Aril reach for her Wish. Their eyes met and Lia had the strange feeling she had been in the exact situation before, that she had seen it all happen.

'I've got–' Aril screamed but, before she could finish her sentence, she collapsed. Daria had hit her over the head with the back of her sword. Lia quickly made her Orb disappear again.

'Curse you!' Aril howled and threw lights towards Daria's face but she crouched down to avoid the attack. 'This won't work twice, witch.'

Aril picked up Lia's sword and effectively blocked another blow from Daria. The older woman stood up and, still shaking and bleeding heavily, succeeded in fending off all of her opponent's attacks. The tower was echoing with the sound of clashing metal and the anger in Daria's voice. Aril kept her cool. She was fighting so serenely and so well that Lia wondered if she was even human.

'You are a monster and a thief.' Clang. 'You snatched people and Wishes mercilessly.' Clang. 'You tried to hurt my brother.' Clang. Daria continued to shout and accompany each statement with a mighty blow. Aril was retreating towards the balcony but didn't look worried about it.

'I will make you pay for everything you did,' Daria went on. 'I will make you pay for kidnapping Lia's grandfather.' Clang. 'And for leading the Cardinal to his death.' Clang. Daria had tears in her eyes as she continued to strike. With each blow, Lady Aril was becoming weaker.

One wrong step made her wobble. Daria took advantage of the situation and, with an apt move, disarmed Aril. Lia's sword flew in the air and she managed to catch it back before it hit the ground.

'It's over,' Daria said menacingly and punched Aril who, defenceless, took a few more steps back and fell, unconscious, on the floor.

Daria and Lia could not believe it. The fight was over.

The powerful woman who had them in her hands just moments ago was lying on the floor at their feet. The Wish Thief everyone was looking for was right there. Defeated. The devious member of the Wish Council who betrayed the Cardinal was ready to receive her punishment.

Lia wanted to help Daria tie Aril up and take her downstairs when she saw her friend raise her sword. She was about to hit again.

'No!' Lia shouted and placed herself between Daria and Aril. Daria slowly lowered her hand.

'Don't do it,' Lia pleaded. 'She will face the judges tomorrow and receive the punishment that is right for her. It's the only way to save the Cardinal and...'

She suddenly stopped. She had just realised something. Daria asked her what happened.

'I know now where I saw it before… Aril's look,' Lia murmured and her heart started to beat faster, ready to break out of her chest.

'Was it in Evergreen, in the house of the other witch?' Daria asked.

'No, it was in my own house. And then in the forest on the night we left Raven behind,' Lia said, struggling to articulate her thoughts. 'It was… the look of the people who came for my Wish Orb. It was the look on the Cardinal's face yesterday…'

'Lia, that is impossible,' Daria argued. 'It is impossible because Aril was controlling the Cardinal. And she was controlling your friend and the soldiers who came to take you away in Ostrova.'

'No, Daria! Aril was in the same state as them. I could see it perfectly. I could see it in her face when she looked at me. I could see it when she was fighting you just now,' Lia started speaking faster.

'We have to go! We have to take your brother and go. We have to go now!' she screamed and pulled her friend urgently by the hand.

'What do you mean?' Daria asked and set herself free from Lia's grip. 'We won't leave without her, now that we know she attacked us and kidnapped my brother. You saw all of that, right?' she asked Lia. 'You saw how she used her powers, you saw how well she fought. No, Lia, this was not a person controlled by someone else, I can tell you that.'

'Daria, please, please, let's go now,' Lia begged and started looking around in panic.

'What is wrong with you?' Daria said and shook her gently. 'Lia, nothing will happen to us. The fight is over. We won. We found my brother. We...'

'We will never leave this place,' Lia said. Or, at least, it was her own voice she heard. But her mind didn't produce that sentence, it came from elsewhere. Sharing Daria's surprise, Lia took a step back and covered her face.

'When you want something done right, you have to do it yourself.' It was not her speaking this time. The voice came from the balcony.

When they turned around, they saw the King stepping in from the dark.

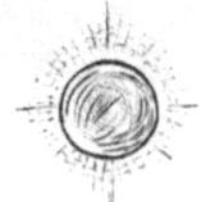

King Alexandru wedded Queen Margareta in 630, shortly after coming of age and dedicating his Royal Wish to the sailors of the Kingdom. The couple were not blessed with any children and this brought the Queen great sadness. It is said that this sadness contributed to her death in 635. The Royal record tells of a brief illness of the lungs, but some blamed the tragedy on a curse placed on the King's house at birth – a story dismissed by the Order as pure superstition. The King did not remarry and remained childless.

(*The Chronicals of Maar*, by Alfred from Ostrova)

Chapter 27. Trapped

Daria and Lia found themselves shoved back in opposite directions, their bodies smashed against the walls of the chamber. The impact was so violent that Lia thought she would faint. But, instead of falling down, she remained fixed on the wall as if held by invisible hands.

They were both unable to move but could still speak, Lia realised from hearing her own moans. She didn't know what to say in any case. Instead, she was mesmerised by the King who had entered the room bringing in snow with each one of his heavy steps.

He was dressed in simple clothes, wore no crown and carried no weapons. He would have no use for them, after all. The only thing he had on his shoulder was a dark leather bag.

Alexandru walked slowly, as if inspecting the scene, careful not to step on any dead bird. He pushed the chair to the middle and, without paying any attention to Lia or Daria, moved towards Lady

Aril who lay motionless on the floor. He turned her around gently, checked her wounds for a moment and, surprisingly, started to laugh. At first quietly then loudly.

'You know that attacking a Cardinal is punishable by death, don't you?' he asked, visibly amused, without looking at either of them. 'But there are worst punishments in this world than death.'

'What will you do to us?' Daria was the first to address him.

The King turned around, surprised to have been asked a question. He took a long look at Daria.

'Such a shame. You could have been a great soldier, Daria. You could have fought for your Kingdom. Instead, you chose to fight your King.'

'I did no such thing,' Daria protested. 'I chose to fight the bastard who imprisoned my brother and stole the Wishes of many innocent people. Am I to blame just because my King is that bastard?' she asked defiantly.

'Oh, how you will hate it then when this "bastard King" makes your Wish for you,' he answered with a smile.

'I will never give you my Wish!' Daria shouted. 'Aril didn't manage to take it and, soon enough, you will be lying there next to her.'

The King's smile grew wider. 'I like a good challenge. But don't forget, child, that I have taken the Wishes of hundreds before you, many of them more valiant and skilled than you are.'

'Why? Why are you doing this?' Lia asked faintly.

'I don't have to explain myself to you,' he said abruptly, turning to face her. 'But if you do care to know, I will tell you. After all, you two are the last and most valuable items in my collection. The two majestic butterflies, pinned to the wall, whose wings are flapping for a little while longer.' He made the sign of wings gently flapping in the air.

'The two brightest lights in the Eastern Kingdom, in fact, in the whole of Maar. How lucky is that?' he asked without expecting an answer.

'I don't know, it doesn't feel very lucky to me,' Daria said icily but the King ignored her. Instead, he opened his bag and showed Lia what was inside. Wish Orbs, a whole pile of them.

King Alexandru was visibly proud of his catch. He took a couple out, as if to inspect them. 'You see this?' he said, showing them to both his captives.

'This is what moves the world. The life energy of the thousands of Wishes of its people,' his voice grew passionate. 'A Wish may look like such a small, insignificant thing. And yet, it can strengthen a life or bring it to ruin. Wishes are power,' he said and raised his fist.

'And whoever can harness their power will rule over the land and everyone in it.'

'But you are already the King, you idiot!' Daria said, unable to control herself.

'I rule the Kingdom, yes. And, before me, another King did. And after me, another King will,' he answered undisturbed, looking melancholically into the Orbs. 'My rule is but the blink of an eye, a small glimmer in the infinite darkness of death.'

'As are all our lives,' Lia said, hoping she might be able to reason with him.

'Your miserable life might be,' the King replied, ending her delusion. 'My destiny is different, Lia. I was born a King for a reason. I had a Great Wish for a reason. And I will not fade away in the dark like the rest of you.'

She saw the madness in his eyes as he continued. 'My Wish is to live and to rule. Forever.'

'You are a fool!' Daria interrupted him again. 'Nobody can make such a Wish, not even you, oh great and mighty Wishfull,' she said mockingly.

'You are right about this,' the King conceded. 'One Wish will never accomplish that. But many, many Wishes will,' he added with unmasked pride. 'And you are calling me a fool, little rascal, when you dream of giving people a second chance at Wish-Making?'

Daria paused. She didn't tell anyone else about this except for Lia, her friends, and her brother. Did the King torture him? Why would this matter to the King, anyway?

'How do I know?' The King sneered. 'Well, I know it just as I know what you are thinking right now. I can read minds, you wretch. Your mind is an open book for me, ready to be read. Ready to be written.' He laughed and the sound made Lia shiver. In contrast, it made Daria even more furious.

'You stay out of my mind, you monster! And away from my Wish. Yes, it is true, I want to give people a second chance at creating their lives. What is wrong with that?' she raged.

'What is wrong is that it is impossible, even for a Great Wish like yours,' the King replied calmly. 'Don't you think I would have done this myself if it was possible? You wouldn't be here today with your friend if that was the case. But it is not. However, nobody forbids taking the Wishes of others.'

'That is impossible, too,' Lia said, trying to reassure herself.

'Technically, yes, it is not possible. Unless, well, unless you control the mind of the Wish-Maker. Then it becomes perfectly possible! More than this, it becomes easy. You want a demonstration?' the King asked. Before Lia could say no, he took an Orb from the bag and smashed it on the floor.

The light inside escaped and started evaporating like a bright mist. In its place, a hideous monster took shape. It was a half-monkey, half-snake, with long, bat-like wings. It looked around viciously, ready to attack. Lia gave a faint scream.

'Bring his brother to the old Royal prison,' the King said. The beast groaned and, with a gush of wind, raised itself in the air and flew out the window.

'See how easy it is?' he asked with a smile. 'And now, this minion of mine will bring me the Wish owner's young brother, who also has a Wish to make. It is not a Great Wish, but it is a Wish nonetheless.'

'Monster!' Daria shouted.

'Why? Is it not good to reunite families?' the King asked with mock naivety and looked down at Dragomir. 'Besides, I know for a fact that the Wish-Maker misses his brother terribly. Remember, I can see deep into his mind.'

'You see what you want to see,' Daria replied.

'Nonetheless, I helped a Wish be made. Do you understand now the brilliance of my plan? I didn't waste my Great Wish on granting myself more Wishes. That would have been in vain,' King Alexandru said, giving Daria a look of pity. 'Instead, I granted myself access to the minds of others and, through this, to their Wishes. Isn't that much better?'

'It's unlawful, unwise and criminal!' Daria shouted. 'You were supposed to give your Wish to the Kingdom. Isn't this what Kings do? And why they are Kings?'

'Oh yes, of course. Officially, my Wish blessed the Kingdom's rivers and lakes and helped our fishermen and tradesmen sail safely through them,' he said with the tone of someone bored of repeating the same thing.

'And probably it did, who knows? Sometimes simply believing helps things come true. The Cardinal certainly believed the Wish was made – I helped him a little, of course. You see, tradition says that the Cardinal is the King's main Witness. Well, tradition doesn't say anything about the King not controlling the mind of the Cardinal.'

'You used the Cardinal and you are letting him die for you,' Lia said bitterly.

'Aron will give his life for me, yes. He would have wanted it anyway. He loved me like a father loves a son, you know? And I loved him in return.'

Daria laughed but the King just continued.

'And what greater sacrifice can a person make for the one he loves? The Cardinal pays the price for my sins, as you would call them, it's true. But you cannot have Wishes disappearing for years from the Kingdom without anyone noticing it. Someone needs to pay a price.'

'Why did you become so greedy? Why did you start stealing so many Wishes? And why do you still need ours?' Lia asked. She felt exhausted, defeated. 'Didn't you know this will be the end of the one who loved you so?'

'I am glad you asked this,' the King replied almost cheerfully and, moving to where he placed the chair, he sat down, as if ready to tell a story.

'You see, normal Wishes can keep one going. With their help, I managed to perfect my skills and test many of my ideas about Wish-Making and the human mind. But this was only preparation,' he said gleefully.

'The aim was always to get to the two of you. Yes, you may feel flattered to know that two peasants such as yourselves, growing up in the middle of nowhere, were on the mind of your King for a very long time. Ever since the Cardinal informed the Council that two Great Wishes had been found, two Wishes brighter than anything he had ever seen.'

'Daria and me,' Lia muttered.

'Yes, the two of you. And, naturally, he wanted to place you under his close supervision. I agreed with that. It was important for you to grow up safely and for your Wish Orbs to become more mature, to swell with the energy of your dreams.

'The Cardinal tried to bring you both to the Order. That would have made things much easier for me but, as you know, it failed miserably in the case of this one,' he said pointing towards Daria. 'And was never agreed to by your grandfather, Lia.

'Nevertheless, for as long as I knew you were safe, and I knew where you were, everything was fine. And so, the years passed, you grew up and the time for you to make your Wishes started approaching. Daria, you would have been first. A year from now, you would have had your Rite, Lia the year after that. As you can imagine, I cannot allow this to happen,' he sounded almost concerned.

'Besides, you are both rebellious enough to let accidents happen, like Eduard did. You know what I'm talking about, Lia.' She knew.

'Why? What do you need our Wishes for?' Daria asked impatiently.

'I need them to make myself invincible and immortal,' the King admitted. 'Yes, it is only Great Wishes, the greatest there are, that could accomplish this. Do you see how it all makes sense? How your insignificant lives were meant to serve a greater purpose after all?'

He stood up but did not wait for an answer.

'Daria, you will Wish to make me invincible, safe from any weapon known to men. Lia, you will Wish for me to never get old and, thus, never die, since nobody will be able to kill me. Isn't that perfect?' he asked knowing very well their views on the issue.

'You will not have my Wish, you selfish brute,' Daria protested. Lia said the same.

'But I am not *asking* for your Wishes,' the King reminded them. 'I am *taking* them. I have the power to do this, remember?'

'You have the power, yes, but you had this power all along, why didn't you do it already?' Lia asked, trying to buy time. Will her friends arrive with help? Or did the King send other Wish beasts to capture or kill them?

'That is a good question. You see, the only problem I could not overcome is that I can only enter the minds of the people I meet and, even so, I need to have formed a close relationship with them in order to take full control from a distance. Alternatively, I need to find a way to break their will. Then, and only then, I will have complete power over them,' the King said and tapped his bag full of Wishes.

'The short time Daria and her brother spent with the Order didn't allow me any of this. But the Cardinal and Lady Aril were easy prey. So were the soldiers from my guard. And, when I take control of a person's mind, I can also entrust them with the Wishes of others. It takes a lot of effort to possess two minds so completely, at the same time, but it is possible. You have seen this, Lia.'

Lia almost didn't hear his last remark. Her mind was focused on the question of how the King knew Raven. He must have met him. That was possible. But to have such control over his mind he must have managed to break his will. How? Raven was so determined, so independent.

Until that cursed night, anyway. Then he was possessed by the King. She had seen him trying to get the invader out of his own mind, she saw it. And he knew it all... This is why he told her and her friends not to go to the Order or the Castle and to avoid both the King and the Cardinal. He knew who the Wish Thief was... But then, why didn't he warn her, why?

'Enough with the stories,' she heard the King say next. 'Aril is bleeding to death here and I am not about to lose another loyal Cardinal because of you two.' He almost sounded caring. 'Daria, we can do this the easy way or the hard way, as you prefer.'

'You just set me free and you will see how hard things can get,' she said with resolve.

'I suspected as much,' the King replied and gave a long, theatrical sigh. 'Well, let's get you more mellow, shall we?'

As he said this, he opened his bag and stared at the Orbs as if looking for something in particular. He took one out and raised it in the air like a prize. 'Curing burns, hmm, a noble Wish,' he said.

'No!' Daria shouted. Lia knew what was about to happen. The King held Dragomir's Wish in his hand.

'There's no point curing burns if one doesn't make them first, is there?' the King said, looking at Daria's brother. Then, with a swift move, he threw the Orb towards Daria. She could not move her hands to catch it.

Lia desperately tried to get herself free. She couldn't move either.

The Orb smashed into the wall just beside her friend and broke with an echoing sound. The light it held inside moved freely in the air. Daria and Lia both watched with terror as it became red, revealing the first flames. In the blink of an eye, the flames turned into a tall fire that encircled Daria.

She was not stuck to the wall anymore but trapped by the fire. The King sat back on the chair, visibly enjoying the scene. Lia shouted and twitched her body, if only she could help her friend, if only she could make her Wish and stop this madness.

Daria's clothes started to catch fire. She was clearly trying hard not to scream and give the King that satisfaction. The heat and the pain it brought were unbearable. Daria took a deep breath and jumped as fast and as far as she could.

'Bravo!' Lia heard the King say. Her friend made it to the other side, but she was badly hurt. Her clothes were not burning but she couldn't find the strength to stand up. The fire melted away as fast as it started.

'What does brotherly love feel like, Daria?' the King asked dryly. She did not answer. 'I thought so,' he continued. 'Give me your Wish Orb,' he ordered.

To Lia's surprise, Daria extended her hands and materialised her Wish. Her friend was giving up. No. That was not Daria anymore, it was the King taking over her mind and body.

'No!' Lia shouted in vain. She felt sick to her stomach.

The King ignored Lia's protests and slowly stood up, walked to Daria and picked up her Wish. He took a moment to admire it. The brightness of Daria's Wish Orb was exceptional. Lia had only seen such light in her own Wish. If only she could control her body, she would make her Wish right there.

'Your turn will come,' Lia heard the King say. Then he turned back to her friend. 'We are almost there, Daria. You are becoming the good girl I expected you to be.' The King caressed her hair. 'The Cardinal would have been so proud of you,' he whispered. Daria didn't reply.

She was in a similar state as her brother Dragomir who seemed not to have noticed anything of what had happened, of how his Wish had been used. It was better for him that way…

Lia was sobbing. She felt powerless. She wanted so much to help her friend. Raven, Maxim, Tudor, where are you?

'We are almost there,' the King said again, inspecting the Wish Orb. 'You see, Lia, I could try to make this Wish right now, but it would be a bit risky.' He sounded like Filip before he used to show them demonstrations in class.

'Daria's mind is in my power, but not completely. I can feel this. And then there is a small chance that, as this Orb breaks, her mind won't formulate the Wish correctly. And we can't have that, can we?' he asked, this time looking at Daria. 'A bit more is needed to break your resistance. And I know just the way.'

Lia saw her friend stand up and slowly walk towards Lady Aril. She called her, but Daria completely ignored her plea. She kneeled beside Aril and turned her over. What was she doing? Lia didn't understand until she saw Daria pick up Aril's knife. Was she going to kill her?

'Don't do this!' she shouted.

As if listening to her, Daria stood up again, with the knife in her hand. She turned towards Lia, who felt chills running down her spine. Was Daria going to torture her?

No. Instead, Daria walked across the room and stopped in front of Dragomir. The King nodded. Daria didn't look at her brother, just lifted the knife. Dragomir didn't look up either, he went on staring into the void.

Lia's screams were amplified in the empty room and carried down the tower. She wanted so badly to move that her muscles hurt, ready to explode. Daria could not hear or see any of it.

Holding the knife, her hands started shaking. The King ordered her to do it. The knife's blade, shining in the light of the torches, came down quickly. It pierced through flesh. Its red mark grew wider and wider.

Lia could not believe her eyes. The King could not either and he let out a roar of absolute rage.

Daria's body quivered. Then she fell slowly over her brother, who did nothing to catch her. She fell by the staircase they had walked up only an hour before. The blood from her wound started dripping down the stairs. Lia saw the Wish Orb in the King's hand vanish. As its light went out, she was also engulfed by darkness.

Wᴉsʜᴇs ᴀʀᴇ ᴛʜᴇ ᴄʜɪʟᴅʀᴇɴ of dreams.

(Popular saying in the former Southern Kingdom)

Chapter 28. Hope

LIA DIDN'T KNOW WHETHER she was dead or alive. She couldn't see, hear, or touch anything anymore. Perhaps the King, enraged by losing Daria's Wish, finally killed her as well. All she could feel were tears rolling down her cheeks and the weight of extreme tiredness. It was time to let go.

It wasn't all bad, she told herself. At least he didn't have her Wish. Her body was no longer stuck to the wall. In fact, she couldn't feel her body at all. No more pain from the cuts and wounds of the battle.

Just the pain of losing her friend. There was no escaping that.

But she could cry about it. Maybe she would go on weeping for eternity. The thought didn't frighten her, it was soothing.

Moreover, there was no fear anymore. If that was what death was supposed to be like, then its agonising terror was highly overrated. She was oddly at peace with everything. She had lost Daria and will never see her friends or grandfather again, but at least the King's plans had been ruined.

With Daria and Lia gone, there would be no Great Wishes left to make the King invincible and immortal. And someday, somehow, his evil deeds would bring him to his own end. She knew it. And that was enough.

Slowly, her eyes started to accommodate to the darkness around, but there was still absolutely nothing to touch or hold on to. She was floating around in emptiness. Might just as well keep her eyes closed.

If I am really dead, will I find Daria here? Lia thought but did not ask. Who would she ask this to?

A new idea dawned on her. How about using her Wish Orb to make some light? She focused on materialising it. She opened her eyes. There was no Orb in sight. Lia tried to feel her hands but couldn't.

Her heart sunk. Did she lose her Orb as well? Did the King manage to take it and then kill her? Did she forget it all because he took control of her mind?

More tears fell down her cheeks – this time tears of anger. And, as they fell down, the place on the ground they touched started to change. Initially she only saw a faint light emerge. Then the light became stronger and created what looked like small, growing crystals. Her tears were creating tiny ice flowers at her feet.

The crystals grew larger and followed each other straight down into the darkness. Curious, Lia forgot her sorrow and, starting to feel her body again, began following the crystals.

The ice flowers stopped in front of a thick, black curtain. Lia touched it, trying to find its end. She found an edge and pulled. The curtain moved sideways, revealing a magnificent field of flowers and grass, endless, basking in the warm sun of the afternoon. All in front of her.

Lia smiled for the first time in a long while and stepped into the light.

The flowers and grass seemed real enough. She felt her arms, her legs, her whole body. There were no more cuts and bruises. Just the nice feeling or being caressed by the sun and getting warmer. It had been so long… She could smell the fresh scent of spring, touch the flowers around her, see little insects going about their daily lives as if all was well in the world. Near her, a couple of beautifully coloured butterflies were chasing each other.

And there it was. An urge to leave it all behind, to forget it all. Lia started running into the open field. She felt her body fully now and she was in control of it. She was herself once more.

She could run, jump and shout in the beautiful landscape that reminded her of Ostrova, of the hills behind Grandfather's house. Some of the flowers even looked the same, many others were different, either in colour, shape or size.

In fact, on closer inspection Lia couldn't recognise any particular plant, insect or bird. Seen from afar, the birds looked like the parrots she admired in her grandfather's books. But, at the same time, they had butterfly-like wings. The butterflies, in turn, were covered in tiny feathers.

Am I going mad? Lia wondered.

'You are not,' was the answer she received. 'But you certainly are forgetful in the extreme.'

'Who spoke?' Lia asked, startled, looking around.

'As always, you look up to the sky and forget to see the ground,' the voice retorted.

When she turned her eyes towards the grass around, she couldn't see anyone or anything at first. Then her eyes fell on a tiny salamander attached to the red petals of a wild flower.

'It's you, isn't it?' she said excited. 'You look a bit different.'

Lia remembered having met a talking salamander in the cave close to Ostrova, in that other world. But that was a black and yellow one. The salamander in front of her was bright red with a few spots of green – this new costume made it even harder to notice it in a field of grass and flowers.

'Well, hello to you too,' the salamander replied in a tone that tried to sound friendly.

'Where is your master?' Lia asked.

'Here we go again. I have no master, you silly girl,' the little creature said scornfully. 'And I am very close to refusing to talk to you if you continue asking such silly questions.'

'Alright, alright, I am sorry,' Lia was quick to apologise, fearing she might be left alone. 'It has been a long time since we met and many things happened since then.'

'I know,' the salamander said and left it at that.

An awkward silence followed and neither Lia nor the salamander wanted to break it. Lia was thinking about what exactly the tiny creature might know but didn't want to antagonise it further by asking. So, instead, she decided to ask something else that was on her mind.

'Do you know why my Wish Orb doesn't appear anymore?'

'It's simple. You have no need for it here,' the salamander answered.

'Right, right… because this is the World of dreams, isn't it?' Lia said, trying to remember what she had learnt during her last visit.

'Call it what you want but it is a world different than your Outer world of Wishes,' the salamander confirmed. 'And its Kings, Cardinals, grandfathers, and friends,' it continued, as if knowing what was on Lia's mind.

'Am I dead?' she asked her next pressing question.

'You are not dead. Nor are you alive simply because there is no time in here,' the salamander clarified. 'But why do we have to still go over all of this, girl? Didn't you learn it by now?'

As it finished scolding her, Lia saw the salamander become distracted by noises from a bush of roses nearby. Or rather, they looked like roses, except they had little colourful tubes instead of spikes. She too wondered what could be hiding there.

Out of the bush came a little boy, seven or eight years of age. Lia was relieved to see a fellow human being.

'Hello,' she said as sweetly as she could. The boy ignored her and came close to her only to pick up the salamander and place it on his shoulder. Lia recalled the little creature sitting on an old man's hat. She assumed that, if the tiny beast didn't enjoy this treatment, it would react vehemently. The salamander kept quiet.

'So, who are you?' she asked, trying to catch the boy's attention.

'Short memory, what did I tell you,' the salamander puffed.

'You are the old man I saw before' Lia said tentatively, hoping she would get at least one thing right. It was clear to her now that everything was possible in the Dream world and, if this was the case, why wouldn't the man grow younger instead of older?

As a reply, she heard the child murmur a song. Lia didn't understand what he was saying at first but then, suddenly, it came back to her.

Dreams show you want was, is, or will be
It is not what you wish for, but what you came to see

What did she want to see, after all? No, she wanted to stop seeing things.

And if your travels take you to places far and wide
Remember who's beside you, and those you left behind

Tears came back to her eyes. In the other world, there was nobody left beside her. Daria was gone. Raven had abandoned her. Tudor, Matei and Clara could not follow her. And she never did find Alfred.

Beside her was only that monster they called a King, a wounded Cardinal, and a hypnotised boy who didn't even know he had lost both his Wish and his sister… That was not the world she wanted to be in!

The song grew louder. It was not only the boy singing now, but also the salamander. And the butterflies, the birds, even the thick bush of roses.

The Outer world loses its shine,
As Wishes wilt and people pass.
He looks for you and if you're found,
Your Wish will fade, and his will last.

'No!' she screamed. 'His Wish will not last. Never! He will pay for this, he will pay for everything he has done,' Lia shouted so loudly she didn't notice everyone around her fell silent.

And started disappearing. The blades of grass, one by one, started turning black. The sky became darker. The roses and the flying insects started blending into the surrounding night.

'No, no, please don't go,' Lia pleaded anxiously, as she tried to reach the young boy and the salamander. She grabbed the boy by the hand and held on tight. Everything around them was dark once more. Only the tiny salamander was glowing brightly.

'I don't want to go back, I want to stay here,' she said as tears dripped down her cheeks once more.

'You still don't know what you wish, do you?' the salamander noticed. It was comforting to hear even its sarcasm. And it was true. She did not know what she wanted, much less what she wished for. All she knew was that she had to stop the King and make him pay for his deeds.

'That is a start,' the salamander continued. She was by now used it hearing her thoughts. So Lia asked, in her mind, how to defeat the King.

'Look around you, Lia. And listen. Didn't you hear us sing just now?' The voice didn't seem to come either from the salamander or the boy.

'I did and the song said he will win,' Lia answered.

'The song said no such thing,' said the voice. 'It told you to look at what is around you.'

'There is nothing around me,' Lia said, growing desperate. 'Well, except you two,' she didn't want to sound ungrateful.

'What else?' the voice insisted.

'I don't know… the King?'

'He looks for you.'

'And if I'm found… I need not to be found. He must not reach me,' Lia said, feeling she was getting close to getting her answer. 'If I am here, I am both with him and away from him. He cannot enter the Dream world, can he? My mind can travel, right?' She did not wait for a reply. 'And if he can enter my mind then, perhaps…'

'I told you we shouldn't lose hope,' the salamander said, this time addressing the young boy. The boy looked at the glowing little creature on his shoulder and smiled. There was something so innocent and carefree about that smile that Lia felt touched by it.

She could not let go of the Outer world. She could not abandon her friends and her grandfather. She could not leave Dragomir in the hands of the King. Daria would never forgive her for it.

'I am ready,' she said. 'Thank you both.'

'There is nothing to thank us for,' the boy answered politely.

'It's time for me to go. Or, actually, it's time for you to go,' she replied. And, as she did, both the boy and the salamander started fading away into the darkness. Lia found herself completely alone once more.

She closed her eyes and started breathing loudly, to calm herself. With her eyes closed, she could still sense light and movement around. Somebody was moving back and forth in front of her.

The King was pacing restlessly, cursing. When he saw Lia had opened her eyes, he was both relived and angered by it.

'You! You came back, you little brat. Did you see what your friend here chose to do?' he said and pointed to where Daria was lying, next to her brother. 'This miserable creature decided to take her own life rather than surrender her Wish. Idiot!' he shouted at Daria.

Lia kept silent. She wanted to see and hear rather than think and talk.

'Well, if you think I am defeated, you are sadly mistaken,' he went on. 'I can do without her wretched Wish. I will harvest others, many others, and I will make myself invincible bit by bit. It will take longer, but I have all the time I need. All the time you will give me,' he said, looking directly at Lia.

'Your Wish will keep me young and healthy forever. And if you think-' He stopped all of the sudden.

The King came close to where her body remained trapped on the wall. He took her head in his hands and looked into Lia's eyes. She looked back without saying a word.

'What happened?' he asked. 'You have nothing to say or think about? You imagine this is how you will stop me from taking control of your mind?' His voice grew menacing.

'You forget that I have many weapons at my disposal. Your friends, for instance, or your grandfather.' He paused again, noticing his words had make an impression on her. 'You still care about them, don't you Lia?' he asked. 'I am ready to make a deal with you. I promise you nothing will happen to them if you give me your Wish Orb, how about that?'

Lia answered calmly: 'You promise? Only a fool would trust you.'

'Well, let's put it this way. You have no other choice than to trust me. Don't forget that I have enough Wishes at my disposal to create an army of monsters that will hunt down your friends inside the Castle and shred them to tiny pieces. Is that what you want?' he asked angrily.

'No,' Lia replied.

'Then obey me now,' the King commanded.

Lia closed her eyes. Her Wish Orb materialised at her feet. When the King saw its shine, his eyes glittered and his smile turned into a malicious grin. He picked up the Orb.

'You are a good girl,' he said, grabbing Lia's cheek. 'I might even let you live when all of this is over. Of course, you will have to be imprisoned with the rest of them. Some are still alive, you know. Others will join you in the old prison. You will always have company there.' He seemed to be trying to convince her of how good things would be.

'Look at it! What a magnificent Wish this is,' he continued, this time focusing on the Orb. 'It reminds me of my own…'

'Your own selfish Wish?' Lia asked coldly.

The King was too content to take offence. He told Lia the Wishes of Kings are always selfish.

'Even those who go through the Rite, do you think they care for their Kingdom and their people? No, they sacrifice their Wish for the power to rule. They Wish to rule over others. I simply found a more efficient way to do it,' he explained.

Lia continued breathing, listening, and trying not to think.

'This is the best thing I could have done for myself and my subjects. Imagine a Kingdom with the strongest King on this earth. The Eastern Kingdom will take over the whole of Maar again. Finally, the Northern Stronghold will fall. The South will be conquered once and for all. And the West will follow. And we will send ships over the Endless Sea to the furthest corners of the world. They will all know me, fear me and obey me,' the King said with great satisfaction.

Breathing. In and out. In and out.

'And it will be thanks to you. You will make history today, Lia. You really should be more cheerful on this special occasion,' he looked at her, faking disappointment. 'After all, you don't want to make a Wish anyway, do you?'

Go on. Go on breathing.

'Your dear Professor Filip told us that before he was sent to jail. I am afraid you won't be seeing him again, Lia, but you don't mind it that much, do you?'

'You are a murderer,' she said bitterly. She couldn't help it. 'And you are mad. The Kingdom will stand up to a wicked King. You will never win.'

The King laughed for a long time before he raised her Wish Orb and showed it to her.

'I've already won.'

Just that moment Lia heard herself say 'I Wish…' and was startled by it. She did not want to make a Wish. Especially the one she was about to make. She closed her eyes and tried to clear her mind again.

And if you're found. She could feel him looking for her.

'You insufferable peasant!' the King shouted. 'You think you can escape me? Now that I am so close, I am not letting you slip through my fingers.'

As he said this, he opened his bag, took a Wish out and placed the bag in a corner. He swiftly smashed the luminous Orb on the floor.

In its place, Lia saw a huge black lizard appear. It was enormous, her own height. Standing on its back legs, it looked intensely at Lia with its bright, red eyes.

'Let's see how fast you cooperate this time,' the King said and pushed the lizard's head into Lia's face. She closed her eyes and tried not to scream. She could feel the foul breath of the beast and its slimy tongue rolling down her cheeks. The lizard's sharp teeth were trying to grab her head.

'Let go,' she heard. It was a voice inside her head. 'Let go and it will all be fine. You will live.'

She did not care about living. She was not…

A swirling noise and the lizard gave a deep growl that startled her. Then its weight collapsed on Lia and, with its claws, it tried to grab on to her shoulders. It couldn't.

The next thing Lia saw was the beast lying at her feet, twitching and turning to reach an arrow that had torn through the back of its neck. It was pointless. A final spasm ended its torment.

Both the King and the girl were equally surprised. The arrow came from the balcony. They turned and what Lia saw made her heart jump.

Raven was placing another arrow in the middle of his bow.

WISH-MAKERS ARE ALL EQUAL, even if their Wishes are not. Some people have a stronger Wish to make and they are called Wishfulls. And they are rare. Even more rare are those born with no Wish Orb at all. The difference between the Wishfull and the Wishless doesn't reside in strength or in virtue, but in their upbringing. Love, from before birth, nurtures the energy of Wishes. Its lack destroys Wish Orbs and forever shames the family of the barren child.

(*The Book of Wishes*, secret appendix added by the
Wish Order in 455)

Chapter 29. The Fall

LIA WANTED TO CALL out to him, but the words refused to come. The King, on the other hand, took a long look at Raven and said, both surprised and amused: 'Your friend decided to join us.'

The second arrow shot by Raven was meant to pierce the King's chest. With a simple wave of the hand, he changed its course.

'You have to do better than that, Alex.'

It was the first time Lia heard his name. Alex. She was so exhausted she only managed to whisper it. Raven had come to rescue her. She wasn't relieved but frightened. She knew what the King was capable of, she had seen it. Did Raven know it as well?

Apparently, he did, because he quickly moved out of the way when the King lifted Daria's sword from the ground with his telekinetic powers and sent it his way. The sword flew past him, through the open balcony and straight into the night. Raven took out his own sword.

'Drop it,' Lia heard the King say. And, a moment later, Raven let his sword fall. He made no move to pick it up. Or maybe he couldn't.

Lia tried hard to escape and place herself between the two but there was no chance of that. She shouted at the King to let him go.

'Oh, my dear, but the fun has just begun,' the King said softly, turning towards her. 'And, if I get rid of this rotten fellow, you should be the first to thank me. You have no idea what he is capable of.'

'Shut up and fight,' Raven said angrily, still unable to move.

'What's the matter, Alexandru? You don't want this young girl to know who you really are? You don't want her to know that, this very moment, you are trying to kill your own father?' the King asked loudly.

Silence followed. Lia heard the King's words but could not grasp their meaning. Raven was the King's son? Raven, the one who wandered endlessly through the Kingdoms of Maar with nothing more than what he could hunt or steal? Raven, the one who saved her Orb from being stolen, was the son of the Wish Thief?

'If you are going to repeat this, you better kill me right now and spare me the misery of hearing it ever again,' Raven said bitterly.

The King laughed wholeheartedly.

'I am not going to spare you any misery, you filth,' he replied. 'You already murdered your mother at birth and now you are coming after me, you swine. You, who have made me so ashamed by being born Wishless. Yes, did you know that, Lia?' he turned towards her once more.

'I… I don't,' she muttered.

'You don't know what Wishless people are? Because if you don't, I present you one,' he said and pointed to Raven whose eyes were burning with anger. 'He was not born with a Wish to make, you know? My son. The son of the King. Barren! I had to get rid of him as soon as possible, before everyone in the Kingdom started talking about it, started doubting me.' The King was beginning to lose his temper.

'Why would they do that?' Lia could not understand.

'Because a Kingdom is only as strong as its King. And a King's strength is measured in its heirs.'

'That is absurd,' she said and looked at Raven. She wanted to comfort him, to tell him she doesn't care about any of that. That she knew the King was mad. That everyone will know it as well.

At the same time, she felt ashamed for being there, for unwillingly learning Raven's secret. For seeing him humiliated by his own father.

'I bet he made you believe that bird of his was his Wish creature, right?' the King said mockingly. 'Where is the old crow anyway?' he asked Raven. 'I am in the mood to twist its neck and add its corpse to the rest of the family,' he said, pointing to the dead birds lying around.

'Zyron will feast on your eyes before the night is over,' Raven replied ominously, but his answer only managed to make the King laugh harder.

'I will never die!' he said and raised Lia's Wish Orb. Raven knew it.

He once managed to save it from the greedy hands of Lady Laurnic, a woman who shared the same dream as his father. Who would have thought fighting the witch would be so easy, compared to the Thief, Lia wondered. Of course, Raven did know. He told her to go into hiding, not to look for her grandfather, not to go to the Order or to the Castle. She didn't listen...

'Let him go,' Lia intervened. 'I will grant you my Wish if you let him go.'

'If you do that, you will never see me again!' Raven shouted at her from across the room.

'Silly little girl, you are in no position to grant me this Wish. I have it already, remember?' the King replied and pointed to the Orb in his hands. 'All I need is for you to cooperate and I can see you are not yet ready. You still harbour the will to fight Lia, don't you?' She did not deny it.

'Well, if a fight is what you want, why don't we oblige?' he asked with a smirk on his face.

The moment he finished his question, Raven was free to move again. Regaining control, he quickly picked up his sword from the ground.

The King kept Lia's Wish Orb in his left hand and, with his right one, summoned Solia. The thought of seeing Raven killed with her own sword, a sword she received from him, was unbearable. She pleaded again with the King to stop, but he did not listen.

'You are not going to play dirty, old man?' Raven asked, circling him.

'Not as dirty as you will,' the King replied and attacked first.

Their swords met in a violent blow. The tower trembled with the loud echo of clashing metal. The King and his son were evenly matched. Raven was agile enough to avoid most of his father's blows, but the King was stronger, despite his age.

Several times his sword was close to piercing through Raven's chest. Lia could not watch anymore. She felt powerless, crushed. Was it even possible for Raven to win against his father? And why was he fighting his son instead of her? Was he trying to punish her for not giving up?

Lia realised the King could read her mind. She made an effort to chase her thoughts away. *Your Wish will fade, and his will last…* Never!

'I expected more from you, son,' the King told Raven when he managed to escape yet another mighty blow that hit the wall instead, making sparks fly. 'You have quite a reputation as a thief and murderer in this realm.'

'If I do, I learnt from the best,' Raven replied curtly and launched his own attack. He managed to make the King lose his balance for once and almost drop Lia's Wish Orb from his hand.

'You want this, don't you?' he asked Raven. 'You would have liked to have an Orb of your own. You are not normal, and you will never be. And there is no Wish in the world that can save you from that.'

Raven hit the King's sword with such rage that it flew from his hand and went down the stairs. Lia's heart jumped with joy. Raven had won.

The King, on the other hand, didn't show any concern. On the contrary, he looked calmly towards the staircase and then at his son.

'You are not as useless as I imagined,' he said. 'And I am generous enough to let you take this little victory to your grave.'

Raven dropped his own sword again and covered his head with his hands. 'Get out!' he shouted. 'Get… out…' The King started moving around his son like a vulture circling its prey.

Raven's body shook uncontrollably, as if possessed by an evil spirit. His father was torturing him.

'I almost had you in my hands that night, remember Lia?' he asked his other prisoner. 'If only this useless boy of mine could have finished the deed, I would have had the pleasure of making your Wish much sooner.'

'You are a monster, that is what you are,' Lia replied, distraught to see Raven in such pain. His body was not trembling anymore, but his face looked struck by terror.

'If I order it now, he will kill everyone here,' the King continued, without paying any attention to Lia. 'He could finish Aril off,' he said, walking past her. 'He would murder Daria's brother,' he pointed to Dragomir in the corner of the room. 'He would even kill you, Lia,' he said, looking directly at her.

'That is a lie,' Lia replied. 'You would be the one killing each of us. You are responsible for Aril being wounded, for Daria's brother standing there, for Daria…' Her blood was boiling with anger. 'And, if I ever get a chance to fight you, I would be sure to avenge all of them. Including Raven. It's not his fault he has such a heinous father,' she said defiantly.

The King stopped.

'You love him,' he murmured, then turned his gaze towards Lia's Wish Orb, as if looking for confirmation.

Lia was stunned. She didn't know if that was the case. Was the King capable of seeing something she herself did not know? What did this monster know about love, anyway?

The King turned to Raven slowly. 'You will be useful after all, my son,' he said chillingly and, with a move of his hand, sent him flying in the air.

'No!' Lia shouted, as her friend was being violently thrown against the walls of the tower. He was killing him. Killing him for her, because of her. Lia wanted to scream but had no breath left for it.

With his hands alone, the King kept moving Raven through the air, dropping his body to the ground and raising it the ceiling again. Every time there was a drop Raven remained silent. Was he unconscious? Dead?

'I will make the Wish for you, just stop it,' she begged, 'I will make your Wish!' The King remained deaf to her cries and anguish.

He only stopped when he got bored of torturing his son. And, as he did, he dropped him on the chair in the middle of the room. It broke into many pieces with a loud, echoing noise.

To Lia's surprise, Raven was still able to move. He tried to lift himself up from the floor but couldn't do it at first. When he did stand on his two feet, Lia saw the terrible state he was in. His head was bleeding heavily, and his right arm looked broken.

'You didn't have enough?' the King asked dryly. Raven did not respond. He was breathing with great difficulty.

'Stop it, please, I beg you.' Lia was in tears.

'We are almost done,' the King said, looking into her Wish Orb. 'There is just one last thing.'

And, as he said that, he pointed to the staircase. Raven was pushed once more. Lia could only catch a glimpse of his eyes before he fell off the edge and down the dark void of the tower. She could not save him. Raven's look – full of defiance, sorrow and affection – was all she had left.

She had lost him too.

Lia didn't notice the King approaching her. She only saw him when he was standing right in front of her. She knew the time had come. She heard his voice inside her head, searching, trying to find her and crush her will.

You won't, she told herself. I will be the one coming for you, Lia thought and stared right back at him.

The King frowned. He saw Lia facing him, asserting herself. She was pushing inside his mind. Nobody ever tried to do that. He was the one in charge, the one who Wished control over the minds of others.

The King dropped her Wish Orb. Freed from her enemy, she made it disappear mid-air. He wrapped both his hands around her neck. Out of breath, Lia knew she needed all the strength she could muster. She had to escape him. To become him.

When she looked next, she jolted. Lia could see her own eyes staring back at her. And the hands extending in front of her – the hands of the King – holding her by the neck and squeezing tighter and tighter.

She didn't have the energy to make him stop or loosen his grip. Her mind began to wander inside the King's. It stumbled upon a memory.

In a flash, Lia could see her hands extended, trying to strangle another. The look in his eyes reminded of her own. It was her grandfather.

'If you are not ready to obey me, you will die,' she heard herself say, with the King's voice. She felt the anger the King experienced seeing Alfred's defiant gaze. He had been badly beaten, Lia realised.

The King kept asking him where she was hiding, but her grandfather refused to talk or surrender his mind. The King ordered him to help find her, but he shook his head. She could feel her hands pushing harder against Alfred's neck. Lia wanted to scream, to make the King stop, but there was nothing she could do. She was trapped inside the King's mind.

'I had enough of your stubbornness, old man,' she told her grandfather, memory and real life mingling. 'If you don't tell me where she is, you will never see her again,' she heard herself say with the angry voice of the King. It was the first time he couldn't penetrate the mind of a person standing in front of him.

'I would rather die than know her in your hands,' Alfred managed to whisper before she felt the King's grip intensify.

He did not stop. He did not stop when he saw her grandfather was struggling to breathe. He did not stop when he saw he became unconscious. He only stopped when he was certain Alfred had died.

Her grandfather had been killed. Lia knew it, she had just witnessed it inside the King's head. The man who raised her, who loved her above all else. The man she travelled for was gone, had been gone long before she arrived.

A rush of emotions came over her. Despair. Anger. Lots of anger. More than she had ever felt. Lia was ready to kill the King with her own hands.

Her emotions had an impact on his body. She saw the hands extended in front of her let go of her neck. She finally managed it! She was inside his mind and, for the first time, she was in control.

Lia knew this wouldn't last long. Her body was still fixed on the wall. His powers did not wane and, if he found her, if he got her out, that would be the end. She had only one chance to do this.

First, she looked at the room through his eyes. The whole place seemed smaller, seen from his height. There were no weapons left around to use.

She was running out of time.

Then Lia looked in front. A gust of wind came from the open balcony. She started moving him towards it. Every step required an enormous effort, as if she was carrying a heavy load. In time, the burden softened. He was walking now in the snow, on the balcony.

In the distance, the first rays of sun were showing behind the mountain crest. Looking down the tower, way below, Lia could see the inner yard of the Castle. The guillotine was still there.

Her heart was beating so strongly she could hear it in the silence of the dawn. Or was it his heart?

She didn't think about it. Just bent over. A little at first, then more, until she knew her feet – his feet – were no longer touching the ground.

The air of the morning was so cold it felt like tiny knives piercing through her. Falling fast through the air had made the knives cut deep marks into the skin. She felt a deep fear that was not hers. Falling, faster, faster.

Lia was ready for the crash. She welcomed it. All she wanted was to reach the ground and be done with it.

Next thing she felt were her arms and knees hurting badly. She had fallen but not from the tower, from the wall. Her head was bleeding.

When she looked up, the King was no longer beside her. The rays of sun were coming in, giving the room a strange hue of orange.

As she managed to raise herself up, the first thing Lia did was walk slowly to the edge of the staircase. She was trembling, afraid that she might lose her balance and trip over.

Luckily, she stopped before the edge and gradually looked down. Lia did not want to see what she knew she would.

The staircase was dark but, with the rising sun, she could perceive clearly the bottom of the tower. Her friends were not there. But neither was Raven. She took a deep breath and closed her eyes.

After a while, she gathered enough strength to move towards the balcony. It was more painful to do so. Lia looked down the tower with the same feeling of dread, but for a different reason.

What if he wasn't there either?

She didn't expect to feel pity when she saw the King's deformed body smashed on the ground, surrounded by crimson coloured snow.

It was over. It was cold and silent. A silence broken by the sound of weeping coming from inside. Dragomir had woken up and had found his sister.

'WHAT IS THE MEANING of justice if not to reward those who do good and punish those who are evil?' asked the apprentice.

'It is neither. Justice should show us the meaning of care, not that of right and wrong,' answered the master.

(A Dialogue; text forbidden by the Wish Order
in the 5th century)

Chapter 30. The End

LIA'S FRIENDS RAN UP the stairs and were struck by what they found. Tudor was fast to catch Lia before she fell. Clara sat down, comforting Dragomir and watching over Daria. Matei walked around, checking if the lizard on the floor was dead and if Aril was still alive.

Tudor tended Lia's bruises and wounds. He told her they had tried to reach the King's chambers but were chased away by a group of soldiers. Just like she had seen in her vision, back in the cave…

It was Tudor's Wish Compass that helped them escape. It led them to a secret underground prison where they found the missing Wish bearers. They should have thought about using the Compass before. None of the seven people in the dungeon had their Wish Orbs anymore, they told Lia.

'I know,' Lia whispered. Her friends fell silent.

She pointed to the bag on the floor and asked her friends to check how many Wishes it contained. Matei picked it up and found four Orbs. The Thief had used the other three.

She couldn't tell them Dragomir had lost his Wish. And certainly not what the Wish was used for. Dragomir didn't care either. He was on the floor, hugging his sister's body tight while Clara hugged him.

Lia asked Tudor to help them get downstairs. 'First, we need to make sure the Thief won't wake up,' Matei said, pointing to Aril.

'The Wish Thief is dead,' Lia responded with great difficulty. She was interrupted by the sounds of commotion coming from the Castle's yard.

'Daria is still breathing! Help me, quick, quick,' they heard Clara shout over the noises from outside.

Lia found it hard to keep her eyes open.

***

When she woke up, she had no idea where she was. The room had a high ceiling and looked vaguely familiar. The curtains were half pulled and there was barely any light coming in from the grey winter day. Lia couldn't figure out if it was morning or evening.

Then her mind was flooded by memories of the night before. Strangely, she remembered first the lizard hovering close to her face. Then the King's eyes. And then it hit her: her grandfather was gone.

She wanted to get out of bed but her body was aching everywhere. She only managed to lean on her elbows.

Raven. She remembered Raven fighting. Then falling. Was he dead as well? No, she didn't see him at the base of the tower. Nor did her friends find him. And just before she fainted, she clearly heard Clara say that Daria was still breathing.

Lia was greatly relieved but instantly felt guilty for that. Her grandfather had been murdered. He died trying to protect her until the very last moment. Lia could not bear the thought of never seeing him again. She couldn't even bring herself to understand what it meant.

Then she noticed she was not alone.

A woman was sitting in a chair not far from her bed. She had been there all along, looking at her. Realising she'd been seen, the woman stood up. For a moment she looked exactly like Lady Laurnic. It was Aril.

'Don't,' she said as she saw Lia trying once again to get up. 'You are too weak for that.'

Aril was not the Thief, she had never been. She was actually one of the many victims of the King. Lia knew that but could not bring herself to feel it as well.

Aril had been nothing but hostile with them from the start, particularly with Daria. Maybe she was forced by the King to fight her friend, but somewhere, somehow, she must have enjoyed it as well.

'What do you want?' Lia asked curtly.

'I wanted to check on you,' Lady Aril said and stepped into the light. Lia could see she was wearing a dark purple cape and had a big bandage around her left arm. What surprised her more than the enormous bruise on Aril's face was her general demeanour.

She was no longer the person Lia knew. Lady Aril looked sad and embarrassed as well as visibly tired, maybe as tired as Lia was.

'How… how are you?' Lia was surprised to hear herself ask.

'I am fine,' Aril replied thankfully. 'And your friends are also well,' she said, anticipating Lia's next question. 'The Cardinal's sentence had been revoked. He is now being taken care of.'

'Taken care of?' Lia asked.

'Yes,' Aril hesitated. 'I am afraid these recent events affected him greatly. His ability to remember and reason are greatly diminished. But I can assure you that we are–'

'What about Daria?' Lia interrupted. 'Is she alive?'

Aril lowered her eyes. Lia's heart jumped – what if her friend had died after all?

'She is alive but barely so. Her state is critical. We have the best doctors tending her, Lia, people whose Wishes give them extraordinary healing abilities.' Lia thought of Maxim's Wish. 'She is being well taken care of and I hope she will wake up soon, but we don't know when.'

'Do you really hope that?' Lia asked reproachfully. Lady Aril was stung by the remark. She was quick to say how brave both Daria and Lia had been and how the entire Kingdom owed them a great deal.

'Myself included,' Aril added after a brief pause. Although a different person than before, Aril was still stiff and formal. Maybe her attitude was not the King's work after all, Lia thought with a smile.

Lady Aril must have seen her smile differently because she started behaving even more awkwardly. She told Lia that the body of the King was going to be incinerated without any festivity and the ashes scattered in the wind instead of being placed in the Royal crypt with those of ancient Kings and Queens. Lia was not interested by such things.

'What happened to the other Wish bearers?' she inquired. 'I think my friends said they found them last night and that several of them were alive.'

'Yes,' Lady Aril confirmed, happy to change the topic. 'Seven of them to be more precise. And four of them had their Wishes returned. The other three…' She paused.

'What will happen to them?' Lia wanted to know.

'They have been given the option to stay on at the Castle or at the Order and work for us. They refused,' she admitted with visible discomfort.

'I am not surprised,' Lia replied. 'If I was given the option, I wouldn't stay here either.' She could see on Aril's face that she was ready, in fact, to make her a similar offer.

'I mean, we have been through so much here. It is impossible to see this as something other than the place where we were tortured and lost friends and family.' Her grandfather. As painful as it was, Lia had to ask.

'Did you find where the King hid the bodies of all the people he killed?'

Lady Aril was not surprised by the question. She told her that a common grave was found under the abandoned Royal dungeon. 'And…'

'My grandfather's body lays there,' Lia said, taking a deep breath.

'Yes,' Aril confirmed without looking at her. 'And your grandfather along with the other victims of the King will receive the highest honours of this Kingdom, they will–'

'I want my grandfather's ashes returned home, to his garden in Ostrova,' Lia interrupted again.

'Naturally,' Lady Aril agreed on the spot.

'I will take them back myself,' Lia said.

'We can help you with this. You and your friends will be escorted by our soldiers on your way home. We will of course provide a carriage,' Aril added quickly.

'No need for carriages or soldiers. Only horses will do. Plus our weapons and the things we came with,' Lia replied resolutely in order to prevent Aril from insisting. They both fell silent.

'How was this possible?' Lia said in a low tone, as if to herself. Lady Aril avoided her gaze again.

'How was this possible?' she asked, this time looking directly at Aril. 'The King is supposed to be the one who protects the land and its people. The Order is meant to ensure that.'

'Yes. We have failed. As you probably know, the King made a forbidden Wish. He was then able to read and control minds. Able to make Wishes for others. This is the greatest crime in Maar. And he managed to do it right under our noses,' she took a breath.

'His first unlawful act was to confound the Cardinal and the Royal Watchers and make them believe he had dedicated his Wish to the Kingdom's prosperity. Now they were able to remember that none of them actually attended his Rite,' Aril explained.

'And he was not alone in making such a Wish, I'm afraid…' she continued, then stopped. Lia intuited what she was thinking about.

'Lady Laurinic made a forbidden Wish,' Lia stated rather than asked.

'Yes… Yes, she did. She and the King might have made their Wishes together for what we know,' Lady Aril said reluctantly. Lia knew from Raven that Crina gave her Wish to the forest, but didn't want to tell Aril.

'Laurnic lived in the Castle?' she asked instead.

'Yes,' Lady Aril confirmed. 'But as you told us, she is now dead. Even in death, the two of them are joined in disgrace and will be forever damned.' She spoke with more anger than she previously allowed herself to show.

'Were you friends with Laurnic?' Lia asked before Aril could change the topic.

'She was my older sister,' Aril said without hesitation. The conversation with Lia was not going as she had expected.

'I see,' Lia said. 'You two look alike. I am sorry for the death of your sister, even if she was not a good person.'

'She was not,' Aril said and fell quiet again. 'But thank you,' she added in the end.

Lia imagined the King played a big part in that too. He and Laurnic must have been accomplices, perhaps lovers, before becoming enemies. They were after the same thing and couldn't both have it. They wanted to live forever, to be forever young and powerful. And they had found a way to take the Wishes of others to accomplish this.

'Who will be the next King?' Lia asked Aril, trying to spare her further thoughts of her sister.

Lady Aril was visibly grateful for this new topic and answered more enthusiastically than expected. 'We don't know yet. As the King had no direct heirs, the Order has the duty to find the new King. We will be stricter than ever. We did learn our lesson.'

There was always Raven. Or, rather, Alex. Alexandru. The son of the King who wore his father's name and was unknown to them all. This was, at least, how the King wanted it to be. He was too ashamed to have a Wishless child. And he was willing to murder his own child in order to get what he wanted, after condemning him to live the life of an outlaw. The King had been rotten in every way. Lia could not feel sorry for him.

But what if she told Aril the truth, she thought all of the sudden yet stopped before opening her mouth. What would that accomplish? Raven would probably refuse to be King. Like those who had lost their Wishes in that wretched place, he understandably wanted nothing to do with it.

No, she understood she must not reveal Raven's secret. It was not her right to do so. He probably knew the King was dead. If he wanted to claim his birth right, he could do it himself. She smiled imagining Maxim as Royal adviser, taking care of the Court, and working closely with Aril, the new Cardinal. Now that would be a sight worth seeing!

'There is one thing I would like to ask for,' Lia said.

'Yes, anything,' Aril replied. 'Would you like to stay with us during this process and see it from up close?'

No, Lia did not want that, it had never occurred to her. 'I would like to ask for clemency for someone,' she said instead.

'Clemency? For whom?' Aril asked, surprised.

'Before I left Ostrova, there was a boy in our village called Eduard, who made an unwise Wish. Well, one that Professor Filip called unwise. I am afraid the previous Cardinal might have agreed.' Lady Aril was listening intently. 'He Wished to be able to fly. He Wished himself a pair of wings,' Lia continued.

'And why would it be deemed unwise?' Aril asked.

'Because he was the son of a fisherman and went against his family's hopes and the Wishes of the community. But I think you and I can both agree that being able to fly is not a bad thing, is it?' Lia asked, sensing Lady Aril's reticence.

'It is a form of bodily change and you know the Book of Wishes is very strict regarding this, Lia,' she replied. 'Was your friend Eduard judged?'

'He ran away. Or, rather, flew away. You can imagine he was under a lot of pressure from everyone,' Lia pleaded. 'Professor Filip is… was an impossible headmaster, he would have made life very difficult for Eduard. My grandfather would have helped him, but he cannot anymore. As the Cardinal, you have the power to redeem him.'

'This power needs to be used wisely, Lia,' Aril replied with a stern look.

'This power needs to be used charitably,' Lia said, increasingly annoyed. 'The Order has been the prosecutor and judge of so many people. It never really listened to any of them, to their dreams and hopes.'

'Wishes are not dreams,' Lady Aril said didactically.

Lia was instantly reminded of the strange man and his talking salamander. She would probably not be there if it wasn't for her ability to dream. But she didn't want to share that story with anyone, least of all Aril.

'Where did this strictness lead you and the Order?' she asked instead. 'You punish and isolate people, you manage to break families apart and create outlaws of everyone who is remotely different.'

'The King also wanted to be different,' Lady Aril responded.

'The King didn't want something different from what the Order wants. Both want to be eternal and all-powerful!' Lia shouted and, with a push, finally managed to sit up. She was shaking. Lady Aril chose to keep her distance.

'You want my Wish just as much as he did, only in a different way,' Lia said and saw she had touched a nerve.

'If you cannot see the difference between the Order and the Wish Thief, I am afraid you have misunderstood what we do,' Aril said. 'You are free to use your Wish the way you want. But don't expect our blessing for everything you might Wish for.'

She paused.

'I will look into Eduard's situation and will try to help him as much as I can within the limits of the Law,' she said, her voice softer now. Lia turned away and moved to the window, then drew the curtains wide apart.

It was snowing heavily and, just as with any winter day in the north, it was hard to say what time it was. She asked Lady Aril about it, deliberately not thanking her for "trying" to help Eduard.

'It is midday,' Aril answered.

'I slept for so many hours,' Lia said quietly. Lady Aril heard her and specified that she slept for a day and a half and that she still needed to rest.

'What!?' Lia cried. 'But what about my friends?'

'The funeral for the King's victims is today,' Lady Aril answered. 'And I will bring your friends to accompany you.'

Tudor and his cousins entered the room soon after Aril left. They asked her how she was feeling and whether she talked to the new Cardinal. Lia told them she felt better despite having talked to Lady Aril.

***

They found Dragomir at the gate, waiting for them. He had been beside his sister and her doctors until that moment but wanted to join Lia and her friends for the funeral. Everyone who was found dead in the dungeon, including Lia's grandfather, was to be honoured and the whole Royal Court would attend. All eyes were on Lia.

Dragomir thanked Lia for everything she had done for him and his sister. She didn't know what to say and gave him a hug instead.

Lia wondered how much he remembered from two nights before. Probably not much and it was better that way. She asked about Daria and learnt she was still unconscious but her state was stable.

Dragomir and Lia walked hand in hand, accompanied by Matei, Clara and Tudor. The funeral place was outside, on a mount usually reserved for royalty.

While her grandfather's remains and those of others were each engulfed by flames, Lia's eyes stayed dry.

She had been hopeful and fearful for so long that it felt good to say goodbye and to let him rest. Her life would never be the same again. She knew that very well. But she was not alone, not since it all began that late summer day.

Holding Tudor's hand, Lia found the contrast between the brightness of the fire and the whiteness of the snow enchanting and comforting. Everything around was movement and sound. The people's chants, the dancing snowflakes, the living flames.

With the corner of her eye, she saw a dash of black and turned towards it. It was a raven, gliding silently above the snow.

WISHES ARE NOT INSIGNIFICANT lights in the infinite darkness of the universe. They carry with them the light of all those who came before in the world.

(*The Book of Wishes*, Advice for Young Princes)

Chapter 31. The Beginning

After the funeral, Lia and her friends passed by Daria's room. Seeing the fearless warrior who led them into battle lying in bed, motionless and silent, broke Lia's heart. And yet, Daria's gentle breathing, the support of her brother, and the care of the nurses made her feel hopeful.

She will talk to her friend again. And they will remember the night that changed everything, and they will laugh, and cry, and travel together, and fight new evils, and win… And Daria will make her Wish one day, and Lia will be there to learn from her.

That evening, Lia got to meet the seven young people rescued by her friends. They were four girls and three boys, around her age, brought to the Castle from across the Kingdom either by the Order's soldiers or through the King's machinations.

She enjoyed their company and, although the post-funeral dinner was sombre, it was also a festive moment for all those who met the

King and managed to survive the encounter. Lady Aril was present for the first half of the dinner. She was friendly but awfully tired. Lia could see that the past few days had taken a heavy toll on her.

Nobody mentioned the fact that four of the people at the table had lost their Wishes. Lia knew who they were. Matei pointed them to her during the funeral, but she would have figured it out anyway. While most of those present were happy to return home the day after, the Wishless four – Dragomir, Flavia, Rivos and Mariana – were mostly silent and kept to themselves.

Clara decided she was in charge of keeping Dragomir company even if he was eager to return to his sister's side. She wanted to lift his spirits and it seemed to be working. Lia was glad to see Clara so animated and notice Dragomir smile more than once.

Rivos, Flavia and Mariana all seemed to have made peace with the fact that they had lost their Wishes. Only Flavia mentioned that she worried about how her family in Serex would receive her. They had such hopes for her that they sent her to the Order for protection. If they had known they were sending her directly to the Wish Thief…

Mariana from Voroi, the winemaking region, had been kidnapped by one of the King's flying monsters. The tallest at the table, she was also the most talkative of the three and Lia had the impression that, under different circumstances, she would have been the liveliest of them all but that title was, once again, reserved for Matei.

Rivos was a tall and thin teenager, with broad shoulders and a warm smile. He was from the south, like them, from a small village bordering the Southern Lands. Although people there were mainly farmers, Lia discovered they had many things in common with Ostrova. They were even blessed with the equivalent of Professor Filip, according to Rivos, who had his own history of fighting tyrannical headmasters.

Rivos was already there when everyone else was brought in. He was among the first to be locked up and tortured by the King. He was not particularly eager to return home and share his story but had no other place to go.

Lia felt that fate had brought them together and that, despite all the losses they shared, they were together for a reason.

A thought started forming in her mind. An idea that would upset Lady Aril. All the better.

She and her friends should be the ones taking Rivos, Flavia and Mariana home! Tudor could use his Wish Compass and guide them along the way. Besides, she and her friends had to return to Ostrova, if only to scatter her grandfather's ashes.

Most of all, she wanted to meet their families, convince them of the fact that their children were perfectly valuable members of Maar, even without a Wish to make. After all, Raven was born without a Wish and he was one of the most wonderful people she'd ever met. If she could, she would share her own Wish with all of them, they would know better what to do with it.

When the dinner finished, Lia ran her proposal by Tudor, his cousins and Dragomir. It was received enthusiastically by all of them. She wanted to check especially if Dragomir minded being left at the Castle with Daria. They would come back to visit, that was certain. He agreed with the plan, saying Lady Aril behaved impeccably towards the two of them. Lia hoped things would continue that way.

They didn't have to wait until morning to talk to the others as Mariana and Flavia had their room next to hers and Rivos's was just across the corridor. Lia feared they might have reservations about the whole thing. After all, they had met only a few hours before and might be more comfortable travelling with an official escort.

They not only accepted but felt relieved to return home with Lia and her friends. Mariana joked that Lia was now famous across the whole Kingdom and it would be useful to have her around to distract her parents. Lia smiled and promised to do just that.

Lady Aril, predictably, resisted the idea. Early in the morning, she formulated tens of reasons why it was best for all of them to accept her offer of travelling with the Order's soldiers. Lia rejected each one of them tactfully.

She finally won the argument when she mentioned the debt of the Order towards those who had lost their Wishes because of its failures. Lady Aril conceded and offered Lia horses and supplies for the road ahead.

***

The morning air was crisp and the day sunny and unexpectedly warm for winter. The snow reflected so much light it was difficult to see properly. As the group of seven left the Castle and entered the forest, the shade and the cool air made for a welcome change. Tudor checked his Compass and led the way while Lia travelled beside him.

'It seems like it's been a lifetime since we last travelled together,' Lia said pensively.

'Yes, it does. Even if we only entered the Order a week ago,' Tudor replied.

'We entered a week ago, but we are a world apart from that time. A week ago we still hoped we would find my grandfather. And I was almost certain the Cardinal was the Wish Thief. It was a world in which Lady Aril didn't exist, neither did the King and his infamy. A world that was happier,' she concluded.

'No, we were not happier back then, just more naïve. We thought that Kings always cared for their people. That nobody can make a Wish for someone else. That good people always win the day and escape unharmed.' Tudor said and fell silent.

Lia's grandfather and Daria were on both their minds.

'There are many things that I would be happy to be naïve about,' Lia said after a while.

'But, despite everything, I would still do it all over again. I would leave Ostrova with you to look for my grandfather. I would still reject Raven's offer to travel with him to the South and I would still follow Daria into the Castle,' she said confidently. 'And I know she would do the same. Just like my grandfather would try to protect me no matter what.'

Tudor smiled.

'I am sure your grandfather is very proud of you, Lia,' he said.

'Of *us*. I couldn't have done it without you, Clara and Matei. You know, when I thought the King would kill me up in the tower, one of the things I regretted most was not seeing you again.'

Lia extended her hand and Tudor held it in his. After everything had changed, he was still the same, and this made all the difference in the world.

And, even if Raven was not there, she knew he was watching over her. She did not know why he was hiding but perhaps he had been badly hurt when he fell inside the tower. Or he could not face her because she learnt the truth about him.

Doesn't he realise that all she wanted was the chance to comfort him? That she understood him, perhaps better than anybody else?

Tudor was talking about the road they were taking, checking both the map and his Compass. They were heading first to Rivos's village, close to their home. They would pass through Ostrova for Lia to spread her grandfather's ashes in the garden, as she wanted. As he would have wanted.

'It will be strange to be back, won't it?' Tudor asked.

'It will be different, that is certain,' Lia said, her voice full of melancholy. 'And it will be a chance to close a chapter in all our lives. Who knows if we will ever live there again.'

'We are not closing a chapter, we are opening a whole new book,' Tudor replied. '*The Adventures of Lia and Her Friends*. No, *The Adventures of Lia the Brave and Her Almost as Brave Friends*,' he laughed.

'Ha, it's the other way around,' she said with a smile. 'But you are right, we were four when we left and now we are seven. We didn't know much about the world then, and now we have friends almost everywhere in the Kingdom. We hated the Cardinal and, well, we still do, but maybe a bit less,' Lia replied in jest.

'And we are ready for whatever comes next!' Tudor said loudly. The others heard him and cheered.

It was a sunny winter afternoon when they started going down the mountain. In the distance, the Castle looked like a tiny pile of stones upon a dark, lonely rock. They were on the road again. Just like before. Like always.

The forest carried the smell of fresh snow and green moss, of the coming spring and of new beginnings.

V LAD GLAVEANU IS A Romanian psychologist living and working in Dublin. He is Full Professor of Psychology at Dublin City University and the author of numerous books on creativity, imagination, wonder, and human possibility.

Some of his titles include *Wonder: The Extraordinary Power of an Ordinary Experience* (Bloomsbury) and *Creativity: A Very Short Introduction* (Oxford University Press).

The Wish Thief is his debut novel, an invitation to reflect on the power wishes have to shape our lives and the lives of others.

Outside of fiction and psychology, Vlad enjoys visiting the local farm with his wife and three young children, long sunsets, drag shows, and sour cherries.